BLOOD IN THE COTSWOLDS

Thea Osborne and her faithful spaniel, Hepzie, are house-sitting in the quiet village of Temple Guiting, and Detective Superintendent Phil Hollis is looking forward to visiting for a night or two, but a slipped disc puts an end to their romantic weekend and Phil is forced to take sick leave, with Thea as an unwilling nursemaid. A few days into their stay a skeleton is found at the roots of an old, uprooted beech tree. Among the locals theories and rumours abound, as Thea and Phil try to prevent another murder investigation from threatening the quiet solitude they hold so dear.

BLOOD IN THE COTSWOLDS

BLOOD IN THE COTSWOLDS

by

Rebecca Tope

Magna Large Print Books
Long Preston, North Yorkshire,
BD23 4ND, England.

British Library Cataloguing in Publication Data.

Tope, Rebecca
    Blood in the Cotswolds.

    A catalogue record of this book is
    available from the British Library

    ISBN   978-0-7505-3018-7

First published in Great Britain in 2008 by
Allison & Busby Limited

Copyright © 2008 by Rebecca Tope

Cover illustration © ThreeSixtyGroup.co.uk

The moral right of the author has been asserted

Published in Large Print 2009 by arrangement with
Allison & Busby Limited

Magna Large Print is an imprint of Library Magna Books Ltd.

Printed and bound in Great Britain by
T.J. (International) Ltd., Cornwall, PL28 8RW

For Paula

Author's Note

Temple Guiting is a real village with real claims to a Knights Templar connection. The Manor and the village shop are real, but just about everything else in the story is imaginary.

CHAPTER ONE

June 7th, at last! Phil Hollis hummed a broken medley to himself, in sheer boyish exuberance at having reached the long-awaited date without any last-minute impediment. Even the sun shared his sense of a holiday deserved, as it rose over the hills and warmed central England to Mediterranean levels.

Thea would be waiting for him in the house she had described as 'quaint', just outside Temple Guiting. She had already been there for two days, taking charge of a rare collection of tropical fish indoors and two horses outside. 'And that's not all,' she'd said on the phone. 'You can have the complete inventory when you get here.'

He hoped to stay the whole of Sunday, including the night, leaving first thing on Monday for a full week's work. He had not enjoyed a free Sunday for the past five weeks, thanks to complex work patterns combined with a massive emergency in Worcester a fortnight earlier, involving a cache of ricin and great political fallout. Despite one or two lone voices, asserting with complete authority that ricin was not an especially dangerous substance, utter panic had resulted from the overwrought reporting and the police had been expected to find those responsible in a matter of hours. The small pockets of calming reason were ignored and their message unheeded. Like many other chemicals or

11

plant derivatives, they insisted, ricin could cause damage and death if administered directly into the body, but simply having it scattered in the vicinity wasn't going to hurt anybody. Detective Superintendent Hollis did his best to keep an open mind, but knew he was unlikely to succeed. When everyone around him used the word 'ricin' as if it were the greatest killer substance of all time, it was impossible to believe it was no more harmful than asbestos dust or the sap of the giant hogweed. Much more prevalent was the idea that it was as poisonous as polonium or some sort of 'dirty bomb'. Besides, Phil knew the real danger came from public panic, regardless of the actual objective level of risk from the material in question.

The only balancing words of scepticism he ever heard were those uttered by Thea, his girlfriend. Thea Osborne did not take newspaper headlines or politicians' utterances seriously. She understood the pressures on the police, and sympathised, not least because her daughter was in the Force. But she had grown up in a family that regarded law enforcement as something that should remain in the background, not affecting people's lives unless they demonstrably transgressed. Surveillance, pre-emptive arrest, holding people in custody without charge – it was all quite obviously wrong in her eyes, and any attempt to justify such practices earned him her scathing rebuttal.

But this weekend, he was smugly confident that Thea would be entirely focused on the weather, her dog, the house-sitting commission and her feelings towards himself, perhaps not in that order. Approaching their first anniversary as 'an item', they were resolved to devote themselves to consolidating their relationship in the isolated charm of Hector's Nook. Phil had not brought his own two dogs, and hoped that Thea's spaniel would refrain from being too effusive. It wasn't difficult to have too much jumping up and licking, however lovingly meant.

Thea's directions were clear, and he wound through the village with the sunlight flickering through the wooded areas on each side of the road. Accustomed to the skewed levels of many parts of the Cotswolds, he dropped his speed enough to admire the succession of tree-capped hills to the right and the sweeps of upland to the left. He glimpsed water between the trees and remembered that this was yet another village built on the River Windrush. He anticipated a long riverside walk later in the day, with perhaps a meal in one of the characterful pubs the area boasted.

The trees were striking and he took a moment to analyse what it was about them that he found so significant. It came to him that they had a special air of age to them. Twisted and mossy, rooted in uneven stony ground, they gave the appearance of having been there forever, witnessing aeons of human folly. Uncharacteristically fanciful on this sunny day, he imagined the scenes they must have observed over the years. This village was on the way to nowhere, secluded and ignored, like dozens of others in the area, until the taste for English heritage took hold and busloads of tourists found their way to

Gloucestershire to admire the colour of the stone and the neatness of the gardens.

DS Phil Hollis had spent most of his life in the Cotswolds, and knew his way around. But he could still make new discoveries, and only since meeting Thea had he realised the depths of his ignorance as to the history of these places. She had made him aware of wool as a great economic and political force, and the sheer aesthetic brilliance of turning its profits into sumptuous yellow buildings that showed every sign of lasting several times as long as the venerable trees that surrounded them. Just such a building loomed ahead on a modest promontory, a classically breathtakingly beautiful manor house, basking in the sunshine with complacency oozing from every stone. He mentally saluted its claim to be just as complacent as it liked. Anything as lovely as that deserved to be pleased with itself.

He was aware of a need to remain steadfastly optimistic, given the setbacks he and Thea had endured over the past year. Her role as house-sitter had plunged her into a number of adventures, most of them dangerous. The mere fact of a home owner disappearing for two or three weeks frequently appeared to activate malign forces in the neighbourhood. 'But,' Thea had asserted recklessly, 'not this time. The sun is going to shine, the house will be a haven of tranquillity and you can come both weekends to share it with me.'

Both weekends had already dwindled into one definite Sunday and one possible thirty-six-hour period a week later. 'And I might manage to come over for an evening now and then,' he had added, with crossed fingers. 'That leaves you with an awful lot of time on your own.'

Thea shrugged bravely. 'I'll be OK,' she said. 'I've got Hepzie, don't forget.'

'Oughtn't you to think about asking someone to join you, like last time?' he insisted. Thea's daughter Jessica had been with her in Blockley, a few months previously, and her sister Jocelyn had shared part of an earlier commission. 'One of your relations or something.'

'They're all busy,' she said. 'Besides, I wouldn't know what to do with an "or something".' The feeble joke landed face down and the subject was changed.

The approach to Hector's Nook was a bumpy bendy track between high hedges, plunging alarmingly downhill for the last fifty yards. The house stood on a levelled shelf, facing the drive, in full morning sunshine. It was the mellow hue of every old stone building in the area, greyish-yellow, with woodwork picked out in a dark orange. A steep garden rose on one side, and a large shed or garage occupied another plateau on Phil's right. In a lopsided curve around the corner of the house, at the foot of the sloping garden, there was a lawn, partially shielded by a few shrubs and some tall willow trees. The willows were a narrow-leaved variety, with a delicate semi-transparent tracery presented by their upward-thrusting branches. On a windy day they would flicker and dance delightfully, he thought. The whole place had an unplanned, careless air which he found refreshing in the self-conscious Cotswolds.

He parked his car next to Thea's red hatchback,

got out and paused to savour the sight before him.

Thea had come to the door with her dog. She stood there, the light in her face, smiling broadly. Her dark hair was longer than he had ever seen it, the ends flipped up where it reached her shoulders, giving an impression of youth and innocence. She wore a sleeveless top, dark red, and white cut-off trousers. Her bare arms and calves looked brown and warm. But it was her face that held his attention. Thea was a beauty, by any standards. Large deep-set eyes, an elfin chin, slightly pouting mouth – it all added up to a picture that people liked to simply contemplate for its own sake. But for Phil, there was a lot more to it than mere contemplation. This was *his* woman and had been for nearly a year, despite cool times and angry times and periods of mutual suspicion. He would have only himself to blame if things went sour between them now, and he was entirely committed to ensuring that no such thing could happen.

He climbed slowly out of the car, mirroring her smile. 'Here I am,' he said. 'As promised.'

'So you are,' she nodded. 'Congratulations.'

She meant it genuinely – that much he had learnt about her from the outset. Thea Osborne did not do sarcasm or barbed remarks with critical subtexts. She was sincerely applauding his achievement in escaping from work and arriving when he said he would.

But nonetheless he laughed, a trifle uneasily. He could still hear the distant tones of his ex-wife, uttering the same word, loaded with venom and bitterness. He still felt the strain of the two conflicting demands on his energy and attention. He still believed, deep down, that senior policemen ought not to even attempt to engage in serious relationships. Even his dogs would have endorsed that sentiment, deposited as they so often were with his sister in Painswick.

'Coffee's brewing,' Thea added.

He stepped quickly towards her, his arms held wide. Her smile went soft and her eyelashes fluttered. As he enfolded her to his chest, a voice spoke from inside the house.

'He got here then,' said a woman. 'Just like you said.'

He tightened his grip on Thea in his shock, and angled his head to see who had spoken. The shadows in the hallway revealed nothing more than a bulky silhouette, until the figure moved further into the light. A very large person emerged; a woman he guessed to be around thirty-five years in age and close to twenty stone in weight, with short chopped hair and the oddly similar features of all fat people: small half-buried eyes, rosebud mouth, multiple chins and long plump cheeks.

Phil waited for enlightenment as to who she might be, making no attempt to guess.

Thea pulled herself free, but kept one arm curled around his waist. 'Oh, sorry,' she said. 'Phil, this is Janey. She's from the village.'

'Hello, Janey,' he said with deliberate pleasantness.

The woman responded with a complicated smile, acknowledging her size, her borderline

17

claim to being fully human, her willingness to pretend that normal social intercourse was possible. He sensed the effort that even such a simple exchange required of her, the effort that virtually everything required, simply to shift twenty stone of flesh from place to place. He felt the exasperation that he supposed most people felt, confronted with such an example of rampant lack of willpower, or perverse refusal to link food with body weight.

'Don't worry, I'm not staying,' she said. Her voice was musical, rich. He imagined it bubbling through double cream or melted chocolate. She looked at Thea. 'Thanks for the chat,' she said, and began to walk away. Her feet, Phil noted, seemed tiny, and not at all burdened. Almost, she seemed to walk on tiptoe, though surely that wasn't possible?

The couple watched in silence until she had turned the bend in the rutted drive. Hepzie, the cocker spaniel, had followed her a short way, but Janey ignored her. Now the dog came back and devoted its entire attention to Phil, sniffing his legs for evidence of Baxter or Claude. 'She's putting on weight,' he said, innocently.

'Hey! Mind what you say,' Thea protested, glancing up the drive to where her visitor had walked. 'She might hear you.'

Phil blinked, and then laughed. 'Not *her*. Hepzibah. She's getting broad in the beam.' He patted the dog's rump.

'Nonsense. It's her coat. She always gets more hair in the summer – and loses it in the winter. She's on the Australian calendar, I think. Besides, cockers are meant to be boxy. Hepzie's always been too rangy until now.'

'So, who exactly is Janey?' he wanted to know. 'And why? And *how?* I mean – *how* is it possible...'

'Poor thing. It must be awful on a day like this. She's walked at least a mile to get here, and a mile back again. It's already hot.'

He raised an eyebrow, awaiting replies to his questions. But Thea shrugged Janey away and began to talk about the house, its owner, the fish and the hitherto undisclosed creature in the shed at the end of the garden. 'A snake!' she said, wide-eyed. 'There's a python out there, and the dratted woman never told me, in case I was phobic.'

'Grounds for refusal to do the job, if you ask me. You're not, are you?'

'Not what?'

'Phobic.'

'Not in the least. I like them. I think they're fantastic, in fact. So strong and supple. Sinuous, muscular. I'm only sorry I'm not allowed to take her out and play with her.'

His eyebrow kinked again. 'You are, I assume, aware of the Freudian undertones in what you've just said?'

Her grin spread right across her face. 'I am,' she said.

The button had been pressed, and wordlessly they went indoors and indulged in half a morning of intimacy, which took in three of the house's rooms as they moved from urgent foreplay in the main living room, then to a wood-panelled dining room from which stairs led to two upstairs bed-rooms. The stairs were narrow with a sharp turn

19

halfway up. Phil had an impression of a cosy house full of plants and mellow old-fashioned furnishings. In the living room he had glimpsed a row of fish tanks, one containing large bright orange fish like something out of a picture book.

Thea had been given a generously sized bed in the second bedroom, with a plump feather mattress that felt like sleeping in a cloud. Only after an hour or more did Phil come to his senses enough to comment.

'This mattress is outrageous,' he said. 'I've never met anything like it.'

Thea ignored him, stretched naked on her back, watching the leaves of a tall willow make patterns against the blue sky. 'We ought to be outside,' she said. 'We're wasting the weather.'

He swallowed the implied insult, which she surely hadn't meant. His own preference would have been to sleep soundly until early afternoon and then wake to a late but very tasty lunch in a riverside hostelry. Senior policemen, like dairy farmers, were habitually, inescapably tired. They snatched sleep whenever they could find it, and learnt strategies for resting mind and body even when forced to remain awake.

'So tell me about the person who lives here,' he invited, hoping to keep her beside him for a while longer.

'Miss Polly Deacon. Mid-sixties or so. Retired civil servant. Plenty of money. Lived here all her life, and her parents before her. Never saw any reason to move, but likes to travel. She's gone to Argentina for nearly a month. I'm only needed here for part of the time, because her brother,

Archie, is taking over from me. Archie's wife has just kicked him out, being a selfish bitch and a spoilt cow. Or perhaps it was a selfish cow and a spoilt bitch. Anyway, we don't like her. Miss Deacon wears tailored slacks and expensive shoes, and has red dyed hair. She goes to local history classes and hoards magazines. And cultivates house plants. You might have noticed the house plants? And the fish, of course.'

Phil had only the haziest impression of greenery on a number of surfaces in the rooms he had passed through on the way upstairs. 'Mmm,' he said. Then he summarised: 'She's a character, then.'

'You'd like her. She's the last of a dying breed.'

'Must be. Sounds as if she's in the wrong generation entirely. Apart from the dyed hair. That doesn't seem to fit with the rest of it. Not to mention the snake.'

'Oh, that's Archie's. The wife kicked it out as well. But Miss Deacon has always liked them, and bought in a consignment of mice for it to eat.'

Phil gulped. 'Mice?'

'Dead ones – they're in the freezer. They breed them specially, apparently, for people to feed to exotic reptiles.'

'That's disgusting!'

'Yes,' said Thea equably.

'What time is it?'

'No idea. Nearly twelve, I guess. We could go somewhere for lunch.'

'Just what I was thinking,' he said, with only a flicker of disappointment.

21

Thea had not fully researched local pubs, apart from establishing that Temple Guiting did not possess one. 'Just a shop and a church,' she said. 'The shop's a bonus, although it's not open all the time. A local collective runs it on a rota system.'

'Quaint,' said Phil.

'Oh, yes. Everything round here is quaint,' Thea confirmed.

They used his car to drive to the next village, which was Guiting Power. There, the Hollow Bottom offered an acceptable bill of fare, and they ate outside, chatting easily. The pub had an unmistakable affinity with horse racing, which neither Phil nor Thea found particularly atmospheric. 'We'll try the Farmer's Arms next time,' he ordained. 'It has a much better view of the village. Which, I have to say, is quite a lot prettier than Temple Guiting, unless there's a part I haven't seen yet.'

Thea tilted her head. 'They're completely different. Temple Guiting's got a lot of trees. It must be very dark on a dull day. And there's not really a proper centre like this one has. But it feels *older*, somehow. More history. Not least the Knights Templar, of course.'

Phil sighed gently. 'You mean all that tedious Dan Brown stuff, I suppose.'

'It can be tedious, but not in the way you mean. The mythology that's grown up around them is completely idiotic. But if you research them properly, as a real historian, you get a whole new angle on the Middle Ages.'

'And you've done that? Researched them properly?'

She shook her head. 'Not my period, but I did have a bit of a trawl on the Internet, just to get myself clued up. And Miss Deacon's got stacks of books and magazines all about it. I'll be able to sit outside in the sun, reading for long lazy afternoons. It'll be blissful.'

'You're right about the oldness,' he said, after a pause. 'I felt it right away. As if the trees are the real inhabitants and the people are just recent intruders.'

'Very romantic,' she approved. 'And exactly how I felt when I first saw it. Guiting Power is quite different from Temple Guiting – there it's all about the people and their buildings. I suppose they both feel a need to be different – given how confusingly similar their names are.'

Phil nodded and changed the subject.

'And that Janey – is she going to be a regular visitor? She seemed to think you were best buddies already.'

'She's been twice so far. She likes Miss Deacon's horses. She's one of those people you find yourself talking to about personal stuff after ten minutes.'

'She doesn't *ride*, does she?' He entertained a grim image of the wretched animal sagging helplessly as the vast woman landed on its back. 'Or are they Shire horses? That might just work, I suppose.'

Thea giggled. 'Stop it,' she said. 'Don't be so nasty.'

He looked at her steadily, making her giggle again. 'It isn't really something you can just ignore,' he said. 'Is it?'

'Maybe not. But there's a lot more to her than her size. She's a very nice person.'

'Well, as a local friend, I'm sure she has much to commend her,' he said primly.

Thea turned her attention to the spaniel sitting patiently in the shade under their table, and said, 'Hepzie likes her, as well. She took to her right away.'

Phil was unimpressed. 'Hepzie likes everybody,' he said.

Hector's Nook boasted a small courtyard at the back of the house, facing south-west and filled with more pots of exuberant plants. One in particular caught Phil's attention. It had large palmate leaves and a cluster of ripening seedpods in a striking shade of pale terracotta. 'That's a castor oil plant,' he said, his voice oddly harsh to his own ears.

'So what if it is?'

'The seeds are used for making ricin.'

Thea grinned. 'My God! Miss Deacon's part of the supply chain for al-Qaeda. Who'd have guessed it? Do you think she has a little chemistry lab in the cellar? Has the Government banned these plants? If not, why not?'

'It's not funny, Thea,' he snapped.

'You're wrong, my lamb. It is actually *very* funny. There must be thousands of old ladies with one of these plants on their patios or even in the front room. It's a handsome thing – I bet the Victorians loved them. Besides, I thought we decided that ricin isn't especially lethal anyway. Didn't we?'

He screwed up his eyes, struggling to reconcile the two extreme bodies of opinion in his daily life. As a police officer, he was expected to anticipate and prevent all activity that might present a threat to the general public. He was supposed to take the worst case scenario and act as if it was certain to happen. But Thea threw doubt and even mockery over much of what he was obliged to take seriously. With feigned interest, she cross-examined him on the precise method of extracting ricin from the plant, and just what damage it wreaked on the human body. To his irritation, he found he could give only the vaguest answers. 'It can kill,' he repeated doggedly. 'It killed that Bulgarian. The one that was stabbed with an umbrella.'

'Oh yes,' she recalled. 'And Miss Deacon's got an umbrella – probably. I can't say I've seen it, but there's sure to be one. So we can agree that ricin is dodgy if it's injected into you. That's true of quite a few substances, isn't it?'

'Stop it!' he ordered, laughing in spite of himself. 'You make everything I do look ridiculous. I don't know why I tolerate it.'

'It's not you,' she soothed. 'It's this idiotic Government. You're just the helpless instrument. Just obeying orders,' she added, less flippantly.

Phil was not much reassured. He had watched her becoming more and more enraged by the latest round of legislation further curtailing individual freedoms, sometimes floundering for the words with which to explain how sinister it all was. He worried at the wedge it threatened to drive between them. When sitting at one of the many briefings he received at work, he tried to give space in his head for Thea's point of view, with increasing difficulty. *The innocent have nothing to fear*, came the official line. *These measures are designed specifically to protect the innocent.* But he wasn't stupid. He could see some of the dangers for himself. When he visualised 'the innocent' they were pink-skinned, rural-dwelling, unambitious zombies. Anybody brown or clever or angry or unusual raised suspicions. And it didn't stop there. The police were supposed to keep a close eye on people who behaved irresponsibly in their cars, who smoked or drank too much, who cast a lustful eye on young girls or accessed the wrong sort of websites on their computers. Surveillance was everywhere, and sometimes it seemed to him that it wouldn't be long before half the population were being employed by the police to keep a close eye on the other half. He knew it was possible, that there were unpleasant precedents in countries not so very far away.

But he couldn't let any of this spoil the day with Thea. The long lazy Sunday afternoon stretched invitingly ahead, slowing the pace of life almost to a standstill. There were scents of ripening grass and warm wood on all sides, sounds of distant lawnmowers and bleating sheep. 'It could be a hundred years ago,' said Thea. 'Except for the lawnmowers.'

'If this is global warming, bring it on,' said Phil, aware that this was something he said slightly too often, and with a lurch of guilt every time.

'Easy to say,' she reproached mildly. 'But you

know perfectly well it isn't something to celebrate. All the same, it's hard to argue with regular long hot summers. The Edwardians had them, after all.'

'And what about the Knights Templar?' he wondered. 'Did they have good summers, as well?'

She shook her head. 'I haven't the faintest idea,' she admitted. 'But I'll look it up and let you know.'

They walked a mile or so along the Windrush, much to Hepzie's joy. The sense of perfection persisted for all three of them. Landscape, buildings, weather – it all came together to bathe them in a pure sensory harmony that combined with the physical delights of the morning to reinforce a growing conviction that they too belonged together. Phil could hear Thea's thoughts, hoping perversely that she wouldn't utter them. Nothing needed to be said, as they meandered with linked arms, pressed closely together, savouring the best that England could offer. If niggling recollections of the working week ahead, the existence of malevolent forces, the fragile edifice of civilisation teetering on the brink of some cataclysm intruded into his thoughts, he firmly pushed them away. *Stay in the moment*, he adjured himself. Whatever might happen, there'll always be this glorious afternoon to hold on to.

CHAPTER TWO

They got back to Hector's Nook shortly after four, and sat outside with mugs of tea, watching Miss Deacon's two horses in a good-sized paddock behind the garage and extending up to the road. Thea had checked that there was water in their trough, and given each a pat on the neck, before going to make the tea. Now she and Phil were lounging on the small patch of lawn at the corner of the house, surrounded by low maintenance shrubs, the willows screening them from the front. 'Miss Deacon doesn't like gardening,' Thea remarked. 'She says it's pathetic. Those willows were just sticks that she bought on a whim. She rammed them in, along the edge of the grass, and in three years they were trees.'

'Pathetic?' The word had snagged his attention. 'How does she work that out?'

'Something about it being a substitute for real creativity and a forlorn attempt at immortality.'

'You seem to remember a lot of her quotes. How long did you have together before she left for Argentina?'

'A couple of hours. She does talk a bit like a book of aphorisms. I liked the way she's obviously thought about everything, and not just adopted other people's ideas.'

'Like you,' he said.

She looked at him, eyes wide. 'Me?'

'Thea, I don't think I've ever heard you utter a cliché,' he smiled, reaching for her hand. 'You're an original, same as this Miss Deacon.'

'Oh.' She swilled the last drops of tea around the bottom of the mug. 'Nobody's ever told me that before.'

'You're surprised?'

'A bit. But in a nice way. It must be good to be an original – I suppose.'

'Of course it is. It makes you more real than most people.'

She shushed him with a wave of her hand. 'There's a car coming down the track,' she said. 'What a nuisance.'

'Perhaps they won't see us if we keep still,' he suggested.

'Too late.' Thea tipped her chin towards Hepzie, who had gone trotting towards the sound, long tail wagging in welcome. 'She loves new people. Besides, whoever it is'll see our cars and know we're both here.' The car engine was loudly evident now, the tyres crunching on the gravel in front of the house.

'You go, then,' he said ungallantly. 'You're better with visitors than me. I'll watch from behind the laurel.'

Pulling a face at him, Thea got up and followed the spaniel. The slam of the car door reverberated just as she rounded the row of shrubs and set eyes on a tall dark man fondling the long ears of the excessively hospitable dog.

He was impossibly handsome. Words like *chiselled* and *debonair* flittered through her head. He had deep-set eyes, full lips, straight black

29

brows. He looked to be in his mid-forties, perhaps, with no trace of silver in his hair and a supple body as he bent down to the dog. He wore a thin shirt, with at least two of the buttons undone, and cream trousers that made her think of cricket.

'Hello?' she said.

'Good afternoon.' It was a Noel Coward drawl: easy, assured, slightly amused. 'I'm so sorry to intrude, but I've come to find Miss Deacon. Is she in?' He glanced at the two cars parked tidily side by side in front of the garage.

'No, she's away. I'm her house-sitter. Thea Osborne.' She almost held out a hand for him to shake, but something stopped her.

'Hi, Thea Osborne.' He paused, looking at the upper storey of the house, as if checking the veracity of Thea's words. 'I'm Rupert Temple-Pritchett.' The scattering of plosives in his name made it sound military and intimidating. Thea silently repeated it to herself, wonderingly.

'Temple,' she said. 'Something tells me that's not a coincidence. This being Temple Guiting, I mean.'

'Well spotted,' he smiled. 'A scion of the oldest family in the area, that's me. Very much diluted, it has to be admitted, since the Temple bit derives from my mother, and I'm afraid the female line carries rather less clout – deeply unjust as that may be.' He twinkled at her, conveying his aware-ness of latter-day sensitivities on gender issues. 'So – the old girl's away, is she? That's a disap-pointment.' And it did look as if he was at a loss as a result. 'I always like a chat with Polly. Sets me up for weeks, it does.'

'She's not back until the very end of the month.' She bit back further information with an effort. Discretion did not come easily to her, but she had learnt a certain caution over the past year. Already there was something about the man that raised a wriggle of alarm in her insides. His manner was old-fashioned, languidly careless, but not genuinely relaxed.

'Oh dear. Well, I should go then. Hot, isn't it,' he added irrelevantly.

'Yes,' agreed Thea. 'Oh – would you like a drink? My friend's here – do you want to come and meet him?'

'How kind. But no, I've taken up too much of your afternoon as it is. It was lovely to meet you. And your dear little dog.' He made an odd little quirk with his mouth. 'Pity about the tail, though,' he added. 'Makes her look a very peculiar shape.'

Thea had had this conversation a score of times since she'd acquired a cocker with an undocked tail. Country people in particular thought it an outrage. 'I like it,' was all she said.

She watched him turn his low-slung car and retreat up the track, before returning to Phil. 'Rupert Temple-Pritchett,' she said. 'How's that for a name?'

'Impressive. What did you mean by asking him to stay for a drink?'

'Common courtesy. Did you hear the whole thing?'

'More or less. What was that word – the thing he said he was? Not a Zionist, surely?'

'A scion. He said he's a scion – how about that?'

Phil shrugged. 'He's welcome, whatever it is.' He glanced at his watch. 'What should we do now, do you think?'

'Why do we have to do anything? I'm all right here for ages yet. We can see without even getting up that the horses are fine, and the snake doesn't need feeding again until Tuesday. This is a sinecure, compared to the other places I've had to look after.'

Phil sighed and slumped back in the garden chair. 'You're right,' he said. 'Of course.'

They drifted through to nine o'clock, when the sun finally disappeared and the house was an enclosed haven surrounded by trees and silence.

Preparation for bed carried a slight awkwardness with it, thanks in part to the unaccustomed house, but also to the fact that the number of nights they had spent together was still low enough for it to be a novelty. Phil had spent a total of six weekends in Thea's Witney home, plus perhaps a dozen snatched nights, or part-nights. Their bodies had become familiar to each other, but the rituals were slower to establish. Each was more used to solitary sleeping, with pillows and windows set just so, the easy spontaneity of putting on the light to read at three a.m., or going to the loo at five was not possible with another person in the bed. Even more clumsy were the minutes before finally settling together. Phil felt himself to be tense and slightly irritated when they finally rolled into each other's arms, not long after ten that night. Try as he might, he could not shake off a sense that the best moments had already passed. The coming morning, with its many necessities, was already forcing itself into his mind. Afterwards, he could not be entirely surprised by what happened next.

The sex began langorously, with much stroking and kissing. Then, before it had properly got going, as Phil twisted in the suffocating mattress, intending to move Thea from his side, to lie on top of him, there came a pain in his back as shocking and sickening as a badly stubbed toe.

'Aarghh!' he cried. 'Oh, bugger. Aarhh, oohh!' He went rigid against the pain, pushing her away.

'What? Is it cramp?' She herself floundered in the feathers, before sitting up to stare at him in the fading light.

'My back! Something's gone. It's agony.'

'Gone?' she repeated stupidly.

'Slipped. Dislocated. I don't know.' He spoke through clenched teeth. He put a hand to the place, trying to roll sideways at the same time. With another loud groan, he slumped flat again. 'I've never known pain like it,' he gasped. 'It's unbearable.' Tears seeped from the corners of his eyes. 'What am I going to do?'

'Try to relax,' she ordered.

'I need a doctor. An ambulance.' The thought of being forced to move made him go rigid again. 'But I can't be moved,' he wailed. Fear shot through him, as acute as the physical pain. 'What if I'm paralysed? What if I've broken something?'

'Don't be silly.'

He subsided like a shocked child after a slap. Thea got off the bed and stood looking at him, her skin still flushed from the interrupted sex. 'Doctors don't come out these days,' she said.

'Especially not on a Sunday night. Haven't you got a tame osteopath or something? Has this ever happened to you before?'

'Never,' he said. 'Not a twinge.'

'Well, I think we'd better not panic. Give it a few minutes to recover. It might just click back into place if you give it a chance.'

'It's this damned mattress,' he said. 'It's lethal.'

Thea shook her head helplessly. 'Just when everything was going so well,' she murmured. 'I feel as if we're jinxed.'

Phil gingerly tried to pull himself up towards the headboard, digging his elbows and heels into the thick mattress. He discovered that if he kept himself completely straight, some movement was possible. But the procedure was far from painless and he groaned as he inched himself up the bed. 'I feel such a fool,' he complained.

'Yes,' Thea agreed. 'I expect you do.'

'You're not being very nice.'

'I'm a terrible nurse, I admit. Illness always seems such a waste of time. If people were less kind to the sick, I expect there'd be a lot less pressure on the NHS.'

'You're mad,' he moaned. 'I'm in the hands of a madwoman.'

'Well – what are we going to do?' She was brisk almost to the point of aggression. 'I think we'll try and make it through the night, and if it's still bad in the morning, we can get you to a doctor.'

He stared at her wildly. 'In a car? Down those stairs? I can't possibly. I'm *paralysed*, I tell you.'

'No, you're not. You've pulled a muscle, or slipped a disc, and I can see it hurts. But the only

34

other option is an ambulance, and that's going too far. Imagine the drama if we called one now and all the locals saw the flashing blue light. They'd think there'd been a murder.'

Phil managed a tight grimace in place of a smile. 'And we don't want that, do we?' he said.

Thea's plan prevailed, and Phil endured a long tortured night in which he managed to doze from around two to four a.m., lying flat on his agonised back, and snoring loudly. At seven, Thea got up and went down to make two mugs of tea. On her return, she insisted he roll onto his side, and from there to a sitting position on the edge of the bed. 'You'll have to go to the bathroom,' she ordered. 'It'll be a trial run.'

He got himself vertical, with several cries of anguish, and shuffled pathetically to the lavatory. Then Thea forced him into some clothes, the effort of pulling trousers up almost too much for either of them. 'Can't I just wear a dressing gown?' he pleaded, tears in his eyes. 'This is killing me.'

He could see that even Thea was losing her nerve. She chewed her lower lip, and repeated several times a belief that nothing too desperately serious could have happened. 'You can't have *broken* anything,' she insisted. 'How could you? It's not as if you fell off a horse.'

The next apparently insurmountable obstacle was the stairs. They were narrow, with a twist halfway down, and were made of stone. Thea had been especially taken with them on her first inspection of the house, realising that they formed the sturdy core of the whole building, and had not been modified or moved in three hundred years. She tried to distract Phil from his anguish by fantasising over all the human crises the stairway must have seen. 'Women in labour, dead bodies taken out by the undertaker's men, visiting boyfriends tiptoeing down in the early morning.'

'Not to mention crippled policemen crawling down backwards,' he puffed.

And it was true that this had turned out to be the only possible mode of descent. One foot would be lowered gingerly to the next step, sharing the weight of the semi-prostrate body with his forearms, without any jarring or pressure to his back.

'Try to see the funny side,' Thea suggested incautiously. The snarl that met these words was more than a little alarming. Even Hepzie retreated from her concerned position at the foot of the stairs.

Because Thea was obviously going to have to drive, Phil assumed that they would use her car. But then he noticed how small it was, how little legroom it could offer, and thought again. 'We'll have to take mine,' he said. 'I suppose you'll be covered by the insurance.'

'Who cares?' she said. 'Just let's get you in.'

The passenger seat was adjustable in all planes, and they eventually got him into a position that he could tolerate without constant groans and screams. It seemed to him that Thea's driving was unbearably jerky as she mastered the unfamiliar clutch, and bumped them up the uneven drive to the road at the top. Pain tore at him like a mad dog, making him feel sick and tearful.

They arrived, finally, at the hospital in Cirencester, where they were met by helpful paramedics and Phil was gently stretchered into a cubicle in a department that appeared to have nothing else to do that day. Nobody took his agony lightly, or made ominous comments about the impossibility of backs. He was probed and questioned and X-rayed, given analgesia and generally reassured. Thea hovered, waited, smiled and sighed. Phil began to look less drawn and terrified. By ten he was hungry and impatient for something more to happen.

A little while later, a man in a clean white coat, holding a clipboard, materialised and made his diagnosis. 'It's what we used to call a slipped disc,' he asserted.

'What do we call it now?' asked Thea.

'Prolapsed or herniated disc,' he responded with a tolerant smile.

'What happens next?' Phil enquired with unnatural meekness.

'It will almost certainly get better on its own,' the doctor said. 'The pain will subside in a few days, and in three months or so, you'll be back to normal.' He nodded in a bobbing mechanical fashion, as if delighted with his own words.

'Three months!' Phil's voice rose to a squeak. 'Can I work during that time?'

'Depends what you want to do. No lifting, straining or bending.'

'Do I have to stay in bed?'

'Absolutely not. Though you might want to stay reasonably still for the rest of this week. Find a comfortable position on a firm surface and let your body do the rest. Make the most of it, is my advice. With this lovely weather, you could be outdoors. Try an airbed in the garden.' The smile widened. 'Try to treat it as a well-deserved rest.'

Phil sighed and rolled his eyes, catching Thea's thoughtful glance. The implications of the situation were obviously starting to dawn on her.

'Can he drive?' she asked. 'I mean when the worst of the pain has gone.'

'Probably. Give it a go, and see how it feels. We advise people to be as active as they can after the first week or so. Walking, swimming – that sort of thing.'

'And is there any treatment?'

'You could try an osteopath, if you like.' The tone was unenthusiastic. 'That can sometimes reduce the pressure on the nerves, which helps. It doesn't actually hasten the recovery process, though.'

'Meanwhile I have to get him home again,' Thea realised.

'It'll be better now he's had the painkillers,' the doctor assured her, and a few moments later was gone in a flick of the white coat.

Phil and Thea looked at each other carefully. 'Home,' he said. 'Where's that then, I wonder?'

'It's up to you. I've got to stay and mind Miss Deacon's house. You're welcome to be there with me. Or you can go back to your flat and take your chances. Is your sister a good nurse? Because I warn you, I meant it when I said I wasn't. I'll probably shout at you.'

'You can't be worse than Linda,' he said. 'I'll have to phone her,' he realised. 'And ask her to keep the dogs until I'm better.'

Thea said nothing.

'But that mattress will have to go. And I can't face the stairs while I'm like this.'

'There'll have to be some rules,' said Thea. 'Number One – no complaining. Number Two – no self-pity.'

'Aren't they the same thing?'

'Well spotted. All the other rules are on the same theme. Now, let's go before those pain-killers start to wear off.'

She settled him on the sofa in Miss Deacon's front room, and got to work creating a lavish lunch to compensate for the lack of breakfast, having found him his mobile with which to make his excuses at the station and inform his sister of her extended dog-minding duties. She heard his tone from the kitchen, though not the words, and surmised that he was having difficulty convincing his colleagues that his injury was genuine. 'Well,' he was shouting as she carried a tray into the room, 'you'll just have to manage without me. There's nothing I can do about it.'

'Problems?' she asked sweetly, when he'd finished.

'Not really. Fielding calls from the Home Office seems to be the main preoccupation at the moment, with this terrorist scare. They don't need me for that.'

'Although, if they did, you could probably do it from here,' she suggested rashly. 'After all, you can still talk – and think. And read,' she added. 'You're not completely useless.'

'I have to be on the spot,' he said sullenly. 'How can I keep abreast of everything from here?'

She put the tray on a low table, and leant over him, kissing his forehead. 'Poor old Phil,' she crooned. 'It's a horrible thing to happen. We'll have to think of some games we can play. Or perhaps we could find you a wheelchair and I could push you around the village.'

'Don't you dare! I'm not going in a wheelchair for anybody.'

'Why not? It would give you an insight into life as a disabled person.'

'I had plenty of that last year when I broke my leg, remember. Hobbling around on a crutch for weeks was no fun. And this is even worse.'

'Ah, ah!' she admonished. 'Remember the rules. We are going to make the best of this, Phil Hollis, if it kills us.'

He rolled his eyes and reached for a sandwich.

CHAPTER THREE

By late afternoon, Phil had eaten a hearty lunch, had a little sleep in the garden, and persuaded himself that there was something to be said for enforced idleness. Thea had walked Hepzie through the village and back, and was lying contentedly on the grass with a book. 'This is the life,' she sighed. Then she shook her head. 'Though I can't quite believe it. It reminds me of Frampton Mansell when Jocelyn stayed with me.

It was sunny then, as well, and we lazed about in the garden, while everybody around us was killing each other.'

'Not a whisper of any killing here,' he assured her. 'Unless you let that snake out and it terrifies somebody to death. You did say it wasn't poisonous, didn't you?'

'I can't remember what I said, but it's quite harmless. I think it's even quite affectionate in a reptilian sort of way.' She sighed. 'I do love snakes. Isn't it funny how some people are so paranoid about them?'

'Not at all funny when you consider that more people in India die of snakebite each year than any other cause.'

She gave him a stern look. 'Is that really true?'

'Absolutely. It makes more sense to be scared of snakes than of spiders or bats or wasps, and all the other things that freak people out.'

'I wonder whether dogs are frightened of them. Snakes, I mean. I haven't shown Shasti to Hepzie yet.'

'Shasti? Is that what you said?'

She nodded cheerfully. 'Nice, isn't it?'

Phil merely sighed, and went quiet for a few moments. Then he voiced his thoughts. 'I hate to say this, my darling, but I can't help thinking we're going to be horribly bored by about Thursday at this rate. I mean – a day can be a dreadfully long time when you're not doing anything.'

'Not to worry,' she breezed. 'You'll be walking by then. That doctor said you had to keep active once the pain subsided. We can go out and about and do some local history studies. Won't that be fun?'

'I remember it a bit differently. I remember him saying I should rest for a week or so.'

'You will be resting – between short spells of gentle activity, like walking. He said it was good to walk, I know he did.'

'You never ask me how I'm feeling,' he noted.

'Sorry. Do you think I should? I can tell, more or less, by looking at you. And I didn't want to draw attention to it. I work on the theory that distraction is the best cure for almost any ailment.'

'I'm not complaining,' he said quickly. 'It's quite refreshing, in a way. But if I may, I'd like to just mention that it feels easier now. There hasn't been any of that stabbing agony of this morning. And I haven't had a pill since lunch.'

'Good,' she nodded. 'You'll be better in no time at this rate.'

'I'll have to sleep downstairs, though. Lucky there's a loo on the ground floor, or I don't know what I'd have done.'

'Use a pot, I suppose,' she said carelessly.

Phil laughed; even when the tremors revived the pain in his back, he went on laughing. 'Thea Osborne, I love you,' he choked. 'I love you, I love you.'

'Good,' she said again.

Although the day had drifted by slowly, looking back on it, Phil felt it had been far from wasted. His declaration of love had marked a deepening of his union with Thea, despite her apparently unconcerned reaction. He tried to examine his feelings towards her, forcing his mind to the unfamiliar task. He concluded eventually that she made him a better person than he might otherwise be. Not only the veto on self-pity, but the very *straightness* of her. She had occasionally caught him out in small moral lapses associated with his work, and never let him escape reprimand. She reminded him of his mother, who had been equally uncompromising over ethical issues. 'Either a thing is true or it isn't,' she had been wont to say. 'It's not something that can be bent or stretched.'

His life experience as a police officer had demonstrated to him many times that his mother had been wrong about that, but Thea made him understand that he wished she hadn't been. Thea taught him that cloudy morality was a cause for regret, and the best people were those who stepped across the grey swamps of laxity without getting their own feet dirty.

Besides, she was lovely, and funny and clever and sweet. She was more than he deserved, but he was resolved to improve himself and earn her love. He smiled daftly to himself, as he watched her putting away the Scrabble board and taking their wine glasses into the kitchen. Only Thea, he thought, could have turned a day that began with such pain and panic into the one where he determined once and for all that this was the woman he wanted to devote the rest of his life to.

But things felt somewhat different when she kissed him a solicitous goodnight and left him alone on the fold-out bed she had found in a corner of her bedroom. She had lugged it down to the front room and made it up with a sheet and a light summer duvet. Wistfully, he watched her disappear with her dog, wondering whether it had even crossed her mind to remain downstairs with him, perhaps on the sofa.

The house-sit was certainly not arduous. There was still a day to go before the snake needed its frozen mice, and the fish seemed content with a pinch of dry food and an occasional check on their water temperature. The horses had each other and seemed to be pleasingly self-sufficient. Remembering earlier commissions, where Thea had been employed effectively to guard the house against unwanted intrusions, he shuddered. Perhaps the slipped disc was a blessing, ensuring he stayed to watch over her until Miss Deacon's brother arrived to take over. Despite there being every sign that this was to be the easiest, most relaxed of all her experiences as a house-sitter to date, he was still very glad to be there with her.

They had learnt almost nothing about the village since arriving. Left to himself, Phil would not have seen this as anything to reproach himself for, but Thea had insisted that she wanted to find out as much as she could of the history of all the places she found herself in. Frampton Mansell and the Cotswold Canal; Blockley and the strange story of Joanna Southcott; Cold Aston and the Notgrove Barrow – they had all been of the most vital interest to Thea, despite the wide range of historical periods and the peculiar people who conceived passions for their little bits of local history. When the name 'Temple Guiting' had first been mentioned, Phil had paused to wonder just what it might have tucked away in its past that would ensnare his girlfriend's attention. It had not crossed his mind until she mentioned it that the Knights Templar might be involved. And, if he had, he would not have been very pleased. The Templars had links with the Freemasons, and since the episode in Cold Aston, Phil Hollis had striven not to speak or think again about that particular organisation.

His back felt tender and battered, as if he had been viciously kicked. Turning over was still frighteningly painful, in spite of the bedtime pain-killer. He tried to force himself to relax, to simply let himself float away into sleep, where nothing would hurt any more and he would awake in the morning to a dramatic improvement. Instead he found himself listening to sounds outside – an owl close by, and the intrusive cry of a fox. Nasty things, foxes, he mused – the more so now they were so prevalent in towns, raiding dustbins and keeping whole streets awake. His Cirencester flat suffered badly from them and he had conceived a profound dislike for the whole species. He remembered Thea's first ever house-sit, over a year ago, in Duntisbourne Abbots, and the cry she had heard in the night. That cry had, as it turned out, brought the two of them together. His leg had been in plaster at the time. *Am I destined to hurt myself every year from here on?* he wondered muzzily.

First light began to dawn around four, and when Phil next opened his eyes, he could discern the beginnings of the day. The fish tanks were gluggling rhythmically on the other side of the room, but another sound had woken him. He could hear a voice, outside the open window, speaking at a normal level.

'His car's still here. That's odd. She said he'd be away again by now.'

'So?'

'So, he can join in as well. Not a problem.'

The first voice was the melted-chocolate-and-double-cream of Big Janey, unless he was much mistaken. And, although there was no suggestion of threat or subterfuge in the calm tones, he felt at an acute disadvantage. His back had stiffened during the brief sleep he'd managed, and he flinched at the prospect of having to stand up or walk. What's more, his bladder was painfully full, which presented him with a new distraction.

'Thea!' he called, as loudly as he could. 'Are you awake?'

Of course she wasn't awake. It was still the middle of the night to her. But he felt justified on at least two counts in doing his best to rouse her. There were people outside, for heaven's sake! 'Thea!' he yelled.

The curtains had not been closed the previous evening, and now, in the thinning darkness, he saw a face pressed against the glass. The heavy jowls of the woman he had met when he first arrived made inhuman pink shapes against the glass. 'Can I come in?' she called, flapping a hand towards the front door. He tried to remember whether the door had been locked before Thea went to bed. He knew her careless habits, her resistance to keys and burglar alarms, and he could not recall any discussion of the matter.

'If you can get in,' he said to the face outside. 'It might be locked.'

'So get up and open it,' she suggested, eyebrows raised.

'Easier said than done,' he confessed. 'And–' he tried to sit up, but only succeeded in making the flimsy bed wobble alarmingly. 'What are you *doing* here? What time do you think it is?'

'Didn't she tell you? I explained it all to her on Sunday. It's the Festival of St Yvo today and your lady friend said she'd like to come.'

'Saint Eevo?' he queried. 'What's that?' He shook his head tetchily on the pillow. 'Thea!' he called again.

'Oh, this is ridiculous,' came another female voice. 'We're wasting time. Janey, I don't know why you have to recruit total strangers all the time. We don't need any more people.'

At last, Thea must have stirred. He heard a thud at the top of the stairs and claws clattering on the stone steps. Hepzibah scratched at the closed door of the dining room and whined. At least the dog had finally decided to investigate, Phil thought dourly. Some guard she was. But then who ever selected a cocker spaniel with a view to being guarded?

Thea's head appeared around the side of the door, her hair wild and her eyes half shut. 'What's the matter?' she slurred. 'What time is it?'

'Your friend's here,' Phil said. 'I need the loo, and it's just after four a.m.'

'Mmm,' she scratched her head and yawned. 'I was having a lovely dream. There was a white bird, with fluffy feathers like fur... You shouted,'

47

she accused. 'Really loud.' She reached out and switched on the light, which changed everything.

Thea looked towards the window, where Janey was no longer visible. Outside had returned to darkness in reaction to the electric light. 'Friend? What friend?'

Then there was the sound of a door opening, followed by footsteps, and Janey stood in the doorway of the room. 'Hiya!' she trilled. 'Have you forgotten about St Yvo?'

'How did you get in?' Phil demanded. 'This is like a bad dream.'

'Charming,' chuckled Janey. 'Listen, I've got Fiona with me, and she's getting impatient. We have to be at the top of the hill by five at the latest. I did tell you all about it,' she said to Thea. 'I thought you were genuinely interested.'

Thea showed signs of dawning recollection, along with the start of a headache. She rubbed the side of her face. 'Oh yes,' she said. 'It's Tuesday already, is it? That was quick. The trouble is–' she waved towards Phil, 'things have changed a bit. I won't be able to come after all. I'm really sorry, because it sounded so interesting. Come back later and tell us how it went, if you like.'

'Is he ill?' Janey suddenly seemed to perceive Phil properly, and to take in the fact that he was lying on a temporary bed in the main living room.

'Hurt his back. Not exactly what we had planned.' Phil wondered whether he had missed a woman-to-woman wink at the end of Thea's comment. Something in Janey's strangled response suggested he might have done.

The other woman, Fiona, was almost obscured

48

from view by the massive Janey, rather to Phil's relief. Two strange women were effectively in his bedroom, putting him at considerable disadvantage. He watched as a hand was laid on Janey's bare arm. 'We ought to go,' urged Fiona's voice. She moved into view, looking intently into Janey's face. 'I did say...' She glanced at Thea, '...it's better without new people. You *will* keep wanting to bring them in.'

Janey waved a hand in a generalised gesture of apology. 'I can see it was a bad idea now,' she said. 'We'll go. Fiona's going to be cross with me otherwise.'

Phil caught a look of exasperation on Fiona's face. She was like a collie rounding up an errant bullock which was suddenly diverted by a patch of lush grass. 'Come *on*, Janey,' she urged. 'We're already late.'

And they were gone, leaving Phil feeling foolish as he clutched the duvet that was all he'd had to cover himself.

Phil never fully understood the nature of Janey's festival, and who St Eevo might be. Hagiography not being his strongest subject, he felt at something of a disadvantage. Thea's temper had been badly affected by the dawn summons, and once she had organised the shuffling trip to the loo and back, she returned to her bed with an injunction against any further demands until eight at the soonest. Phil was left on his narrow precarious bed to try and get some more sleep, hoping in spite of himself that Thea would be lying equally wakeful upstairs. He had taken two painkillers, which worked well enough for him to shift position without anything more than a dull twinge.

Tuesday, he reminded himself. Nearly thirty-six hours since he had hurt his back. Jeremy, his best detective inspector, had said all the right things about his unscheduled absence, during a second phone conversation the previous evening. 'Give it a good rest,' he'd advised. 'That way, you'll be back all the sooner.' Phil had not troubled himself to report the doctor's words about being as active as possible once the worst of the pain was over. He knew that by the end of the week he would be itching to catch up with what was happening, and chafing at missing new cases that he ought rightfully to be overseeing. By then, the main panic about the ricin thing would surely have died down and something else would have moved to the top of the heap. The West Midlands was a volatile region these days, with tensions between the three main racial groups keeping the enforcers of the law on their toes. People tended to forget the large population of non-Muslim Asians: the Sikhs and Hindus, who were getting tired of being tarred as potential terrorists by the hopelessly ignorant whites. Sometimes Phil suspected that it wasn't really ignorance at all, but something much darker. It was as if the whites had been looking for any excuse to release their pent-up bigotry, to attack anybody with a brown skin on the grounds that they looked like Muslims and were therefore fair game. Phil had a neighbour in Cirencester whose parents came from Goa. They were staunch Roman Catholics, but that didn't protect the family from the same scattergun abuse that every Asian was currently vulnerable to. Why, the feeling went, should anybody go to the trouble of sifting out the different groups, when essentially they were all Pakis?

But here he was in the sheltered, complacent Cotswolds, where such considerations were completely ignored as if they were a thousand miles away, rather than a mere forty or fifty. Here, the people were more likely to get passionate about long-forgotten saints than about anything as crude as racial tensions. It was restful, he had to admit, but it didn't strike him as very *real*.

With a quick mental jerk, he caught himself up. Reality existed in these villages just as violently as it did anywhere else. He knew from direct experience that people could kill each other for reasons that might seem daft or bizarre to the urban criminals of Birmingham, but they ended up with the same miserable consequences for those involved.

But not in Temple Guiting, he assured himself. This little cluster of quaintly pretty dwellings, with its trees and gardens and snaking river, was quietly dreaming its summer away, the birds singing and the lawnmowers buzzing. Dawn sounds wafted through the open window, lulling him into a semi-doze that was almost as good as sleep.

But – surely that couldn't be a lawnmower? Perhaps it was a milking machine, from some early rising dairy farm or was it possible that someone had made a very prompt start on shearing a large flock of sheep? He listened closely for a minute. If he had to identify the source of the sound, he would have said it must be a chainsaw.

51

A chainsaw before six a.m. seemed as unlikely as a lawnmower – it hinted at a crisis of some kind. A tree fallen onto somebody, perhaps. The road blocked. But why would anybody want to get through at this hour? Janey, he supposed, and her fellow festival-goers. Perhaps St Eevo was the patron saint of log-fellers, and they had to cut down a tree as part of the ritual. Entirely possible, he concluded with a wry sigh. Just as it was possible that the whole population of the village was surrounding the events in a large circle, hand-in-hand and singing the national song of Finland as the sun rose from behind the hills.

As minutes passed and the sound persisted, Phil was increasingly anxious to know what it was. But he could not call for Thea again, for fear of her anger. So he threw back the duvet and edged his legs onto the floor. The painkillers were still in control, and his legs moved with an encouraging ease. With more difficulty he pulled on some clothes, and then he stood up and walked shakily across to the passageway leading to the front door. It was much better than he had expected. Provided he avoided any jarring to his back, it was perfectly possible to walk normally. An upright posture, with no bends or twists, was virtually painless. He inhaled deeply, and that didn't hurt either.

Opening the door was harder, because there was a catch at knee-level, for some stupid reason, but he managed it without mishap.

Outside, morning was definitely well under way. A pinkish light lit the sky and, where the trees caught it, every leaf was outlined sharp and clear. Just the ticket for an atavistic bit of rural festivity, he concluded.

The chainsaw, if that's what it was, had ceased the instant he stepped outside, but now he could hear shouts and a motor engine revving. It all fitted with his guesses about fallen trees and trapped vehicles. Harder to work out was the exact location of the calamity. It sounded very close – probably only a few yards from where the drive leading to Hector's Nook parted company with the road running through the village.

He walked slowly and steadily, wishing he could simply teleport himself to the place where the noises were coming from. It was akin to the clogged progress in a dream, everything flowing at the wrong pace, the drama unfolding without him, just around the bend. He wished he had a walking stick to help keep himself straight.

But he got there in the end. The chainsaw started up again, for a few moments, and another motor vehicle arrived. When he finally emerged onto the road, he saw to his left a small group of men, one wearing a hard hat, and a four-wheel-drive emergency services vehicle parked close by.

It was far from clear what had happened. Trees cast long shadows across the road, but there was no sign of any injury or damage. He tried to increase his speed for the last few yards. 'Anybody hurt?' he asked, as soon as he was within speaking distance.

A man in fire service uniform glanced at him, and seemed to debate with himself whether to reply. 'Nothing serious, sir,' he said. 'We're nearly done here now – soon get things back to normal.'

The *sir* was a courtesy; Phil had no expectation that the man could have known who he was. He was wearing a black T-shirt and green shorts, and must have looked the part of a local villager to everybody's satisfaction.

'Yes, but what *happened?*' he persisted.

'A tree came down, that's all. A beech – they do that without warning sometimes. A lady reported the road being blocked and urgent traffic needing to get through.' The man pursed his lips. 'Turned out to be something of an exaggeration,' he added. 'But it's all finished with now.'

The man in the hard hat looked mutinous, as he listened to this speech. 'Who's going to pay me, that's what I want to know?' he growled. 'Double time for unsocial hours. Three hundred quid, somebody owes me.'

'Whose land is the tree on?' Phil asked, incautiously.

'Don't you know, sir? Aren't you local then?' the fire officer asked sharply.

'Just staying a few days,' Phil said. 'Heard the chainsaw and thought I ought to investigate.'

The officer narrowed his eyes. 'You don't look too well, if I may say so. Best get back home and catch up with some sleep. The excitement's over for the day.'

And Phil quite naturally believed him.

CHAPTER FOUR

Thea hadn't stirred when he got back to the house, and he slipped indoors unheard. But the temporary bed held no appeal for him, so he sat stiffly at the kitchen table with a mug of tea planning to wait for her to wake. It was still not quite seven, and already the day was well underway. He felt he'd done more than enough thinking already, so he got up and went on an exploration of the house. His back seemed to be coping well with all the exercise, although it lurked like a troll under a footbridge, just waiting its chance to leap out at him and stab him with a renewed agony. In a small back room, where he had not yet been, there were perhaps fifty stacks of magazines, reaching to waist height. Carefully stacked, clean and orderly, it was far from clear just what they were. Unlike books, there were no spines to read, but it soon became apparent that they dated back several decades. Unable to bend or lift, all he could do was browse from one stack to another, examining the top magazine on each one. He grew more excited as it became apparent that this was a seriously valuable collection. *Country Life, The Lady, Homes and Gardens, Horse and Hound* – the theme being rural life throughout the twentieth century. He found copies of *Country Life* dating back to 1904 in a corner stack, and assumed they went even further into the past if he could only explore properly.

There was a desk and chair in the middle of the room, and he took a magazine almost at random and went to sit with it. His back was throbbing and he had difficulty getting comfortable, but soon he was immersed in the property section of a *Country Life* from 1916. He read every word of every advertisement, the great mansions with a dozen bedrooms or more, offered for sums that wouldn't buy a beach hut less than a century later. Where were they now, these houses? A few, he supposed, were still gracing the pages of the same magazine, handled by the same agents. Knight, Frank & Rutley, for example, had survived the intervening years seemingly unchanged. Other familiar names jumped out at him. The Cotswolds featured prominently, then as now, as a place for the rich to live, and he was intrigued to see Temple Guiting Manor, looking very much as he'd seen it the day before, available for rent. He read articles about the War, carefully worded to give no hint of despair or even undue anxiety. Life carried on back home, people bought and sold houses – and a lot of renting out went on, as well, he noted. Families reeling from the loss of their sons, perhaps, suddenly finding the big house too much for them, but loath to sell it outright. It made him think, almost for the first time in his life, of some of the forgotten consequences of such a catastrophic loss of life amongst the land-owning classes as well as the workers.

Thea found him still reading when she came down at eight. 'Oh, there you are!' she said, staring round at the room. 'What are you doing?'

'Did you know all these were here?'

'We're not supposed to touch them. I thought I told you.'

'But they're amazing. You should be thrilled – don't these count as a primary source for historians?'

'Yes, I suppose they do,' she said carelessly. 'Do you want some breakfast?'

Over coffee and toast, Phil told her about the fallen tree and the buzzing chainsaw. 'Did I dream the bit before that, when the Janey woman turned up?' he wondered.

'If you did, I had the same dream.' She frowned. 'Seems a bit weird, two things happening before anybody else was up.'

'I'm assuming Janey called the fire brigade about the tree, which provides a nice tidy connection,' he said, in a policeman sort of voice. 'Although rather a coincidence. It wasn't the least bit windy.'

'And you walked all the way up the drive?' Her tone was accusing. 'With your back?'

'No, no. I left the back behind on the bed.'

'Ha, ha. Well, if you're well enough to do that, you can jolly well come exploring with me today. I don't want to be cooped up here if I don't have to.'

'Which reminds me – isn't it today you have to feed that snake?'

'How does that remind you?'

'I don't know, quite. Something about coops and cages, I guess.'

'So, we'll go for a little walk, OK?'

He sighed. 'If we can go slowly, I might manage

57

half a mile or so,' he said grudgingly. 'But I already feel it's time for a nap. Do you know who St Eevo is? How do you spell it? What did he do? And *why?*'

'They choose a different British saint every month, and have a little ceremony to remember him or her. I was looking forward to hearing the story of St Yvo. Y-V-O. Janey said it would be better coming to it fresh and learning about him from their ceremony than if she explained in advance. She was really quite excited about it. I got the feeling it's her main interest in life.' Phil clicked his tongue derisively, but Thea merely smiled. 'I think it's rather sweet,' she said. 'I assumed, obviously, that I'd be here on my own and glad of a diversion when she suggested it. I don't remember her saying it'd be four in the morning, though.'

'She probably said sunrise, and you thought it would be about six.'

'Probably,' she agreed. 'Silly me.'

'I wouldn't mind going back for another look at that tree later on. We could drive to the top of the lane, to give us a start, and then stroll past on the way into the village. A big old beech it is. They have very shallow roots, you know. Doesn't take much to fell them, once they reach a certain age. The drought will have had something to do with it, loosening the roots' hold on the soil. I assumed to start with that it must have been dead, but it had quite a lot of leaves. The branches were across the road. Somebody's going to have a nice stack of firewood.'

She raised her eyebrows. 'I didn't know you

knew about trees. Shallow roots, eh?'

He refused to be baited. 'I only know about beeches,' he said with all due modesty.

He took another painkiller before they set out on their walk, already wondering whether he was being entirely too ambitious. Thea had refused to drive the short length of the lane, on the grounds that it would be a waste of the effort necessary to fold Phil into the passenger seat and out again. He agreed, with growing trepidation, that the walk presented no real difficulty. 'We can always turn back if you feel it's too much,' she breezed.

When they reached the fallen tree, it looked considerably more dramatic than Phil remembered from his dawn visit that already seemed a long time ago. It had fallen towards Hector's Nook from the opposite side of the road, plainly causing a total blockage for traffic until the chainsaw man had turned up. Several spreading branches had been sawn away and left strewn across the tussocky field in which the beech had been growing. The road hedge had been wrecked, both by the impact of the tree and the subsequent attentions of the man with the saw. Miss Deacon's land faced it on the opposite side of the road and a few twigs lay scattered on the verge that side.

'It must have been very tall,' Thea remarked, impressed in spite of herself. 'Poor thing. And there aren't many leaves. It must have been sick, don't you think?'

Phil was examining the area of the roots, trying to explain to himself just why it had fallen when it did. 'I'd guess it must have been a good forty feet high. It was growing on a slope, look,' he pointed out. 'It can only have been the sheer force of gravity that brought it down. Pity we can't remember what it looked like before. I never even noticed it.'

'Nor me. You don't notice individual trees, do you? Not unless they're really spectacular. How old do you think it was?'

'Probably less than a century. Seventy or eighty years, maybe. They grow quite quickly, I think.'

They had gone into the field through the crumpled fence, led by Hepzie. 'Lucky there were no animals in here,' said Phil. 'They'd all have escaped.' He was carefully negotiating the uneven surface, which sloped upwards in one of the classic Cotswold undulations that gave the region its charm. His back was making more of a protest than he chose to admit even to himself. *Distraction*, he muttered. *Think about something else*.

The tree's roots formed a perfect circle, ripped violently from the earth and seeming to silently shriek at this unnatural exposure to air, as a fish might do. He reached the rim of the shallow crater left behind, a tilted bowl on the side of the slope.

'Hello,' he muttered. 'What's that then?'

Thea didn't hear him, until he made a louder wordless cry, and went stiffly down onto his knees into the rumpled orange-yellow earth where the tree had been standing for so long. She looked towards him, from where she was resting against the smooth horizontal tree trunk, and started up in alarm. 'Phil, what on earth are you doing?' she shouted. 'Come out of there.'

He ignored her until she got closer, and then held up his find.

It was a human skull.

CHAPTER FIVE

'I don't suppose it could be a sheep, or some-thing?' she said with a crooked smile. He gave her a withering look and said nothing. 'No, I thought not,' she admitted sadly. 'Trust you to find it. I don't suppose it's been there for a thousand years, either?'

Phil shook his head, and held the bone at arm's length. 'Still got tissue and hair attached,' he said.

She wrinkled her nose. 'Oughtn't you have left it where it was?'

'Thea,' he said warningly. 'This is serious.'

'I know it is. I understand that. But I still think it's a valid question. You've disturbed the evidence.'

'No more than having a dirty great tree uproot itself and scatter bones everywhere.' He waved a hand, and she began to see white objects spread across an area of some size.

'Oh, yes,' she said faintly. 'I hope Hepzie doesn't take a fancy to them.'

He put a hand to his back and groaned. 'I might react better to black humour if I wasn't hurting so much,' he puffed. 'Have you got a phone with you?'

She shook her head and grimaced. 'Silly of me,' she admitted in all sincerity. 'We might have needed help to get you home again. What'll we do? I could run back and get the phone and the car, while you stay here. I don't suppose it's terribly urgent, is it?' She looked more closely at the skull, which Phil had replaced gently on the ground. 'Weird to think that was somebody's head,' she added, putting an unconscious hand to her own occiput.

'Can you bring one of my painkillers as well?' he pleaded. 'This is really starting to hurt. I should never have done so much walking.'

'Phone, pills, car – anything else?'

'Just get on with it,' he gasped.

She seemed to be gone for ages, as he crouched on the dry grass edging the new crater, feeling like a sentry guarding his grim discovery. The fragmented skeleton would give rise to a concerted police enquiry, however old it might be. As he contemplated the skull, he noticed a break in the temple, close to the left eye socket. A ragged hole had been torn in the bone. 'I hope that wasn't the cause of death,' he muttered to himself. But already he knew that it probably was, and that somebody had killed this anonymous sexless victim, and then buried the body at the foot of a beech tree in a small field on the edge of a village. And he knew that once again he and Thea would become embroiled in a murder enquiry.

It was still barely eleven when the full entourage had established themselves in the little tilting enclosure beside the small quiet country road, erecting canvas shelters and bands of police tape to deter non-existent sightseers. A forensics team brushed delicately at the soil covering most of the bones, like archaeologists excavating a barrow. A police doctor hovered, peering at the skull and the newly revealed pelvis. 'Male,' he said. 'No sign of any clothes. You'd expect some fragments of cloth at the very least. Not wrapped in anything at all, as far as I can see.'

Phil felt his face contract in disgust as his mind painted an image of soil being piled over the exposed skin, finding its way into all the private crevices, vulnerable to the worms and insects that would rejoice in the bounty suddenly presented to them. 'Barbaric,' he said. 'Everybody deserves a shroud of some sort.'

The doctor looked at him and blinked. He was a short bald man, with dark eyes set deep in his head. His presence was required whenever a human body, or even a small part of one, was discovered, so that he could pronounce life extinct. This could sometimes give rise to some sighs at the silliness. Phil knew him of old, but they seldom exchanged more than the briefest professional remarks. 'What are you doing here anyway?' he asked Phil, with a meaningful examination of the stiff back and casual clothes. 'If I might ask.'

'I was here for the weekend, and slipped a disc on Sunday night. It seemed sensible to stay. I'm in an old cottage down there.' He indicated the track down to Hector's Nook.

'Nasty. Were you here when the tree came down, then?'

Phil nodded. 'Must have been in the small

63

hours. I heard the chainsaw clearing the roadway at about six. I came up to have a look.'

The doctor raised his eyebrows. 'At six? With a prolapsed disc?'

Phil nodded ruefully. 'I was awake, and I just thought it warranted investigation. I'd already been woken up at first light, anyway.'

It clearly sounded strange to the medic, but Phil was past caring. Despite the painkillers he was still suffering, and starting to worry that he had caused further strain to the prolapsed disc with his incautious behaviour. Thea had tried to take him back to the house in her car, but he had felt obliged to stay at his post and oversee the police activity. 'They'll expect it of me,' he said. 'Since I'm on the scene already.'

'Well, I'm going to check the horses and feed the snake,' she had said, turning her back on the bones and everything Phil had chosen to protect. 'I can't pretend I'm happy about all this.'

He gave her a patient smile. 'I wouldn't expect you to be,' he said. 'I'm not entirely jubilant myself. But it is my job and I can't simply ignore it, now can I?'

'You're sick,' she reminded him. 'Off duty. Not obliged to get involved.'

'Nonsense,' he snapped. 'That's nonsense and you know it.' He had watched her go striding off to the car and then speeding down the bumpy track and he sighed unhappily to himself.

But the pain and stiffness in his back ensured that he was of very limited use to the investigating team, and it was with profound relief that he realised that another senior officer had been sent to take control of the proceedings. News of his incapacity must have reached the roster clerk, and his name removed from duties until further notice.

A thin brown-haired woman he had never met before arrived in an unmarked car and stepped briskly over the fallen tree to where he was leaning awkwardly against a fence post. She held out a hand, and shook his whole body jarringly as she greeted him. 'DS Sonia Gladwin,' she announced. 'Just shipped in from Cumbria. We'll probably be seeing plenty of each other.' Her accent was strong – Phil suspected deliberately so. He had heard its like a few times, the words formed deep in the throat, with echoes of Geordie in it. An old-sounding timbre, calling to mind sparsely popul-ated uplands and mysterious practices.

'Sorry I can't be more use,' he panted. 'But I damaged my back on Sunday night and it's still bloody painful.'

'And yet you managed to get up and find all this,' she said, almost accusingly. 'Some people can never give it a rest, can they?'

'Right,' he agreed weakly. If he could avoid an argument with her, then he would. It would be madness to begin their professional relationship as adversaries. How much easier, he found him-self thinking, if it had been a man. Thin women could be so intense and restless. He felt a flash of annoyance with Thea for abandoning him as she had and wondered when she might condescend to come back for him. And would she use the car or force him to walk down the steep bumpy track? Self-pity welled up before he could stop it and he sighed.

'Do you need to be taken somewhere?' the new DS asked him with a close look. 'You don't seem too bright to me.'

'I'm in agony,' he admitted without hesitation. 'The house is just down there,' he pointed. 'I ought to be able to walk it, but...'

'Get in the wagon, for Christ's sake,' she ordered.

The *wagon* proved to be a generously sized Volvo, and Phil somehow rolled himself into the passenger seat with only minimal howls of pain. Already he felt more favourably disposed towards Gladwin. 'Thanks,' he gasped. 'It'll only take a minute.'

The two women inspected each other in time-honoured fashion, each slightly amused at how different they were. 'Will you be SIO on this, then?' Thea asked.

Gladwin paused only fractionally to acknowledge Thea's grasp of police acronyms before nodding. 'Just got here from Cumbria,' she said again. Then she kinked one side of her mouth. 'First week, to be honest – but don't tell anyone.'

Phil watched Thea's seduction with mixed emotions. The conspiratorial wink, the rapid relaxation of defences, the offer of coffee all contributed to the dawn of an unlikely friendship. He had to bite back a plaintive *What about me?* as they left him shuddering on the edge of Miss Deacon's sofa, his back feeling like jelly after the exertion of getting out of the car.

'I can't stop,' Gladwin said. 'I ought not to have

deserted my post at all, but...' she looked at Hollis. 'I couldn't just leave him to struggle back by himself.'

'I would have come for him,' Thea said. 'I thought he'd be happy to stay in the thick of it for a while. And I – well, I didn't really see the appeal. It wasn't me who found the bones.' She gave Phil a glance that was close to accusation.

'Right. The bones. What a business! And what a place! I thought I was leaving tiny rural villages behind when I came down here.'

'It isn't like Cumbria,' Thea told her. 'Except for the sheep, I suppose. There are still a fair few sheep around here.'

Phil sat rigidly, afraid to move. He took a shaky breath and said, 'Not been dead for very many years, the doc thinks.'

'Not one of the Knights Templar, then?' said Gladwin easily, with a smile at Thea.

'Hey! You know about them, do you?'

'Not a whisper until about an hour ago. There's a young detective constable at the station who reacted when she heard the name of this place. Her aunt lives here, or something.'

'Don't tell me her aunt's Miss Deacon,' pleaded Thea. 'That's the lady I'm house-sitting for. I'm looking after her brother's snake, as well.'

Gladwin flinched and glanced around the room. *Phobia* was written all over her. Phil found himself wishing quite strongly that Thea hadn't mentioned the snake – which he still had not encountered.

'Don't worry,' said Thea. 'It's not in the house.'

'If I had my way all exotic pets would be

67

banned,' said Gladwin. 'I did my stint in Customs and Excise and saw some appalling cruelty in the trade that goes on. I could tell you some stories...'

'Well, don't,' said Thea flatly. 'And I hate to remind you of your job, but...'

Phil held his breath at this impertinence. His girlfriend was effectively throwing a detective superintendent out of the house.

But Gladwin didn't see it like that at all. 'Gosh, yes,' she laughed. 'I always did talk too much. See you again.' And she was gone, the Volvo speeding up the track in a trice.

'I liked her,' said Thea, as if surprised at herself. 'She's too thin and probably dreadfully neurotic, but she has a good heart. How old would you say she is?'

'Early forties,' guessed Phil carelessly.

'Wedding ring, I notice. Probably some kids. That would explain the thinness. Never has time to eat.'

Phil knew better than to comment. They had had a few tiffs where he defended every woman's right to pursue a career, whether she had children or not, whereas Thea claimed that it was a child's right to have its mother by its side for at least the first four years of life, and preferably rather longer than that. He took another painkiller and wondered why he felt so exhausted until he remembered the insanely early start to the day. 'Can I have a little nap, do you think?' he said. 'Just here on the sofa. If that doesn't sound too feeble to you?'

She gave him one of her softer looks. 'You can be feeble for a bit, if you like. But it is your own fault for walking up there in the first place. I still can't believe you did that.'

'Neither can I,' he said, aware for the first time that if he had stayed in bed someone else would have found the skeleton and he would never have needed to get involved. 'I wish I hadn't, if that's any consolation.'

'Not much,' she said, with another almost-as-soft look.

When he woke up, she was clattering quietly in the kitchen and he wondered whether it could be lunchtime. Outside the crystal-clear light suggested the sun was beating down from directly overhead. He cleared his throat unnecessarily, hoping to alert her to his return to consciousness. When nothing happened, he began an inspection of the state of his back. So far, the pain was no more than a dragging ache, like a large bruise. He dug his elbows into the sofa cushions and levered himself gradually upright. It hurt, but not desperately.

But the floor looked a long way away, and the various reconfigurations needed to achieve a standing position were daunting. He settled himself down again and waited for Thea's attention.

It was some minutes in coming, but she finally appeared carrying a metal bowl in front of her like a church acolyte serving the priest. 'What's in there?' Phil demanded. 'Not dead mice, I hope?'

She shook her head 'It's for the horses. Miss Deacon said they like cut-up apples and carrots every now and then. I found some just now, and thought I should give them a treat. I've done the mice already.'

He looked at her closely. 'Was it gruesome?'

'Not a bit. Mind you, it doesn't seem much nourishment for such a big creature. She'd have been happier with a small dog, I think.' Thea glanced at Hepzie protectively. 'That sort of size, in fact.'

Phil swallowed convulsively, imagining the jaws parting to envelop the spaniel. 'Surely not,' he croaked. 'It can't be as big as that.'

Thea made a circle with the forefinger and thumb of each hand. 'Must be about that big around,' she said. 'Three or four inches.'

Phil made a mirroring circle. 'Nowhere near big enough to hold Hepzibah,' he concluded. 'But we'd best not let her wander into that shed, just in case.'

He felt proud of himself for conducting such a normal conversation without once mentioning his back, or reproaching Thea for not asking after it. He knew he was earning her approbation with the slightly dark banter that they frequently slipped into. She rewarded him with another sweet smile. 'I don't know about you, but I'm more than ready for some lunch,' she said. 'There's French bread and paté, and some olives and red wine.'

'Very Continental,' he approved. 'And look at that weather to go with it!'

'We're having it outside, of course. I'll leave you to struggle up while I go and lavish affection on the horses for ten minutes.'

It was obvious that he didn't have a choice, but the floor still looked too great a challenge. 'Could you find me a stick, do you think?' he asked. 'Something to take my weight.'

'There's one in the hall,' she said. 'Must be Miss Deacon's.' She was gone for a few seconds, then returned with a handsome old walking stick with a rubber shoe and a handle that followed the natural line of the wood – a right-angle that offered a comfortable niche for curved fingers. It was unpolished, with the bumps and knobs where there had been shoots growing in its original state. Phil ran an appreciative hand down its length. 'Strong,' he noted. 'Should take my weight easily enough.'

Thea didn't stay to watch, but hurried out with her bowl, followed by the dog.

Phil swung his legs slowly onto the floor and, grasping the stick, hoisted himself onto his feet. He felt about ninety-five, experiencing an unsettling flash of what it must be like to be permanently slow and stiff and sore like this. Nothing could be done quickly, and a lot of things couldn't be done at all.

Then the phone began to ring out in the hall, and the shock of the sudden noise jolted him, causing a flare of pain down to his coccyx and up to his shoulder blades. He tried to turn towards the door, but found himself paralysed. It seemed desperately urgent that the phone should be answered. Even when on leave from work, he could never ignore a telephone. 'Thea!' he shouted, aware that his voice was drowned by the ringing. There was a second bell attached to the front of the house, he realised, sending unmissable peals across the gravel to the paddock

71

beyond. Thea could not fail to have heard it.

But she had never shared his obedience to telephonic summons, and did not appear until some minutes after it had stopped. 'Didn't you answer it?' she said innocently, when he expostulated.

'I couldn't move fast enough.'

'Not even with the stick?'

'Not even with the stick.'

The atmosphere had soured, and although he tried his best to find something pleasant to say, he knew Thea perceived him as being in a sulk. He forced himself to move to the downstairs loo, and then out onto the lawn, where she brought the promised lunch on a tray.

When the phone rang again, she got up deliberately slowly and calmly went to answer it. A moment later she was back. 'It's for you,' she said.

'Can't you bring it out to me?'

'Nope. It's an old-fashioned, attached-to-the-wall model. You have to go to it.'

Phil gave up. 'I can't,' he said flatly. 'Could you take a message, do you think? Or tell them to call me on my mobile. Do you know the number?'

'Phil, if you can't even get to a phone, then you really oughtn't to be getting involved at all. Why on earth did you give them this number anyway? I'm going back to tell them to leave you alone for at least another three days.'

'I didn't,' he said quietly.

Thea paused, and tossed her head just enough to send the flicked-up hair flying. 'What? You didn't what?'

'Give them this number. I have no idea what

this number is. Who is it on the phone anyway?'

'A man. I thought it must be one of your detectives. He asked for DS Hollis, as if he knew you.' She frowned. 'They could easily have looked it up. That must be it.'

'Anyone from the station would have used my mobile.'

Impatiently, Thea went back to the house and Phil heard her speak briefly and sharply. He couldn't decide whether she was protecting his interests or merely expressing an irritation that had been slowly expanding since dawn. He was feeling more than a little irritated himself, with the sun too hot on his head and his back refusing to allow any easy movement.

Thea came back holding a small square of paper. 'A man called Stephen Pritchett wants to see you. He heard about finding the body and thinks it could be his son, Giles. He knew you were here because Janey Holmes told him on Sunday. He met you once, about twenty years ago at a Lodge Dinner, but doesn't expect you'll remember him. He left his number, and is sorry to hear about your back.'

'Thanks,' said Phil gloomily. 'I do remember him, as it happens. It wouldn't be easy to forget Stephen Pritchett.'

'And did you know his son had gone missing?'

'No.' Phil scanned his memory. 'And I think I would have noticed the name if it had made any kind of splash at the nick. I wonder whether it was ever reported. How long ago was it?'

Thea consulted her notes. 'Two and a half years. Not very long.'

'So, I have to call him back, do I?'

'That's the message,' she said neutrally. 'It's entirely up to you. I warned him you were off sick. I was quite short with him, in fact.'

'Yes, I heard you. I wonder how he knew about the body so quickly.'

'I suspect that was Janey as well. She seems to know everything that goes on around here almost before it happens.'

'Even when she's off burning sacrifices to St Eye-vo?'

'It's Yvo,' she reminded him patiently. 'And nobody said anything about sacrifices.'

'Oh,' said Phil, who had hoped to raise a laugh.

CHAPTER SIX

'Stephen Pritchett must be related to Rupert Temple-Pritchett, don't you think?' Thea remarked, an hour or so later. Phil had not made the return call, and the powerful solar rays had driven them to set up chairs under one of the willows, which gave a flickering shade. The garden was somewhat poorly provided with anything capable of giving full protection against the elements, in contrast to the generous number of trees elsewhere in the village.

'Very likely.'

'Are you going to phone him?'

'I thought he might give up and transfer his efforts to DS Gladwin or one of her team, if I leave it a bit longer. It's out of order for him to phone me privately, anyway. Who does he think he is?'

'Another scion, I expect. Of the pure blood of the Pritchetts.'

'Hmm. My hunch is that there's more kudos in being a Temple, especially these days. Definite resonance there.'

'He didn't have the same way of speaking. Rupert positively *drawled*. Stephen was more normal. Besides, Rupert said there wasn't much status in being descended through the female line, which I suppose means his mother's a Temple and his father's a Pritchett and they made the double-barrelled name when they got married.'

'You sound uncomfortably interested in them,' Phil chided. 'I thought you wanted to stay out of anything unpleasant this time around.'

'I do,' she agreed. 'But this doesn't have to be unpleasant.'

He widened his eyes at her. 'It does if that skull I just found belongs to Pritchett's missing boy. Very unpleasant indeed, I would say.'

'I wasn't talking about *that*. I only meant that this sounds like an intriguing family and I'm a sucker for complicated family connections. That Rupert man obviously wanted to explain it all to me. Maybe this one will as well.'

'Lord save us,' grunted Phil, eliciting a stony look from Thea.

The silence between them was filled by nothing but the distant overhead drone of a plane. It was too hot for birdsong, and scarcely any traffic used the road through the village in early afternoon.

'He isn't normal, though,' Phil said thoughtfully, after a few minutes. 'You said he sounded normal, but he's six foot three and has the broadest shoulders I can remember seeing in my life. Enormous hands and feet as well. The man's a giant.'

'Seems they breed them big around here then,' said Thea.

He was aware that she was restless, chafing at the enforced idleness. Hepzie lay panting on the grass close by, rolling her eyes every few minutes as if wondering when the next amusement might come her way. Thea had not enquired about the state of his back since ... he realised he couldn't actually remember any questions about it that day at all. And, although her very reasonable defence had been that she could see without asking, it would still have been nice to have evidence of concern. He regretted his recklessness of the early morning more than he cared to admit to himself. The resulting strain had set things into reverse, even without the added complications of the discovery of a decomposed corpse. It made him feel guilty towards his fellow police officers, as well as spoiling Thea's week.

'All right, I'll phone him,' he said, half an hour later. 'Could you find my mobile for me, do you think? It'll be in the pocket of my jacket.'

She fetched it without a word, handing him the paper containing Stephen Pritchett's phone number at the same time.

The man answered on the first ring, his voice breathless with what had apparently been a desperate wait. 'Oh, Hollis, at last!' he wheezed.

76

'Sorry to hear about your back, old man. Sounds grim. And look, I know this isn't kosher – calling you in your hideaway – but I hadn't any choice. You'll understand when I explain. Could I come over, do you think? I'm only a few miles away.'

'What, now?'

'If you're there. I won't get in the way of your lady friend. I could tell she wasn't too impressed, and who can blame her? But I want to just fill you in and help you see why it has to be like this. I remember you, you see. You always struck me as very straightforward. Not like some of the crooks we had on the square in those days...' He chuckled briefly at some distant memory, before lowering his voice again. 'Sorry. I've been knocking back the Old Peculiar a bit since I heard the news. Always makes me flippant.'

Phil knew the drink in question was not ale, but the best imaginable Scotch. He wanted to make a remark about driving under the influence, but wasn't given a chance. 'I'll be fifteen minutes,' said the man, and rang off.

'We've got a visitor,' Phil told Thea. 'He'll be here in fifteen minutes. Sounds like a retired Army Colonel, but I don't think he was in the military. I seem to remember there was something medical about him.'

Thea's mood was unusually hard to judge. She sighed minimally and made no move to leave her garden chair. An open book lay beside her on the grass, but she showed little interest in it. 'You don't mind, do you?' he said.

She sighed again, more loudly. 'Not much use me minding anything, is it? I'm trying not to

77

indulge in any expectations for this week, if you must know. So far, I've got the weather on my side, which is something to be thankful for.'

'And me,' he said childishly. 'You've got me, when you thought you'd be here on your own.'

'Yes, I've got you.' She gave him an unsmiling gaze, and he remembered his joyful proclamation of love the previous day and her lack of response. He had assumed she was pleased, that the feelings were reciprocated, but now he was less sure. She seemed withdrawn – silent and serious. He felt judged by her, given marks out of ten several times a day for the way he handled his damaged back and the unwelcome intrusion of violence and local characters. Which, he couldn't help thinking, was quite unfair of her. After all, hadn't that Janey woman been in the house when he'd arrived on Sunday? Hadn't Thea agreed to go on some crackpot outing to celebrate some unknown saint, without even telling him? Anxiously, he reached out and grasped her hand. 'We're all right, aren't we?' he asked. 'Tell me everything's all right.'

But before she could respond, a large red Mitsubishi Warrior crunched down the track, and Hepzie gave an uncharacteristic volley of barking, and Phil never got his reassurances.

The massive body of Stephen Pritchett emerged briskly from the vehicle and looked around for someone to greet him. 'Here!' called Phil from behind the willows at the corner of the house. Thea had made no move.

'Good Lord, poor old you,' boomed the man when Phil apologised for not getting out of his chair. 'Nothing worse than a bad back. Lucky for me I've got no first hand experience. Imagine trying to shift this carcase around on a board!' He laughed shortly.

He engulfed Thea's hand in a careful shake, and returned his attention to Hollis. There was an implication that he expected Thea to disappear, which she ignored. 'I gather a body's been found,' he began, once he'd settled himself in a canvas chair. His manner and appearance were transformed completely from one minute to the next. Folds of drooping flesh appeared beneath his eyes, and his cheeks grew mottled.

'No use denying it,' said Phil. 'Although I'd like to know how you found out. The police haven't issued a statement yet.'

'You can't close a road and erect police tape without word getting round. Besides, I'm known to have an interest. There was a conclusion drawn more or less instantly.'

'Which was?'

Pritchett sighed shakily. 'Two and a half years ago my son, Giles, went missing. He was eighteen. Just vanished overnight, with no warning.'

'Did you report it?'

'No. We had our reasons not to, believe me.'

'Wasn't that very odd? If there was no prior behaviour to suggest he might be planning to go off – why in the world wouldn't you report it?'

Pritchett shook his big head and glanced fleetingly at Thea. 'Not so simple. We assumed he was in trouble, you see. Drugs or something. We thought he'd gone into hiding, and if we sent out a search party for him, it could backfire – see him

79

landed in gaol, even. His mother could never have dealt with that. We never seriously thought he might be dead – not until just a few months ago, that is.'

'Did you know for sure he was involved in something illegal?'

'We betrayed him,' mumbled the man after a long pause. 'We believed badly of him, when there wasn't the slightest evidence. Just the word of a silly girl who didn't know what she was talking about.'

'I'm not sure I'm following this,' Phil said impatiently. 'If I didn't know better I'd think there was some sort of hold over you. You sound like a parent whose kid's been taken for ransom and they're scared to involve the police.'

Pritchett smiled tightly. 'No, that wasn't it. There was never any suggestion of a ransom. But we did get the idea that some shady characters might be after him.'

Thea could not restrain a snort at this. Both men looked at her in outrage. 'Sorry,' she said. 'But *shady characters* – isn't that something you've read in a spy novel?'

Pritchett's tight smile flashed again. The fact that he said nothing revealed more of his mental state than anything he had told them. He was holding himself in, Hollis judged, keeping his temper and patience despite the provocation.

'Thea – I'd go if I could move – but as it is, can I ask you to fetch us something to drink? Tea, lemonade, anything that comes to hand?'

'This isn't our house, you know,' she said.

'No, but just the same, I'm thirsty.' Phil

straightened his neck and gave her a look that he hoped said *Stop behaving like a teenager and let me and this wretched man get on with it.* Something of his meaning must have got across, because she went off without further argument.

'Sorry,' muttered Pritchett vaguely. 'P'raps I shouldn't have come.'

'Well, now you're here, why don't you start again and tell me the real story this time?' Phil said. 'I think we've got ten minutes or so before Thea comes back.'

'It was a family thing,' the man muttered, almost in a whisper. 'That's the long and short of it. We couldn't involve the police without exposing a lot of very dirty washing. My wife would have paid that price – but I wouldn't allow it. I've suffered for it ever since. Don't go thinking there's anything criminal in the boy. It isn't that at all. It's his *mind*, you see. He was always very unpredictable. Probably attention deficit syndrome.'

Phil narrowed his eyes. 'You're a doctor, aren't you? You make it sound as if it's something quite outside your area of expertise.'

Pritchett puffed out his cheeks. 'Believe me, my friend, it is. I've only ever been a sawbones. I can replace a hip joint before you can sing two verses of "Onward Christian Soldiers", but when it comes to the psychological stuff, I'm completely at sea. Plus it's different when it's your own offspring.'

Phil could think of nothing to say to that. He merely adopted an open expression, inviting further disclosures.

'The boy – Giles – was very fond of his great-grandpa as a little chap. My grandfather, that is. Lived to be ninety-eight, as sharp as a scalpel to the end. Phenomenal memory and quite a scholar. He knew all there was to know about the Templars, when it wasn't a bit fashionable. Anyhow, he fed Giles all this stuff when he was ten or eleven. You know how keen boys get on stories about battles and betrayal and blood feuds when they're that sort of age. Grandpa had this idea that we're direct descendants of one of the Knights – which he managed to prove to general satisfaction. Giles was delighted to have the same blood running through his veins, and got quite boastful about it.' Pritchett sighed. 'I could never see what the fuss was about, for myself.'

'Harmless enough,' Hollis suggested. 'After all, everybody wants to know who their ancestors were, these days. Gives them roots, I imagine – that sort of thing.'

Pritchett nodded. 'Except it turned out the blood feuds had never really gone away. Your Miss Deacon comes into the story, too, silly old bat. You'll have noticed her crazy collection of old magazines and so forth?'

Hollis nodded.

'Well, a lot of it has to do with the Templars through the ages. And she got our young Giles very much too interested for his own good.'

Hollis thought of the stacks of *Country Life* magazines and other similar titles, and frowned. 'I couldn't see anything like that,' he said. 'Nothing going back further than about 1900.'

'You didn't look hard enough,' Pritchett told him. 'It's all there, mark my words.'

'But how does this lead to Giles going missing? Was that stuff about drugs just a smokescreen for Thea's benefit?' Phil frowned sternly. 'If so, I should tell you off for wasting my time.'

'The boy was eighteen,' said Pritchett. 'Of course he was taking drugs. But not enough to worry us. My wife was a child of the Sixties herself – rich and reckless, is how she describes herself as she was then.' He heaved a deep sigh. 'Not like that now, of course.'

'I still don't–'

The man's face reddened. 'Look, Hollis – I can't say much more. All I wanted was for you to find out whether that body was – is – Giles. If it is,' he swallowed painfully, 'then I'll have to come clean. But if it isn't, then I'd have said too much. Do you see? And, to be honest with you, I think it's unlikely. I only came to set Trudy's mind at rest. He takes after her, you know. What they used to call "highly strung", both of them.'

Phil shifted position, with agonising consequences. The radiating streaks of red hot fire occupied all his attention for half a minute. 'Not really,' he panted. 'I don't really see at all. But I'm not on duty, and I would much prefer not to be having this conversation.'

'Sorry. I can see you're suffering. I take it there's no likelihood of a visual identification?' He swallowed again.

'No,' Phil agreed. 'It'll have to be teeth. You might let us have the name of his dentist?'

'Not DNA?'

'Only as a last resort, I would think, although it won't be my decision. DNA tests cost money.

Besides, we'd have to have a sample of someone we think it could be, for comparison.' Phil was still panting, holding himself rigid. It felt exactly the same as it had on Sunday night, and he was gripped by despair at the prospect of inactivity for several more days. Maybe that hospital medic had been wrong. Maybe he'd be like this for the rest of his life. And Thea would dump him – that was obvious. She didn't love him enough to saddle herself with an invalid for the next thirty years. And who could blame her?

Pritchett brought him back from his gloomy thoughts. 'His dentist was in Stow. A private chap. I'll write it down for you.' He took out a small notebook, wrote in it and tore out the page. Phil had time to wonder at a man who carried such a thing in his inside pocket before Thea came back with a tray.

'I made iced tea,' she said. 'Sorry I took so long.' She looked probingly from face to face. 'Back still bad?' she asked Phil.

He nodded and tried to smile.

'I won't stay, if you'll excuse me,' said Pritchett. 'I think we've finished.' He stood up, looming over the others. The top of Thea's head came to his sternum. 'Oh – one more thing,' he said. 'It might help to know that Giles is very tall. Six foot five, poor lad. And just in case you do need DNA, I could give you this.' He held out a small white envelope. 'Some strands of his hair. We've still got a brush he used when he lived with us.' He chewed his lower lip fiercely for a moment, as Phil took the hair. 'So I'll be off then.'

Phil nodded, and lifted a hand in a complicated

signal of comradeship and acknowledgement and farewell.

When he had gone, Thea said, 'Did you notice he said *is?*'

'Hmmm?'

'Giles *is* six foot five. He doesn't believe his son is dead at all.'

CHAPTER SEVEN

After two more painkillers, Phil was able to creep back into the house at the end of the afternoon. The radio, which Thea switched on in the kitchen, told them it had been the hottest June day for fifty years, and Phil felt some burning on his nose to prove it. And it was expected to be at least as hot the following day.

'Imagine living somewhere that had these temperatures all the time,' said Thea. 'Would you ever get used to it?'

'I had a few weeks in Australia just before I got married,' he said. 'Queensland. Everybody wears shirts and ties. The women wear tights even when it's eighty or ninety degrees. At least they did then. I bet they still do.'

'What a waste. And now they're all terrified of skin cancer, so they keep the kids indoors all the time. We won't go and live there then.'

'No,' he agreed. 'I think we can safely say we won't.'

'But a nice relaxed island, where you don't have

to wear anything, would be all right. Where you wake up to bright blue skies, and the evenings have just a hint of a sea breeze.'

'Shut up,' he said affectionately. 'We've got it all right here. Be content with what you have.'

'I am,' she said. 'Although I'm getting very bored with your bad back.'

'So am I,' he said emphatically.

The little fold-up bed looked somehow forlorn as it waited for him in the living room. Narrow and fragile, it seemed to emphasise his disabled status as nothing else could. 'Can't I use Miss Deacon's room?' he wondered. 'There's a single bed in there.'

'I can think of at least two reasons why not. First, you can't go upstairs for at least another day or two. Second, it would be an outrageous impertinence to sleep in her bed without permission. How would you like it?'

'We'd change the sheets. She would never know. She might think it was her brother, if she did notice anything.'

'Well, there's only...' she counted on her fingers, '...five more nights to go, before Archie takes over. You can manage down here until then.'

'Five more nights!' It felt like an eternity.

'Well, maybe you'll be miraculously restored before then. Stop anticipating the worst. And shouldn't you have contacted that SIO woman, whatever her name is, and told her about Stephen Pritchett? I didn't hear what he said to you after I left, but I'm sure it was something she should know about.'

'Don't tell me my job,' he flashed. Then quickly, he amended, 'Sorry, but I know what I'm doing. I'm going to call tomorrow and ask to see the pathology report from the post-mortem. I doubt they'll have done it yet.'

'Post-mortem? On a heap of bones?'

'Right, right.' He smiled. 'Probably not the right word for it. But the pathologist will have found out all he can. In the light of that, I can feed in what Pritchett told me – or not. If the deceased was a man in his fifties, of short stature, I don't have to say anything at all.'

She frowned. 'That sounds a bit iffy. As if you're protecting him from something.'

'No, no,' he sighed. 'Nothing like that. I'm sorry, love, but I'm too wrecked to talk about it any more.'

She helped him into the bed, and within seconds he'd fallen asleep. It was a quarter to nine. The last thing he was aware of was the sound of curtains being closed across the window.

He woke shortly after midnight, the red figures of the digital clock on the DVD player keeping him informed of the time. His back had roused him, protesting sharply at an unconscious movement. He lay as still as he could, thinking of Thea overhead, curled up with her dog, sleeping blissfully. He couldn't blame her for feeling frustrated at his sudden disablement. It was not the week she had planned, after all. Except, he reminded himself, the plan had been for him to be back at work, and Thea left alone in the house. Surely, he thought, it was a bonus for her to have his company, even if he was so useless physically. Was her disgruntlement purely because they couldn't have sex?

The three large fish tanks in the room gurgled relentlessly, and a dim red light had been left on behind one of them. In the midnight hours, every sound was magnified, and the room felt far too noisy for proper sleep. He thought about the discovery of the dead man under the fallen tree, and wondered exactly how it could have got there. It seemed a peculiar place to bury a body, with the roots obstructing any digging. Probably there had been some sort of natural cavity between two roots, which had looked like a ready-made grave. He remembered just such a tree near his boyhood home, in a park. He and his friends had used it as a secret hiding place for their treasures, tucking packets and messages under the thickest roots. But a body was a far larger proposition, and would have to be much more effectively concealed, not least because foxes and badgers and even dogs would quickly have located it and dug it up again unless it was thoroughly covered over.

He tried to visualise the wider terrain: the angle of the slope where the tree had grown, and the distance from the road. The body must have been uphill from the tree, on the side furthest from the road. When the roots had torn themselves away, the resulting crater had been at least three feet deep in places, and the bones were mostly buried lower than that. It had, after all, been a pretty efficient burial, then. A burial, he recalled, of a naked man – which suggested forethought and planning beyond a hasty panic-stricken disposal of a man killed in error. Possibly some of the roots had been chopped through to create a good-sized hole. It was even possible that this had weakened the beech, bringing about its collapse as the forces of gravity worked their inexorable way with it.

He reran the disjointed, patchy tale that Stephen Pritchett had told. The man had only revealed the fragments he thought would suffice to persuade Phil that he feared the body might be that of his son. Because, he realised, if the body was *not* that of Giles, then he, Pritchett, did not want any further enquiries to be made by the police. The resulting delicate tightrope must have required enormous care, and Phil searched in vain for any mistakes. The reference to drugs had been clumsy, and probably solely for Thea's benefit. The corrected version, once she had gone into the house, focused on family disagreements and vague worries about mental illness. Pritchett would know how slow the police could be in searching for adult individuals who went missing of their own volition. 'After all, sir,' Phil himself had said many a time, 'it isn't illegal to run away from home.'

His next conscious thought was many hours later. Sunshine was filling the room, despite the closed curtains, and there was a smell of toast and coffee. He squinted at the DVD player, blinking in disbelief that it read 8.55.

'It can't be!' he said.

At the sound of his voice, Hepzie appeared, jumping half onto his pillow, thrusting her soft nose into his face. The air turbulence caused by her furiously wagging tail was dramatic. 'Oy!' he protested. 'Put me down!'

Thea appeared from the kitchen, holding two large mugs of coffee. 'Awake at last,' she observed. 'I thought you were dead.'

'Alive and kicking,' he said calmly. 'I can't believe it's so late.'

'Best of the morning's behind us already.' She moved to open the curtains, pausing to gaze out at the hills and trees visible from the window. 'I wonder how Janey got on with St Yvo yesterday. I should phone her and ask. I really would have liked to go along.'

'Well, why didn't you? I wasn't stopping you.'

'Yes you were,' she said, without reproach.

'You have her number? Just how matey did you two get before I turned up?'

She shrugged. 'Not especially. She told me a bit about Miss Deacon and the village. She was born between here and Guiting Power and knows just about everybody. It was nice of her to come and see me.'

'Just being nosy, probably. Wondering what a house-sitter looked like. What does she do for a job?'

'She's a farm secretary. Works for most of the farmers in the area, filling in all those forms they get, and working out their tax returns for them.'

Phil tried to imagine the great body wedged into the tiny cobwebby corners that most farmers called the farm office. In his various investigations over the years he had encountered quite a few of them. Even in the affluent Cotswolds where farms had mostly mutated into huge industrial complexes producing grain to the

90

exclusion of nearly everything else, there were scattered family operations still surviving. Besides, even the big ones tended to skimp on office accommodation.

'So where does St Yvo fit in?'

'Just a hobby, I think. Miss Deacon's one of their circle as well – did I tell you that? She was very sorry to miss this month's ceremony, but she's going to lead the whole thing next month. That's going to be St Kenelm on the seventeenth.'

Phil looked at her. 'I'm amazed.'

'Why?'

'Because you remember the name and the date. But I have heard of St Kenelm, you'll be surprised to know. He's got a well and a footpath near here, if I remember rightly.'

'Well, you're one up on me, then,' she admitted. 'But Janey says he was quite a character–' She paused as if afraid of boring him. 'A young prince, foully murdered, apparently.'

'Well, I am genuinely interested in hearing more,' he said, 'but first I've got to get myself out of this bed. Let's see how the back's shaping up today.'

'I didn't like to ask,' she smiled. 'I thought you might have forgotten about it.'

'Very funny.' He swung his legs onto the floor and shifted his weight. 'So far, so good,' he reported.

Thea watched until he was on his feet and taking reasonably normal steps across the room. 'It's going to be even hotter today,' she said. 'We'll have to go out somewhere with some shade.'

'Right,' he agreed, intent on monitoring his

pain levels. 'This really isn't too bad,' he said. 'Surprising what a good long sleep will do.'

'Well, we'd better make sure you don't overtax it this morning, then.'

Something in her tone alerted him. Suddenly he understood that it wasn't primarily the slipped disc that she was cross about – it was his dawn walk of the day before. Somehow that made him feel better – she was blaming him for something he had wilfully done, and not for the unavoidable accident on Sunday night. He might have known, of course. Thea was seldom unreasonable in her apportioning of blame.

He paused and met her eyes. 'No,' he said. 'And I'm really sorry about yesterday. I was very stupid.'

'Yes, you were,' she said, with an expression that warmed his heart.

Breakfast was taken outside, Miss Deacon's horses invisible on a shaded patch behind their barn. Thea described her morning tasks, performed while Phil was still asleep: checking water, patting noses, watering plants, peeping in at the snake.

'Those fish tanks are noisy in the night,' Phil said mildly.

'I imagine they are. But they can't be turned off. I've got strict orders about that.'

He knew when to drop a subject, and concentrated on his toast for a minute or so.

'Um – that hole in the skull...' Thea began. To Phil's own surprise he found himself washed through with relief. He met her eyes and waited. 'It might have been what killed him, don't you think?'

'Quite likely, I'd say.'

'Something heavy and sharp? I keep visualising a pickaxe, for some reason.'

He had not expected her to be thinking about their find, other than as an annoying interruption to their week together. He smiled drily. 'It could have been the exit wound from a bullet. I can't say I examined it very closely. But I think I'd have noticed a corresponding entry wound. So yes, something like a pickaxe might have done it.'

She frowned in distaste, but pursued the thread she'd started. 'Like Jael with the tent peg. Except that went right through and pinned him to the ground. There'd have been two wounds then, as well.'

He screwed up his face in exaggerated apprehension. 'Sorry, but you'll have to explain who it is you're talking about.' Admitting ignorance was not usually difficult; they both accepted that she knew more about literature and the arts than he did, in the very nature of things. His knowledge of human nature came from direct experience, he sometimes reminded her, and not from books, and she was mostly gracious enough to avoid any hint of competition.

Now she simply smiled and explained. 'It's a story in the Bible. A woman called Jael betrayed a soldier – he might even have been the general of the whole army, I can't remember that bit – from the enemy camp, by inviting him into her tent, and then driving a spike through his head when he was asleep.'

'And is she considered a traitor or a heroine?' he asked, looking at the fresh slice of toast he'd just started buttering.

'Opinion's divided, I think. Although she was celebrated at the time, because the war was won thanks to her.'

'Nasty story, anyway,' he said.

'Sorry. I'm being ghoulish. I wonder whether it really was Giles Pritchett. When will we know?'

He liked the *we*. 'I'll phone Gladwin later today and see if the report's through by then.'

'Won't she be cross when she hears you've spoken to Mr Pritchett and not told her?'

'Don't worry about it,' he said again. 'I know what I'm doing.'

She pursed her lips at the implied reproach. 'We need some shopping doing,' she said. 'I thought it would be interesting to try the local shop. They run it as a cooperative, you know. Very unusual. And I gather there's some controversy about it. It's all on the Internet.'

'Isn't everything?'

'Surprisingly not, actually. You'd never know anything about the history of Guiting Power if you relied on Google, for example. There are still great glaring gaps, which have to be filled by books or word of mouth.'

'Do you want to tell me about the history of Guiting Power? Assuming it's different from Temple Guiting.'

'Briefly, yes. There was a woman called Moya Davidson in the 1930s who bought up a lot of the properties and set up a trust so there would always be affordable houses for young people. It's made a huge difference ever since. Janey told me all about it.'

'And this Moya person's not on Google?'

'Not as far as I can see, no.'

'But the shop in Temple Guiting is?' He was humouring her, parodying an interest which in reality was lukewarm. It didn't matter that she understood this. The point was that they were sitting together in the morning sun, relaxed in spite of his back and the discovery of a mouldering skeleton less than a quarter of a mile away. At their age, given his line of work and the general state of the world, they could scarcely hope for more, and they both knew it.

The trip to the shop, which should have been a pleasant stroll, had to be done by car. Phil lowered himself into the passenger seat, and tried to let the upholstery take the strain, with only partial success. The muscles around the offending vertebrae would not let go enough for him to sit comfortably. As they turned out of the drive they both glanced back to the scene of Phil's discovery, noting that a small SOCO team was still in evidence, police tape still zig-zagged around the plot and a large vehicle parked on the verge.

When they arrived at the shop, he insisted on getting out. In spite of himself, he found he wanted to see how the villagers conducted their retail experiment.

The shop was down a small side road, which was shaded on one side by tall trees. The bow window of the shop front gave it a Dickensian air, spoilt by the red Post Office sign above the door.

Inside there were well-stocked shelves and a tiny Post Office in a far corner. Fruit and vegetables in modest quantities were the first wares to be seen as they went in. It proved something of a challenge to find provisions for the coming evening meal, however. 'Lucky I brought my own dog food,' muttered Thea, as she did a double take on the price on one of the few tins on offer.

'It's not claiming to be a supermarket,' Phil muttered back. 'What do you expect?'

He could see she was itching to get into an argument about shopping practices, and deliberately headed her off with a loud, 'I do like the way everything's laid out here,' which amply served the purpose. A friendly but slightly scatty woman served them. When Thea asked whether they sold shampoo, there was a moment of wild panic before the item was located. Phil stood back, examining an unusual arrangement of small wooden drawers, containing assorted items of hardware such as shoelaces and buttons. It made him think of earlier times, as did almost everything about Temple Guiting.

On leaving, with a disappointingly small bag of purchases, their way was blocked by the towering bulk of Janey Holmes, who gave them an unsmiling look. Her face seemed drawn, her step leaden. Phil recalled the lightness of her tread on Sunday and wondered at the difference.

'How's your back?' she asked him.

He did his best to stand straight, but couldn't help putting a hand to the point of worst pain. 'Improving slowly,' he said. 'The doc said to keep moving, but it isn't easy.'

'How did St Yvo's thing go?' Thea asked. 'I was sorry to miss it.' Only then did Phil become aware that Janey's friend Fiona was standing in her lee, quite invisible until she stepped out and smiled coolly at him and Thea.

Janey shook her head bemusedly, as if the question was too irrelevant to be taken seriously. But she managed to reply. 'Not brilliant, to be honest,' she said. 'Was it, Fee? That fallen tree messed things up a bit for us. Made us late.' She narrowed her small eyes until they almost disappeared in the surrounding flesh. 'Pity we came down to you when we did. It must have happened in those few minutes we were at Hector's.' She sighed windily. 'Why it had to happen just then, I don't know.'

Phil digested this. 'You think the tree came down while you were at our place?' he queried.

'I know it did. We drove along the road at ten to four with no trouble, and when we tried to get back at quarter past, there was a dirty great beech in the way. We called the fire brigade, there and then.'

'You know what we found, later on, of course?' Thea spoke quietly, glancing around for listeners in the small street.

Janey and Fiona each gave her a look. 'Oh, yes,' Janey said, as if half choked. 'It was on the news last night – didn't you see it? Not so nice for the village. Makes the St Yvo ceremony seem quite trivial. He is one of the sillier saints, in any case. Fiona likes him, for some reason.' She smiled affectionately down at her friend, to neutralise her words and seemed to gain succour from the returning smile. 'He's more of a myth than any of the others,' she went on, with less hesitation than

97

before, 'and no suggestion he was martyred. Polly Deacon and I wanted it to be a rule that they all have to be martyrs, but now and then a few others get included. He was just a dead body.'

Thea gave a short laugh. 'Just a dead body?'

Janey looked aghast at her own thoughtless words, and clapped a hand over her mouth, like a young child. 'Oh, gosh – I shouldn't have said that, should I?' Again she looked to her friend for support.

'It's true, though,' said Fiona. 'No harm in saying it.'

Janey seemed to relax. 'Well, that's all right, then.'

'You did promise you'd tell me the whole story,' Thea prompted, much to Phil's despair. All he wanted was to sink into the car and be driven home. But not one of the three women appeared to notice.

'Go on, tell her,' encouraged Fiona. 'You know you want to.' Phil heard an intimacy in this that caused him to make a fresh mental note.

'Oh, all right then. Come over here a bit. We'll be in people's way.' They moved across the deserted little street to a wall opposite, where large trees shaded them. Phil unashamedly leant against the wall, letting it take the weight off his spine. 'Well, it goes like this,' Janey began. 'A body was found in the year 1001 near Huntingdon, and for some reason made a big fuss of. Perhaps it was to do with the date – new millennia do odd things to people. Anyway, there must have been a special casket – or something of that sort. They reburied in at Ramsey Abbey and called it St Yvo, thinking it must have been the famous foreign bishop of that name who'd arrived four hundred years earlier. Fiona likes the mystery around it. How did they come to remember him for so long? And what was it about the body that made them think it was him?'

'Gosh!' Thea breathed. 'That's a splendid story.'

Fiona laughed. 'They're *all* splendid stories. That's the whole point. I know it all sounds a bit daft, doing them every month, year after year – but it's important not to forget them.' It was as if she'd waited patiently for Janey to have her say, and now it was her turn. She seemed to expand, wanting to be noticed. Phil realised that he still had not properly looked at her. She was only an inch or two taller than Thea, probably four or five years older. If she was free on a June Wednesday, then it was tempting to assume she was not engaged in full-time employment. But he had learnt better over the past decade – people, especially in this area, worked at home on computers, and could clock up a forty-hour week following all kinds of strange schedules, that enabled them to go shopping in the middle of the morning with no trouble.

But he was intrigued enough to want to stay with the subject of this weird saints thing. 'So what exactly do you *do* for the festival?' he asked. 'Dig up bodies and bury them again?' The echoes of what had taken place the day before were too strong to ignore. 'And why does it have to be at four in the morning?'

Fiona was all forbearance. With a glance at Janey that clearly said, *Let me handle this, dear* she explained, 'We have a little march, from the east, which is where Yvo came from, just as the sun is rising. He had two companions with him, and we've written out a little playlet acting out the local people's reaction. It was the seventh century – the Dark Ages. He was very exotic, dark-skinned, they didn't know what to make of him. Imagine it. Then he died and they gave him a special burial – we made a cardboard mausoleum for that – and then *four hundred years later* some-body finds it and a saint is born.' Her eyes glowed. 'We find it all very moving,' she concluded.

'Are you Catholics?' Thea asked suddenly. 'I mean – they're the ones who have saints, aren't they?'

'We have one Catholic, two Anglicans and seven or eight others who aren't religious at all. Janey and I are in the last group. It's about history and society and human beings, not religion. I'm an historian by profession, and so is Polly. Janey's our inspiration – she's so passionate about the stories and the heritage they carry with them. You realise she's from the original Templar blood, don't you?'

'Um...' said Thea. 'No, actually.'

'Oh yes.' Fiona seemed fired by a personal pride in this fact.

'Hush now,' Janey murmured, with a glance towards the shop. Nobody seemed to be taking any notice of this odd little gathering under the trees. 'No need to go into that. You know it only causes trouble.' She looked at Thea. 'You're an historian, too, aren't you? That's why we thought you'd be interested. You see–' Again there was a

100

glow to her, a rising passion, 'every one of the saints we celebrate has a message for us today, if you know how to read it. The same as fairy tales do.'

'Ah!' said Phil. 'Now I'm beginning to understand.' All three women looked at him with annoyance at the unveiled sarcasm.

'Sorry.' He held up his hands. 'So when was the saints and martyrs club actually founded?'

'Twelve years ago,' Fiona said promptly. 'Midsummer's Eve. It all started as a bit of a game, in a way. We had a retired vicar living in the area, and he was keen on old British saints. Robin discovered St Alban, who was nicely martyred in about 300 AD, and we re-enacted the whole thing.'

'Lovely,' said Phil dryly. 'I suppose the village children got to throw the first stones.'

'He wasn't stoned. He was beheaded. It's no worse than burning Guy Fawkes every November. Some of us feel quite strongly that the old stories of violence and abuse of power have something to teach us today.'

'Oh,' said Phil, wondering just how she worked that out. 'All your saints came to gruesome ends then, did they?'

'Provided we can find one that fits. Sometimes we have to make do with something a bit tamer, like Yvo.' The eyes went dreamy. 'For some reason, I really do love St Yvo.'

Phil refused to be drawn. 'What happened to Kentwyn?' he asked. 'Isn't he next on the list?'

'Kenelm. You mean St Kenelm. Well, the stories vary, but we prefer the one where his jealous

101

sister murdered him. Raises some useful issues about sibling rivalry, you see.'

He had been just about to snort derisively when he realised she was teasing.

'Come over to my place this afternoon,' Janey suddenly invited. 'Both of you.'

Phil remembered that the woman had been at Hector's Nook when he'd arrived. She had latched onto Thea almost from the outset and still seemed intent on maintaining the connection for some reason.

'Thanks,' said Thea quickly. 'That would be lovely. What time? Where are you?'

Janey gave her the details, and then continued on her interrupted progress into the shop. Phil noted that her tread was still sluggish, her shoulders bowed. 'She seems sad,' he said softly.

'But she's got Fiona to watch out for her – and Miss Deacon, as I understand it.'

'Probably the whole village rallies round her. She might be a kind of mascot for them.'

Thea gave him a considering look, as if wondering how to react. He reran the words in his head, checking them for inappropriateness. To his relief, they both seemed to think he had said nothing too bad. All the same, he was left with a sense of irritation that such monitoring should be required.

'We didn't see the local news, did we?' Thea changed the subject. 'It never occurred to us to watch it.'

Phil felt the familiar shudder that always came with the realisation that much of his work was subject to media and public scrutiny, often making everything much more complicated. What and when to feed the news people was a central issue in police investigations, with a dedicated individual handling the whole matter in large cases. And yet it had not occurred to him that the television news would report his find so quickly.

'None of us said anything about the missing Giles Pritchett,' he noted.

'Nor directly about the body. I think Janey finds it too upsetting.'

'Maybe she's related to Giles.' He had a strong sense of a back story that needed to be told, involving these throwbacks to the Middle Ages, with their Templar ancestry and recurring surnames. That Rupert chap had called himself a 'scion' as if it was important. The missing Giles had grown up with the Templar stories from his great-grandfather and a proud belief that it was personally relevant to him. There was sure to be a cache of genealogical tables somewhere, demon-strating just how it all worked, and who was the bearer of the crucial genes. But how did it bear on the death of a man years ago? There was no hint of a connection, and yet Phil could not help thinking there had to be one. The expressions on the faces of Pritchett and Janey, if nothing else, implied that this death was important to them, and they would very much rather it had stayed hidden under the uncooperative beech tree.

Just before they got to the parking area at Hector's Nook, Phil's mobile went off. He answered it while still sitting in the car, mouthing *Gladwin* at Thea, who raised her eyebrows and remained sitting in the driving seat.

The Senior Investigating Officer spoke succinctly, summarising the report from the pathologist.

'Of course he's not finished, by a long way,' she began, 'but this is what he's found so far. The deceased was male, naked, of medium height, aged somewhere between late thirties and early fifties. No obvious signs of disease or old injuries. We're testing for residues of drugs and other substances. They're still examining the scene, with scarcely anything to show for it so far. He was buried in soft soil, about two feet down.'

'Is that enough to keep foxes and so forth away?'

'Barely. It looks as if a layer of dead wood was placed over the grave, which would have helped.'

'Why not go deeper?' Phil wondered.

'Lack of time. Tree roots in the way. It's quite stony, too. Plus we can really only guess at most of this from the effects of the uprooted tree and the slope of the bank. It seems a peculiar place to choose, although the tree would have concealed the whole thing from the road.' She was almost babbling in her hypothesising, painting a picture that Phil knew would stick in his mind for quite some time.

'So, probably not a vagrant,' he concluded. 'How long had he been dead?'

'Impossible to say for certain, but the pathologist thinks around five years.'

'Not Giles Pritchett, then,' said Thea, when Phil related these details to her.

'Not Giles Pritchett,' he confirmed. 'Which leaves me with something of a dilemma.'

'Oh?'

'Whether or not to call the anxious father and put him out of his misery.'

'Not to mention the invisible anxious mother.' Thea's tone was bordering on the flippant, and Phil gave her a probing look.

'You don't appear to care very much,' he observed.

She sighed. 'I care in *theory*,' she said. 'But I can't pretend to take it very personally. Anonymous dead person found, not the missing son of worried village couple. It's a bit of a non-story, somehow.'

'Never say that,' Phil warned her earnestly. 'It's never a non-story. Each man's death diminishes me, remember.'

Thea sighed again. 'I know. Normally I'd be the first to take that line. But somehow I can't help feeling that the real tragedy around here has to do with something other than those bones.'

'You mean Janey,' he said slowly.

'Yes,' she nodded. 'Yes, I mean Janey.'

CHAPTER EIGHT

'How do they date the age of a skeleton anyway?' Thea wanted to know. 'I mean, the time since it died.'

Phil shook his head. 'I'm not familiar with the precise procedure, although I was sent on a course a while ago which filled us in on the latest forensic stuff. There are all sorts of ways, especially when the body's been buried outdoors. It involves insects and plants and worms. Are you sure you want to know?'

'I can probably imagine for myself, if I put my mind to it. It's quite interesting, isn't it? I suppose the calcium leaches out of the bones at a specific rate, so you could get a good idea by measuring how much was left,' she suggested. 'I mean, a very old bone is all white and brittle, isn't it? And marrow – the marrow must all dry up and disappear. I rather like bones,' she added thoughtfully, her eyes on her own bare arm.

'That's because your dog likes them,' he teased.

She ignored the remark. 'I always wanted to have the bones after Sunday lunch. I would suck them for ages and carry them around with me. My mother used to get furious.'

'Disgusting,' he smiled. 'She should never have allowed it.'

'She tried not to, but I was too devious for her. I hid them in my pockets.'

Phil made an exaggerated grimace. 'That's *really* disgusting,' he protested.

He had been about to pick up the phone to call Stephen Pritchett when Thea had asked her question about bones. Now he achieved his goal, and was not surprised when the man answered before the second ring. The image of him sitting like a faithful dog watching the instrument was an unhappy one.

'It isn't Giles,' he said, quickly. 'It's somebody older, who's been dead for around five years.' He shuddered at his own breach of security in imparting even that much information. Why, he asked himself, was it so important to set Pritchett's mind at rest? Could it possibly be the old Freemason bond, still operating in spite of everything?

'Ah.' It was less of a word than an emotional exhalation. 'Thank you.'

Phil was greatly tempted to leave it there, to let Giles Pritchett slide back into whatever fragile oblivion he had found over the past two and a half years, and get on with his own unexpected holiday with Thea. After all, Giles's disappearance was two or three years after the body had been hidden under the tree, which strongly suggested that it had nothing to do with that event. But he was too much of a professional to allow himself to let it lie.

'I can't leave it at that, you know,' he said gently. 'Something's wrong, isn't it?' It was a foolishly trite way of expressing the unease surrounding Giles, but it served its purpose.

'Wrong?' Pritchett attempted. 'In what way?'

'I mean, Giles is still missing. And he could still be dead somewhere. Couldn't he?'

'His mother–' Pritchett began. 'I only came to you because she wanted it. She'll be all right now you've set our minds at rest. Please, Hollis, just forget I ever approached you. He's got nothing to do with any of this business. I ought to have trusted my own judgment from the start. I knew all along – well, never mind that now.'

'Well, all right,' said Phil reluctantly. 'But at least put him on the missing persons register, if only for your wife's sake. Any news must surely be better than none.'

'That's true,' Pritchett said softly. 'You know,

sometimes I don't even feel sure that I ever had a son. I can't picture his face any more. But other times I know he's out there, not too far away. I can feel his presence, if that doesn't sound too airy-fairy for you.'

Phil closed his eyes, and the features of his own dead daughter floated vividly before his eyelids. Always smiling, with that flickering mischief that had been her trademark, hair never quite tidy, waist as slim as a pencil. Surely it would never be possible for the picture to fade from his mind?

'Well, think about what I said, and don't be shy of reporting him missing.'

Pritchett cleared his throat, suggesting embarrassment to Hollis, even down the phone. 'Look, old chap – the fact is I haven't been completely straight with you. He hasn't been missing for as long as I said he was. We did get word of him once in a while, up to last Christmas. He sent us a card, as it happens. But you know what it's like now – no proper postmarks any more. We couldn't see where it had come from. But it was enough to ease our minds. But that was six months ago, and Trudy's getting desperate.'

Phil shifted in his seat, trying to placate the grumbling from his spine. 'So she thinks he could have been killed sometime this year and buried under a tree? Why tell me he'd been gone for two and a half years then?'

'Well, it was true, in a way. That's when we last saw him. And besides that, I thought you wouldn't listen otherwise. Why should you go to the trouble?'

'Well, we like to have any theories about

108

identity when a body turns up. It wouldn't make any difference how long your son had been gone, if you thought there was a chance he was the victim.' Phil's mind was thick with puzzlement. This solid member of the community, Freemason and senior doctor, was playing the sort of game with the police that was more typical of a petty criminal. 'You could have been a lot more straightforward about it, surely?'

'What I told you about our betrayal of the lad was true. We don't intend to make the same mistake twice. All we need to know is that it's not his bones you unearthed yesterday. What's so strange about that?'

'It's strange that you should ever think it might be him. The usual procedure when somebody dies is to have a death certificate and a marked grave and announcements in the paper. You actually believed your son could have been murdered and buried a mile from his own home, with nobody knowing anything about it. Doesn't that sound strange to you?'

He heard a long sigh of frustration coming out of the phone. 'Things *are* strange here,' he said. 'I thought you might have realised that.'

Phil felt this as a put-down, and wanted to give a riposte that reminded the man that he was a senior police detective, a person to be taken seriously, with powers to make life uncomfortable for anybody he chose. But he clamped his lips together until the urge had passed.

'Well, I've given you the news, such as it is,' he finished. 'Now we just have to hope there are other people around who can be of more assistance to us.' A thought struck him. 'I don't suppose *you* have an idea who the dead man is – given that it isn't your son?'

There was a long silence. Then a low 'No' came through, before Pritchett put down the receiver.

It was lunchtime and Thea had concocted an appetising meal from the items bought in the village shop. The sun was relentless, turning the day into something almost frighteningly hot. 'More like Greece than Gloucestershire,' said Phil. He had removed all clothes from his upper half, and periodically fanned himself with a magazine he had borrowed from Miss Deacon's collection.

'Be careful with that,' Thea had warned him. 'You shouldn't take it out of the house.'

'I know, but it's so fascinating, I can't put it down.' He read her a paragraph from the June 1912 issue of *Country Life*, describing a garden party held by a certain baronet and his wife. 'It's a completely different world,' he sighed.

'That's right. Now can you see why I get so excited about history? And that's a primary source you've got there. There's nothing so thrilling than delving about in primary sources.'

Phil looked thoughtful and slightly pained. 'But yesterday you just waved it away as if you couldn't care less,' he reminded her.

'Oh, did I? Sorry.'

'Emily used to do that. Just when I thought I'd got to grips with what interested her, she'd roll her eyes and tell me I'd got it all completely wrong. Very unsettling it is when women can't be consistent for two days together.'

Thea's reaction to the mention of Phil's dead daughter was subtle. She nodded, and pressed her lips together and said nothing. What could she say, after all? Phil knew he was allowed to talk about Emily any time he liked, and there had been one or two long evenings when he had indulged in an orgy of grieving memories, weeping into Thea's shoulder as he described the child he had seen all too little of, as he worked up the ladder of police promotion. He would always blame himself for her death, for not spending more time with her. He had believed it was enough simply to adjure her to abjure drugs, rather than sit down and debate the issue properly. He had never accepted the peer pressures, the need she must have had to find a substitute for her absent father. She had thrown herself into a wild social life and had died stupidly from taking too many Ecstasy tablets, ignoring her body's warnings. For a time, he had thrown himself passionately into a war against all drugs, only to come slowly to understand that Em had been a rare exception, that Ecstasy very seldom killed anybody, and that random luck was the major factor at work in what had happened.

Thea had helped him to see this, little by little, along with her own stalwart daughter Jessica, who never minced her words.

But he had inwardly winced when Stephen Pritchett had mentioned drugs in connection with his missing Giles. He would always wince at any reference to a dead or missing youngster associated with substance abuse. He wanted to prevent any parent enduring what he had endured, but even more he wanted to avoid enduring it again himself. Which he did, vicariously, every time the subject came up.

He set aside the painful memories and kept his mind on Pritchett. 'He's been playing some sort of game that I can't get a handle on,' he said to Thea. 'Obviously the village rumour-mill got going as soon as the police showed up at the beech tree – and it's not surprising that somebody let slip there'd been a body found. A phone call to Pritchett and he's onto me five minutes later. The question is – how much do the local people know about what happened? When I think of the way Janey and her friend were this morning, it feels very much as if they've already agreed amongst themselves not to talk about it.'

'A conspiracy of silence,' said Thea in a melodramatic voice, refusing to be repressed. 'You'll have to apply to the Home Office for permission to torture the truth out of them.'

'Thea!' His warning was seriously meant, the limit of his patience finally reached. 'Sometimes you really do go too far.'

'Sometimes,' she flashed back, 'you don't know how to take a joke.'

'I can promise you there isn't a police officer in the country who would find that comment funny. Not a single one.'

'Well that just proves my point,' she said obscurely, and walked off into the house.

Phil refused to shout after her, despite a desperate urge to do just that. She would be back in a little while, the whole thing forgotten. One of the things she had taught him over the past year was how to let bad feelings go. She never sulked or harboured a grudge. Despite their differences over the politics of law enforcement, their feelings for each other always resurfaced un-damaged. Or they had done so far. Always, there was a lurking anxiety that this time it might change. This time one of them might find it impossible to fully forgive and forget.

He forced his mind back to the subject of Pritchett and the other villagers, visualising them standing in a circle around the unearthed bones, every one of them potentially implicated in a murder. He mentally listed the possible scenarios that had been suggested by what he knew of the place and its people. An ancient family by the name of Temple, connected, apparently, to the renowned Knights who had owned land on this very spot. It was likely, surely, that they would fight to protect the name and all its associations. Secondly, there was a strange club devoted to keeping alive the memory of obscure saints by re-enacting parts of their stories. Stories which were almost always violent. Saints tended to meet gruesome ends, their martyrdom comprising much of the attraction, as he understood it. Thirdly, another family, named Pritchett, whose son was lost, and whose patriarch denied any knowledge of who the dead man under the tree might be. Finally, an unexplained visitor whose name embraced both local families and who spoke as if he existed in a time warp. It amounted to a hazy sense of bygone times still exerting a powerful influence. Tucked away in these folded hills, funded by activities largely conducted in a

113

virtual reality, the people he had so far encountered appeared to have the time and freedom to pursue their passions uninterrupted by the usual contemporary constraints. They did not rush for early trains to London, or juggle childcare and shopping and housework and aged parents like most people did these days. They spent a few hours at a computer keyboard, made a few phone calls and money fluttered down on them from the sky. Property deals, futures, currency trading, even buying and selling goods on eBay – it all brought in cash with almost no physical effort. Phil found the whole business bewildering and close to offensive. This, at least, was a point of agreement between him and Thea.

Thea did come back, her usual sunny self again, and they sat for a little while in the flickering shade of the willows. The subject of Stephen and Giles Pritchett refused to go away. 'So,' Thea summarised, 'for all we know Giles is still alive and well somewhere. And you don't have any proper grounds for trying to find him.'

'That's right.' Phil sighed. 'It's a familiar feeling – the nagging sense that you know where the explanation lies, but you can't follow it up because there's no hard evidence to justify it.'

Thea nodded, with a small crinkling of her brow. 'And it's Gladwin's case, not yours,' she said. 'Don't forget.'

DS Hollis smiled in genuine amusement. 'She's welcome to it,' he said. 'But unfortunately it doesn't quite work like that. I'm involved, whether I like it or not. I'm here on the ground, and people are going to talk to me every time I show my face outside this house. And Gladwin's at even more of a disadvantage than usual. She's new, and there's much too little back-up for her, with all this ricin business taking up everybody's time.'

'Chances are it'll turn out to be a tramp that nobody missed, when it comes to it,' Thea said. 'Killed miles away and randomly dumped here. Nothing to do with the good people of Temple Guiting after all.'

'Even if it is, it still has to be thoroughly investigated. They'll be going through all reports of missing persons, trying to match him up. Tedious business. And of course you can't trust anything anyone says about events five years ago. We might never have an identity for him.' He paused. 'But Pritchett's given the game away, don't you see? By coming to me as he did, he more or less told us he thinks it's a local matter. Something must have been going on here, bad enough to involve murder and secret disposal of the body.'

'Oh, well.' She tossed her head, the long hair flying lightly, her expression sceptical. 'Why don't we go out somewhere before we have to be at Janey's? Can you cope with a drive, do you think?'

'I can if it's in a good cause. Where did you have in mind?'

'Naunton, or maybe the Slaughters. Both if you can stand it. I thought I might take some photos.' She fished for her new digital camera and brandished it. 'I told Jocelyn I'd try to get some shots that she can use for her folksy cards. She's really getting into it this summer.'

'Folksy,' Phil repeated. 'Is that your word or hers?'

'Oh – mine. She thinks they're fine art. She's being ever so clever with montage or collage, or whatever she calls it. I can email the raw material to her, and she plays with it on her computer. She's got some amazing software.'

'And people buy the result, do they?'

'Evidently. She's got a contract with three or four places, including one of the London museums. You know how people always buy cards, if nothing else, in those gift shops.'

Phil liked Jocelyn and worried about her. Thea's younger sister, she had five children and a tormented husband who behaved very badly at times, although the last Phil had heard there were signs of real improvement. It was pleasing that she had found an outlet that sounded both absorbing and mildly lucrative.

'Good for her,' he said. 'I suggest we do Naunton first and see how it goes. Backwise, I mean.'

'OK – but I would like to make a little detour to Lower Slaughter, if there's time. Did I tell you I had an email yesterday from somebody wanting a house-sitter there in the middle of August? There's several animals and the house is medieval.'

Phil groaned. 'No, you didn't tell me. I suppose you've already said yes?'

'Well, I told them I was probably free,' she said. 'Why wouldn't I?'

Phil spread his hands speechlessly, and found himself thinking that with Thea's track record, a place called Slaughter was probably very appropriate.

His slipped disc behaved moderately well, with only one seriously agonising moment when he turned too quickly to follow Thea's line of gaze. Naunton was unarguably lovely, in the hot afternoon sun. Shadows were deep, and he was impressed by Thea's skill at using them in her compositions. 'Waste of time, really,' she said when he commented on one of her efforts. 'Joss can remove them completely if she feels like it. It's like what you said about five-year-old memories – you can't trust the camera remotely these days. Nothing is as it seems in the finished picture.'
'Except I don't suppose she can create shadows where there never were any, can she?'
'I'm not sure. Probably.'
'You should send her some shots of that snake. That'd add an exotic element,' he suggested.
Amicably, they mooched around the little settlement of Naunton in the sweltering heat. They encountered scarcely any other people, and not a single dog. 'They've got more sense than to be out in this,' said Phil. 'I'm glad I brought my hat.'
'I love it,' Thea said, as if slightly surprised at herself. 'It's exactly right for a holiday.'
'Except you're not on holiday – you're working. And I'm on sick leave. We shouldn't be enjoying ourselves.'
She stared at him, trying to read the level of seriousness behind his words. They shared a thread of puritanism which made them uneasy if life was proving too enjoyable. 'I'm sure it won't

last,' she said eventually. 'It never does, does it?'

They drove slowly eastwards the few miles to the Slaughters, and found themselves behind two well-filled charabancs. 'Touristy here,' Phil commented. 'Much less peaceful.'

'Well, that would make a nice change then,' said Thea determinedly.

Janey Holmes lived in a handsome Georgian house standing on elevated ground overlooking the Windrush. 'My God!' Phil breathed. 'Does she have all this to herself? I thought she was just – well, certainly not landed gentry. Look at this place – it's incredible.'

'She was married,' Thea remembered. 'She told me that on Sunday. Must have been his.'

'And got to keep it as part of a divorce settlement?' Phil was sceptical. 'Who was he – MD of British Aerospace, or what?'

'We'll have to ask her, won't we?'

Again they had used the car to cover the mile between Hector's Nook and Janey's house. There were two cars standing with their noses to a high stone wall, wisteria cascading along it, the mauve flowers almost finished.

'I've seen that one before,' Phil observed, frowning at a big red Mitsubishi.

'Isn't it Stephen Pritchett's?' Thea suggested ingenuously.

He smiled. 'Doing my job for me again,' he acknowledged. 'Where would I be without you?'

'I got a better view of it than you did, that's all.' How could he not love someone so casually generous, so uncompetitive and honest, he wondered fondly.

Janey let them in, quickly declaring that Stephen Pritchett was a fellow visitor. 'I gather you and he have already met,' she added.

They followed her through a large square hall that contained the stairway. The ceiling was two storeys above their heads, light flooding through a window that Phil suspected might be termed a 'solar'. There was a seductive scent of summer flowers and beeswax. Everything gleamed as he looked around at the solid antique furniture and two bright modern paintings hanging on the wall above the stairs.

'Lovely house,' he said, in all sincerity.

'And gorgeous *things*,' contributed Thea.

'Yes,' said Janey. 'I'm very lucky.' Her tone implied that she felt rather otherwise, but was uttering the words expected of her.

Phil had the word *bovine* nudging at his mental tongue, but it actually didn't fit Janey at all. For all her weight and bull-like neck, she was not slow moving, nor slow thinking. Bovine only in the sense that a Cape buffalo was bovine, he corrected himself. The most murderous animal on the African continent, which could eye you thoughtfully, chewing a rhythmic cud, and then casually blast you into Kingdom Come with a sudden thump from the horn across its brow. Phil liked Cape buffalo a lot, and conjectured that this Janey Holmes person might demand the same sort of respect. But she was too fat to be seriously respected, his politically incorrect self insisted. Her body was *her*, when it came right down to it. It was within her power to alter it to something

119

more acceptable. He found himself engaged in a circular internal argument which grew more and more uncomfortable as he walked behind the woman, marvelling at the sheer quantity of flesh. He could hear the mocking voices of male colleagues, the carelessly unkind things they would say about Janey if they saw her, the crude jokes about her as a potential partner in bed. However strenuously the arbiters of behaviour might try to outlaw the very word *fat*, he knew there would never really be a better way to describe her.

She led them into a genuine original Regency conservatory at the back of the house, where a hundred potted palms and vines and fruit trees crowded the cluster of chairs and low table into a small clearing against the house wall. It ought to have been unbearably hot on such an afternoon, but all the windows were open, and the huge plants offered shade. A fan whirred exotically overhead, making Phil think of India or Singapore in the 1930s. He might not be as good a reader as Thea, but he had consumed the works of Somerset Maugham at one time, and suddenly found himself inside one of those stories.

A classic country garden could be glimpsed beyond, between the fronds and flowers. Stephen Pritchett was slumped easily in a wide cane chair, but jumped briskly to his feet as the newcomers entered. Thea was sandwiched between the two giants, looking like a fragile child as a result. Phil had to repress a smile, as his hand was seized and shaken by Pritchett.

'I'll go and get the tea,' Janey said. 'You can chat amongst yourselves for a few minutes.'

'We meet again,' said Phil to Pritchett.

'So it seems,' the man nodded. 'Janey's a hospitable soul. Likes to share this place with the less fortunate among us.' He smiled weakly, knowing that it was a poor joke to characterise himself in such a way. 'Funny, though, how little one's material wealth matters in the end. We cling to it so tenaciously, terrified of losing it – or even a bit of it – and yet it can't really shield you from tragedy.'

Phil could see Thea shaping up to disagree and decided to give her a free field. 'But surely it cushions things?' she challenged. 'After all, if you were homeless and addicted to drugs and in trouble with the police, and then one of the only people you love disappears or dies, you'd be utterly annihilated. There'd be nothing left at all. If you've got a house and a bank balance and a car and a passport, you can find some sort of consolation for your misery.' She looked at him. 'Sorry – I expect that's a bit rude of me, but I do think it's true.'

'I find, my dear,' said Pritchett ponderously, 'that it doesn't do to make comparisons when it comes to suffering.'

Thea was visibly shaken, and Phil badly wanted to wrap his arms around her. 'I am sorry,' she said again. 'I spoke without even thinking.' She looked slightly wildly at Phil. 'I forgot,' she said in a thick voice. 'I actually forgot Carl while I was saying all that.'

Pritchett raised his eyebrows, silently asking Phil for elucidation. 'Thea's husband died, two years ago in a car accident. We've all had our

121

share, I suppose.'

'But you're right,' Thea told the big man. 'It's wrong to make comparisons.'

They retreated from painful matters for the few minutes until Janey returned pushing a wheeled trolley loaded with a Worcester tea service, cream cakes, homemade biscuits and a dish of perfect glossy strawberries.

'Wow!' breathed Thea.

'Good old Janey,' chuckled Pritchett. 'Always knows how to make a person feel better, eh?'

The sheer unapologetic *style* of the surroundings rendered Phil speechless. He would never have imagined there were still people who lived in this way. And hadn't Thea told him the woman was a farm secretary? With all the images of muck and disarray and financial hardship that went with his idea of farming, there was a discrepancy that was causing him a growing unease.

'I thought I'd show you some of the background to the Saints and Martyrs,' Janey said, addressing Thea, once the tea and food had been duly distributed. 'I've got quite a good collection.'

'Saints and Martyrs?' repeated Phil. 'Is that what you call your club?'

Janey nodded. Pritchett uttered a melodramatic groan. 'Oh – she's got you onto all that nonsense already, has she? Sometimes she can be exactly like the Ancient Mariner, boring your socks off with her silly old saints.'

'I don't think they're silly,' said Thea, gravely. 'I think Janey's right, and they have a lot to tell us. If nothing else, they give us insights into how the medieval mind worked.'

Pritchett blew out his cheeks in a wordless acknowledgement that he'd been told off.

'Pre-medieval in most cases,' Janey corrected her. 'But thanks for the support. I knew you'd be interested as soon as I met you.'

Thea smiled sceptically. 'Only because you already knew from Miss Deacon that history was my thing.'

Pritchett groaned again. 'Polly's even worse than Janey about it.' He looked to Phil for some backing. 'I mean to say – grown women charging about the countryside pretending to slaughter some forgotten character from a dusty history book. It's not natural.'

Phil admired him for sticking to his guns, despite Thea's obvious disapproval. 'It's typically British, though – don't you think? Harmlessly eccentric. And it does seem a good idea to try to preserve some of these old stories.' He preened slightly at his own diplomacy – surely everyone would calm down now?

'It's not just women anyway,' Janey muttered. 'There's Robin. *And* Jasper, when he's in the country.'

'What about Rupert Temple-Pritchett?' queried Thea, making her usual meal of the name. She giggled. 'I love saying that. Rupert Temple-Pritchett,' she said again. Then put a hand to her mouth with a look at Stephen. 'Oh – he must be related to you? Sorry.'

Stephen Pritchett was watching Janey with a look of real anxiety, and Phil concluded that Thea had said something very much not to their liking. 'Um,' said Pritchett, confusedly, to be interrupted by a very forced change of subject by Janey. 'Let me show you my collection,' she said with a limp smile. 'Much more interesting than trying to work out the local family trees.' She shot Pritchett a look that clearly said, *Don't talk about it any more.*

Thea turned to Phil. 'Are you coming as well? It sounds interesting.'

He hadn't intended to. The seat was comfortable, and the tea not quite finished. It seemed a pity to leave Pritchett all on his own. But then he caught Thea's glance and began to lever himself out of the chair.

Janey escorted them into a room that could only be termed a library. A large Victorian desk occupied the middle of the floor, and shelves filled two walls. 'Most of these belonged to my grandmother,' Janey said, waving at the books. 'Duller than ditchwater, some of them. But these are anything but dull. They're the ones I wanted to show you.' She tapped a shelf on which stood a row of brown-covered volumes that looked to Phil every bit as uninteresting as their neighbours.

Janey took one down, and proffered it at Thea. *'Lives of the Saints – January'* she read. 'By S. Baring-Gould.' She shook her head slightly, to indicate lack of recognition.

'It's an amazing achievement,' Janey explained. 'Sixteen volumes. Nobody had made such a thorough job before. It took him years – though not as many as you might think, considering all the work that went into it. Grandma inherited them from her father. All first editions of course. And some of the entries are terribly funny. I read them to cheer myself up.'

Phil watched as Thea opened the book at random. It was as if the reference to Rupert had never happened, the whole incident skilfully swept away. '*S. Pega, V. About AD 718,*' Thea read. '*After her brother's death, she used all her endeavours to wear out her life for the love of Christ by still severer austerities. She therefore undertook a pilgrimage to Rome* – da-da-da – *and she there triumphantly departed, on the sixth of the ides of January.*' She looked up. 'What does the *V.* mean?'

'Virgin,' said Janey automatically. 'It's the *Ms* we try to stick to: Martyrs. Let me see that. I don't remember her.' She took the book from Thea and re-read the half-page. 'I suppose she might count,' she murmured. 'British, and ended up dead.'

'Don't they all end up dead?' said Phil, who was already wishing he'd stayed in the conservatory.

'She killed herself deliberately for the love of Christ,' said Thea. 'Isn't that a bit weird? Doesn't the Church disapprove of suicide?'

Janey flapped an impatient hand. 'Oh, we don't ask questions like that. It's the *story*, don't you see? Can't you *feel* the wit behind those few words? You've never heard of Baring-Gould?' She seemed to find this a source of some regret. 'He was a most interesting man. Incredibly energetic.'

'If there's a story like that on every page for sixteen volumes, I can see why you find it all so exciting,' Thea smiled. 'I can almost see St Pega trekking down to Rome in bare feet, not eating anything, and *triumphantly departing* once she got there. Silly creature.'

'Yes!' Janey enthused. 'But I have to admit

they're not all that good. You opened it at a lucky page. There are quite a few dull old bishops who did nothing to warrant sainthood. Even so, there's plenty to keep us going. At least Fiona thinks so. I'm beginning to think we've done all the best ones.'

'You're talking about your club?'

'That's right.' Janey hugged the book to her massive chest, like a beloved pet.

Phil found himself quite unable to share their glee. 'I think I'll go back to Pritchett,' he said. 'Splendid collection, Janey,' he added, glancing around the room. 'Must be pretty valuable, too. Hope you're fully insured?'

'Phil!' Thea protested. 'Stop being such a policeman.'

He forced a smile. 'Sorry. But as a policeman, I think I ought to go and talk to a man who's lost his son. Don't you?'

'Don't you dare!' flashed Janey, shocking in her sudden anger. 'Not in this house. I don't allow any talk like that here. It all has to be kept nice, do you see?' she continued on a softer note. 'I like to maintain a feeling of a haven from all the horrors of the world outside. Is that too much to ask? Besides, Giles isn't really lost. Everyone knows that. He certainly isn't ... *dead*.' She forced the word out as if it physically hurt her to do so. 'So please don't talk about anything so horrid any more.'

Phil wanted to stop and cross-examine her, demand to know what she meant and what evidence she might have for saying what she had. Instead he fixed his gaze on the book in Janey's hand, full of stories of violence and death. 'OK,' he said, and walked stiffly out of the room.

'Sounds as if you got told off in there,' said Pritchett when Phil went back to him. 'Janey can be a bit funny sometimes. We do our best to humour her. Everybody loves Janey, you see.'

Phil took the hint, at least for the moment. 'So,' he said, lowering himself gently into his seat, 'who owns this place then? Did Janey manage to get it as a divorce settlement?'

The question bordered on the impertinent, he knew. But having been reminded of his status, he found himself firmly in policeman mode.

Pritchett showed no sign of offence, but shook his head vigorously. 'Nothing to do with the Holmes chap. She's got more to worry about from he-who-must-not-be-named. You saw the way she froze when your lady friend mentioned him. I won't say any more now, but there's a whole bucket of worms under the carpet where that bloke's concerned.'

Phil glanced at the door. 'Really? Surely he doesn't own the house?'

Pritchett also looked at the door. 'No, no. There's a trust that was set up forty-odd years ago by Janey's grandad. It's got all kinds of conditions and so forth – I don't know the whole of it, but for the time being, she lives here rent free, all the maintenance taken care of so long as nobody rocks the boat.'

'Sounds too good to be true?' Phil cocked his head. 'Trusts usually have some sort of bad news attached to them as well, in my experience. Those conditions sound a bit ominous.' He looked around at the flamboyantly anachronistic conservatory. 'Does she have to keep everything just as it was in 1933 or something?'

'Something like that,' Pritchett nodded quickly, as if seizing the suggestion. 'But then – we're tucked away from the hurly-burly here anyway, aren't we? Might as well be 1933 as far as we're concerned. Your terrorists in the big city don't worry us here.'

Phil looked at the man, ducking his chin as if to peer over non-existent spectacles. He had remembered, as if waking from being hypnotised, that he and Pritchett had spoken of matters that should by rights have been relayed to DS Gladwin in connection with the unidentified body.

'But you know as well as I do that nowhere's immune,' he said softly, aware that Janey might object to what he was going to say, if she heard him. 'And I'm sorry, but I can't pretend I've forgotten the conversation we had only a few hours ago. I still don't like to let it all drop.'

Pritchett wrestled visibly with conflicting emotions. His eyes skipped from side to side and a frown drove a vertical crease between his eyes. 'I told you – leave it, man. No good can come of it now.'

Phil snorted impatiently. 'I ought to have reported everything you told me about your son. Instead I let myself get distracted.' He shook his head as if to clear it. 'I don't really understand why.'

'What's a day more or less?' said Pritchett easily, taking a sudden new tack. 'Nobody's going anywhere, after this long time. Leave it until your back's better, why don't you? Enjoy the extra holiday while you can.'

Phil's head felt tight with frustration and self-reproach. But they *might* be going somewhere, he thought to himself. Once the news had got out that the bones had been found, the killer might have gone into hiding. This case, he thought, was like no other he'd come across. Far too little pressure from any direction on the police to solve it. The media had virtually ignored it, there were no relatives howling for closure, no chief constable threatening dire consequences if it was not cleared up immediately. And yet there was a sense that the village was only pretending to be unconcerned. A vibration in the air, a sense that everyone was studiously looking the other way or eagerly chattering about some other subject, instead of taking due notice of the bad smell right under their noses.

'Don't talk about it here,' Pritchett said in a quiet but steely voice. 'Janey will tear you into shreds if she hears you. Pass it on to the chap in charge, if you must.' He sighed. 'But it won't get you very far, I can tell you that for nothing.'

Chap? Did Pritchett not know that the Senior Investigating Officer was a woman? Had nobody interviewed him? He shook his head. Why would they? Without a name for the dead man, there were all too few questions that could meaningfully be asked. There would be no door-to-door enquiries in a straggling village like Temple Guiting. Only Janey and Fiona, who reported the fallen tree, and the owner of the field – and Phil had no idea who that might be – containing the beech tree could expect to be interviewed.

The visit had given them a mass of things to talk about, rather to Phil's relief. The house; Janey's resistance to anything 'nasty'; Pritchett's hints and evasions; the Saints and Martyrs; the whole unexplored family connections between most of the people they had met – it all kept them occupied for the rest of the day. Thea seemed to have recovered from her subdued mood and was eager to talk.

Phil was feeling more confident of his back after a day of relative painlessness, which had the effect of activating his conscience. 'I've been a real slob,' he accused himself. 'The world's in flames and I've just been sitting here ignoring it all.'

'They seem to be coping well enough without you,' she observed. 'Not a single call since you got here. Maybe they've caught the ricin-makers and neglected to tell you.'

'I don't think so,' he said coolly. 'I prefer to think I've got everyone so well-organised, they can get on with it without constantly needing me to nursemaid them.'

'Do you worry you might be superfluous?' she teased.

He smiled. 'No, my love, I don't worry about that. I have no doubt at all that my desk will be stacked a foot deep with paperwork when I get back. But the ricin-makers, as you call them, are the focus of a far bigger team than my little section. I've never been more than one tiny link in the chain. If I'm out of action, they'll work around that without much difficulty.' He sighed lightly. 'But I doubt if I'll ever get back into it now. I'll find something completely different in the in tray when I get back.'

'What a shame,' she said insincerely. 'Meanwhile, you could see how you get on here, working out why Pritchett wishes he'd never said anything about his missing son, and why Janey won't have him mentioned. And why a dead man got stuffed under a tree, seemingly not missed by anybody.'

'Except there's already a perfectly capable DS working on that.'

'She won't mind,' Thea said, with certainty. 'She's just waiting for you to come to her rescue.'

Phil laughed. 'Thea, Thea, Thea,' he murmured. 'You don't really get it, do you? The way the police force works, I mean. If I rescued Gladwin, she'd never live it down. She'd hate me for the rest of her career and do everything she could to sabotage me and my cases. A lot rides on how she performs over this business – her first in the new job. If I wanted to rescue her, I'd have to do it subtly, invisibly even.'

Thea seemed to like this idea. 'You mean – drop clues in front of her and let her think she found them all by herself? Like helping a child win at chess?'

'Not really,' he said. 'More like – let her do it all on her own, and stay out of the whole business.'

CHAPTER NINE

'I think it's time I met that snake,' Phil said, as the evening started to feel a trifle long. It was nine o'clock, too early for bed, too late to start a game of Scrabble. 'I feel it's a hurdle I have to jump.'

She looked at him. 'What? Are you scared? You kept that well hidden, I must say.'

'Not scared, just – apprehensive. It sounds so dreadfully *big*. And Gladwin was right, you know. It's an awful business, keeping these wild animals shut up in cages, thousands of miles from their rightful homes.'

'Yes,' she sighed. 'But it's here now, and probably doesn't know what it's missing. At least it's got the right sort of weather. I expect it's as happy as a snake can be.'

'And we have no idea how happy that is,' he laughed. 'Funny how seldom one hears that word these days,' he added. 'We all seem to have got so *miserable* over the past few years. Or is it just me?'

'It's your job,' she assured him. 'All that violence and greed. You get a distorted view of the world.'

'Right,' he nodded. 'I see a violent and greedy world out there, no mistake about that. But it's also terribly *sad*.' He stroked an invisible beard reflectively, and searched his mind for some reason to be cheerful.

The snake looked peaceful enough, coiled untidily in a far corner of the generously sized cage. There were stones and hunks of wood to deceive it into thinking it was in its rightful habitat. The scales were large and symmetrical and very decorative. He couldn't see its head.

'Not much of a life,' he said. 'Not much of a pet, either, as far as I can see.'

'Archie takes her out a lot and lets her ride on his shoulders. She weighs something incredible, though, so I doubt if it lasts for long.' Thea put her face close to the fine wire mesh. 'You can see her breathing, look. Don't you think she's gorgeous?'

'Handsome,' Phil conceded. 'Definitely handsome. And very boring. I can't imagine anyone being scared of something so placid.'

'Nor me.'

'You exaggerated, though. There's no way that creature could swallow Hepzie. I expected something much bigger.'

'I wouldn't like to put it to the test.' Thea frowned consideringly. 'You can see there's a lot of slack skin, look. Just waiting to stretch around some tasty little mammal.' She frowned more deeply. 'I hope she's warm enough. They like it really hot and humid. I'm supposed to spray her every now and then, as well.' She indicated a plastic bottle with a trigger device at the top. 'But she's been drinking her water very nicely, so I thought she was probably OK.' She sighed. 'It's a big responsibility, you know, making sure she's just right. You don't think she could get cold, do you?'

'Thea, it's been close to thirty degrees here today. It isn't possible to be cold in this weather. It must have been sweltering in here with the

133

door and windows shut.'

It was a new wooden shed, with two windows, and an airlessness that Phil was finding uncomfortable. 'In fact, I think you ought to open a window for her. She'll suffocate otherwise.'

'Not in the night, though? Doesn't it get chilly at night?'

'Do it first thing in the morning,' he instructed, wondering why he was allowing himself to get involved. He leant against the doorpost, fighting the growing pain in his back. Unassisted standing was still difficult, and he let the post take his weight, pressing his upper spine against it, in an attempt to relieve the lower muscles.

Thea noticed the odd stance and raised her eyebrows. 'Too much standing,' she diagnosed. 'Bye bye, Shasti. Sorry to disturb you.'

But the snake showed no sign of caring whether they were there or not.

They finished the day with a sense of much achieved, Phil's back having cooperated magnificently with everything he demanded of it. 'We could go out again tomorrow,' he said bravely. 'And on Friday. The forecast says this weather is just going to go on and on.'

'Last year it ended in a thunderstorm,' Thea recalled. 'But that was later in the summer. I can't ever remember a June like this.'

'It's not natural,' he said in a tone of mock doom.

'Don't start that again,' she said. 'I'm going to bed.'

Thursday morning dawned red and fiery, but by half past eight there were streaks of cloud approaching from the west and a sudden breathy wind that fluttered the willows in Miss Deacon's garden. The horses seemed restless in their paddock and Phil reported a night much interrupted by the relentless gurgling of the fish tanks. 'I want to sleep upstairs with you,' he whined. 'I'm sure I can manage it now.'

'You might manage the stairs, but you won't like the feather mattress,' she reminded him.

'Well, we could take the fold-up bed and put it beside yours. At least we'd be in the same room.'

'Yes,' she smiled. 'That would be nice.'

His heart leapt with boyish optimism. 'It would, wouldn't it!' he agreed.

His disturbed night had been filled with interwoven thoughts of Gladwin and Thea and the bones he'd found and the significance of ancient history to modern Temple Guiting. There was a powerful duty on the investigating team to identify the body and how it died, and a lesser duty to establish what had become of young Giles Pritchett. It was possible that there was no connection apart from the accident of location, but he was increasingly sure that there was, especially after the way Janey had behaved the day before.

'Tell me about St Kenelm,' he invited, having settled himself back into the garden chair under the willow trees for another sunny morning. 'Isn't that the Saint of the Month for July?'

'Goodness, you have been paying attention,' she congratulated him. 'But I'm sorry to say I

135

know nothing whatever about him.'

'He's got a well near here, for a start.'

'Has he? How did you know that?'

'It's at the end of St Kenelm's Way. It's a long distance footpath. There was some trouble at the Worcester end a year or two ago.'

'We could invite Janey over and get her to tell us.'

Phil put up his hands. 'No, no – please no!' he begged melodramatically.

'But she'll be full of useful local information.'

'In which case Gladwin can have her. She'll have spoken to her already, I shouldn't wonder, what with it being her who called the fire brigade to move that tree.'

Thea was quiet. 'What are you thinking?' he prompted.

She wriggled her shoulders. 'Oh, something about villages and what they can tell you about people through the ages. Just the way the houses are positioned, and the boundaries drawn can conjure up whole social systems if you know how to look at them. Even now, I suppose, we're revealing things we don't realise.'

'Oh?'

'That new wall, for example – did you notice it? A perfect, handmade dry stone wall in bright yellow. On the way here. On the face of it, it's in perfect vernacular, maintaining traditions, keeping things looking the same. But dry stone wallers are highly paid experts now. The landowner isn't doing it himself, or getting his sons to gather the stones. He's paying a fortune for somebody else to do it. It's artificial. There won't be any animals behind that wall, unless they're highly bred and utterly useless horses. There's a complete loss of *integrity* to the whole thing.' Her eyes opened wider, as a new thought struck her. 'That's what bothers me so much about the Cotswolds. I've only just managed to put it into words. Nothing's genuine any more. It's all done for appearances.' She sighed. 'And yet it's all so amazingly beautiful. Even the air is lovely.'

'Right. And I'm not sure what the alternative might be. What should they do instead of that wall? Wire netting? A wall is still the most durable and effective barrier there is. Besides, there are still small working farms around here. There's one just the other end of the village.'

'Mmm,' she said. 'It probably isn't as bad as I think. When the stock market bubble bursts, as they generally seem to do, I suppose all these second homes will be sold to people who need somewhere to live, and the place will come to life again. It's all just being kept on hold at the moment.'

'Preserved in aspic,' he smiled. 'Which has to be better than letting it all go to ruin.'

'That's all right then,' she grinned back at him. 'Now what else can we put right in the world?'

He shifted gingerly, and was sufficiently free of pain to hold out his arms to her. 'Come here,' he invited. 'It's time for a hug.'

It was mildly embarrassing to realise they were being watched, five minutes later. 'I'm sorry, I couldn't make you hear me,' came a female voice from the edge of the lawn. 'This is rather nice, isn't it?' She scanned the scene, bathed in bright morning light, and extended her arms as if to savour the warm air on her skin. 'I hate to say it, but if I didn't know better I'd think that bad back was just a fib to gain a bit of extra holiday.'

Thea extricated herself gracefully and laughed. 'You'd better believe it,' she said. 'The back is bad enough to cast quite a shadow. I still haven't forgiven him for going up to look at the tree on Tuesday. It made everything worse by about a million miles.'

Sonia Gladwin pulled a rueful face. 'Some people just don't know when to leave well alone,' she agreed. 'And now we've got the oddest murder investigation I've ever met. Do you mind if I talk to him about it for a bit? To be perfectly honest–' she threw a worried glance over her shoulder as if seeking for hidden listeners, 'I'm already rather out of my depth.'

'Help yourself,' Thea said. 'I'll go and find some refreshment.'

Phil understood that things had to be badly getting to the new DS if she had been driven to swallow her pride and intrude on him like this. It was barely nine o'clock, and she looked as if she hadn't slept since he'd first met her forty-eight hours before. He felt no irritation with her, and he had detected none in Thea. The woman was only trying to do her job. Besides, as everybody kept saying, Phil had brought the whole thing on himself to begin with.

His only unease stemmed from the knowledge that Pritchett had told him things that he had yet

138

to pass on to the Senior Investigating Officer. This was quite out of order, and only felt worse for his lack of any good reason for the omission. He hoped it wasn't because Pritchett and he had both been on the square, many years ago, and the old loyalties and concerns still held a grip on him. Freemasonry was a brotherhood that bonded more strongly than was generally realised. Even Phil, a refugee from the seamier aspects, could not escape entirely.

'We're held up waiting for all the forensic reports,' she said. 'We made rather a mess of the scene, between us. It's impossible to say now just where he was buried, and how deep.'

'Not your fault,' he said. 'The tree threw everything up in the air more or less literally. Plus the chainsaw gang must have trodden all over the show before any of us got there. Anyway, I'm not sure it matters, does it? There's such a thing as getting too bogged down in the detail. Isn't it enough to know he had his head bashed in and the body dumped? Having a date is the crucial factor, surely?' He was being deliberately deferential, according her the seniority, granting her the case on a plate, with as little interference as he could manage. He found it wasn't difficult.

'How are you feeling, anyway?' she asked, leaning forward slightly. 'I should have asked that first. I know how crippling a bad back can be – my father had one for years.'

'I'll survive,' he said lightly, doing his best not to compare this moment of real sympathy with Thea's cavalier treatment. 'It's a lot better than it was.'

'Well, it's good of you to let me pick your brains, just the same,' she said.

'You didn't give me much choice,' he pointed out. 'Besides, I owe you a rather large apology. I've been withholding information from you.'

She cocked her head, unsure how to take this. 'Oh?'

'A man named Stephen Pritchett has been talking to me. He thought it might be his son – Giles he's called – buried under that tree. It turns out from your description that it can't be him after all – which is why I didn't confuse things by telling you about it.'

'When did he tell you this?' She seemed un-surprised by the revelation, almost *expecting* it, if that made any sense.

'Yesterday. Oh, and Janey Holmes let drop that she thinks Giles is alive and well. In other words, Giles Pritchett is probably a red herring, and nothing to do with the case at all.'

'Is Stephen Pritchett a friend of yours?'

Hollis shook his head. 'I met him once, years ago, that's all. It's a small world around here.'

'Not as small as Cumbria, believe me,' she said. 'I heard something about Pritchett last night, as it happens. There's a family of them. The name of Giles has come up more than once already. That's your man's son, I take it? Early twenties and very tall? Last known address here in the village, but that was a few years ago now.' She was consulting a strange-looking electronic notepad.

Hollis nodded. 'That's the one.'

'So, you haven't kept back anything we didn't already know,' she summarised, sitting back more

140

comfortably in the canvas chair. 'God, this weather's nice, isn't it? I can't get used to it – it feels as if every day's a holiday.'

He inspected her chestnut hair and freckled skin, which didn't look unduly susceptible to sunburn. 'You've got the colouring for it,' he said, and was disconcerted when she blushed.

Deftly she returned to the subject under discussion. 'We're trawling through all the missing persons reports, of course. Three or four names have come up which might be worth looking into. But the pathologist – what's his name? Peter?' Phil nodded, and she carried on, 'He's raising some questions about the cause of death. He thinks the damage to the skull could have happened post-mortem, after all. He's sending slivers of bone from around the wound to the lab for microscopic analysis, but he thinks we might never be totally sure. There aren't enough traces of blood and tissue to work on. You can understand the difficulty,' she smiled, with a flash of typical police humour. 'Every bit of the brain's been gone for a while now. Must have been a feast for an army of creepy-crawlies.'

'So, a stone or tree root or something might have made the hole after he was buried? Is that what he thinks?'

She shrugged. 'There's no exit wound, which might have helped to work out what happened.' Phil remembered Thea's reference to Jael and the tent peg and nodded.

'But it's still a crime, of course,' Gladwin went on. 'You can't just dump a naked body under a tree and leave it, even if you haven't killed it first.

141

And there are anomalies. Some of the long bones are broken.'

He looked at her acutely. 'That sounds interesting.'

'We're not sure what happened, yet. I won't say anything until we are – if that moment ever comes, of course. I hope that's OK.'

Again he felt put down, sidelined. She was treating him like an unreliable amateur, not a highly experienced superintendent. 'Don't you trust me?' he demanded.

'It's not that. Of course it's not. But without you being in on all the briefings, it's not so easy to keep you up to speed with the details. If I tell you something now that turns out to be wrong, I'll have to be sure to correct it later on. You're here, amongst the people who are likely to be most closely involved. That's really useful, especially if they get talking on a friendly basis. But it's my case.' She gave him a straight look. 'I have to have everything at my fingertips, and keep track of who knows what. I'm not keeping any secrets from you, Phil. I'm just trying to avoid telling you something that hasn't been fully confirmed. OK?'

'OK,' he smiled. 'Very professional.'

'Thank you. Now – has anyone else told you anything that might be relevant?'

He recounted the visit to Janey's home, the Saints and Martyrs Club and the trust which financed her lifestyle. Gladwin wrote with an electronic pencil on her fancy modern gadget, recording everything she was being told. Hollis found himself fully engaged with the process of

recalling each and every detail. His back forgotten, it was ten minutes before he paused and
realised how fiercely his mind had been working,
and how much more than mere facts he had
relayed. He had listed avenues of enquiry, ranged
across such hypotheses as family feuds over
property and other issues, neighbour disputes,
drugs and jealousy.

Gladwin looked up and smiled. 'You enjoy your
work, don't you,' she remarked.

He half closed his eyes. 'It saved me, a while
back,' he admitted. 'When my personal life
imploded, it was work that kept me going.'

Again she cocked her head, eyeing him like an
intelligent bird. 'Not the other way around then?'
she probed. 'I mean – personal life usually
implodes for a copper *because* of the work.'

'There was an element of that,' he conceded.
'How could there not be? But I'll always be grateful for the job. It literally gave me something to
live for.'

'Your daughter died,' she nodded matter-of-
factly. 'Of a drug overdose. Can't have been easy.'

'You looked me up? Found it on my records?'

'Nope.' She shook her head. 'Three different
people told me about it within two hours of my
arrival on Monday. Does that surprise you?'

His eyes closed all the way, as he held the
feelings in tight check. 'Not surprised,' he said.
'But not particularly pleased. Do they think
that's what defines me, even now? Does it make
me vulnerable? Unreliable? Or what?'

She pressed her lips together, and put a finger
against them. 'I've said too much,' she whisp-

ered. 'And here's Thea back with refreshments. I'll just stay a few more minutes.'

It had to have been half an hour since Thea had disappeared into the house. Phil held her searching gaze for several steady seconds, unsure of what she was trying to discover. 'Finished?' she asked sweetly. 'I'm getting rather good at this, aren't I? Leaving you to discuss murder while I kick my heels in the kitchen.'

Gladwin took her up swiftly. 'Are you cross about it?' Again the genuine sympathy, the instant understanding. 'I wouldn't blame you if you were.'

'I am a bit. I know it's his job, and he loves it. I don't even want him glued to my side every moment of the day. But I guess I wouldn't be human if – well, you know.'

For Phil it was utter déjà vu. His wife had struggled and kicked against his divided interest, his inability to make or keep firm promises. All the usual clichés had been there, including the pleas from him that she accept it, as fishermen's wives and farmers' wives and soldiers' wives all seemed to do with so much less of a fight. What was so special about the police that it made marriage almost unworkable?

Thea had tried to explain it to him. 'It's because you *think* about it all the time,' she had said. 'And it's such dirty work. Dealing with people who've become subhuman, so much of the time. That's what I hate about Jessica joining the Force. She mixes with the dregs of society – addicts and prostitutes and street gangs, and I know it's going to rub off on her eventually.'

He hadn't denied it. He hadn't argued with her

144

characterisation of criminals, either. There was no denying that they had mostly lost any vestiges of civilised values. There was scarcely any honour amongst thieves any more. The arguments were far better employed in establishing how and why it had happened and what might be done about it.

But now Thea had crossed a line she had baulked at so far. She was acting like a neglected wife, and he was saddened by it. 'You didn't need to leave us,' he said. 'We would have been happy for you to stay and join in.'

'I didn't want to,' she said simply. 'Besides, I've found something about St Kenelm in Miss Deacon's magazine collection. He was murdered too, you know. By his sister, according to one story.'

'Sister?' repeated DS Gladwin. 'That's unusual.' Her eyes lost focus. 'Where have I heard the name Kenelm already today?' She scratched the side of her face. 'I know – that woman, Janey Holmes. She's doing some sort of festival for him next month. And of course, she's a sister, too.'

'Is she?' Phil and Thea spoke almost together.

'Oh yes – didn't she tell you? She's got the same blue blood that everybody around here seems to think is so important. Her brother is a bloke called Rupert Temple-Pritchett. Except,' she added with a small frown, 'we don't seem able to find him.'

'But we've seen him,' said Thea. 'He came here on Sunday, looking for Miss Deacon. Is he really Janey's brother? That's incredible.' She looked at Phil in puzzlement. 'Janey never said anything about that. She even changed the subject when I said his name. They certainly don't look remotely similar.'

Gladwin listened closely. 'Did you notice any-thing else about him?'

'He's got a sporty sort of car and talks like Noel Coward.'

'Did he say where he lives?'

'No. I suppose it might be some distance away, because he didn't know Miss Deacon was on holi-day. I wouldn't think he'd be too hard to trace.'

'Well, he isn't easy,' said Gladwin.

Phil looked at her. 'How hard have you tried?' he asked.

She shrugged. 'Phone book, Google, not much else. There's no real reason to question him as yet. We just wanted to place him in the picture. If you see him again, could you try and get an address out of him?'

Phil nodded and Thea shook her head in con-tinuing amazement. 'Brother and sister, eh?' she said. 'You couldn't hope to find two such differ-ent people. Are you sure you've got it right? Who told you?'

Gladwin didn't answer directly. She simply smiled patiently and said, 'Oh yes, it's right enough. You can take my word on that.'

CHAPTER TEN

He had sent Gladwin off with the firm advice that she ferret out as many hard facts as she could. Thea's introduction of a long-dead saint into the equation had been interesting but surely not relevant. The unearthed body was a matter for urgent present-day detection, not a romantic mythology of long ago.

Thea was in a bustling mode, watering plants, feeding fish, swabbing every surface in the kitchen. 'I still haven't been outside to check the horses,' she said. 'Everything suddenly seemed to need attention in here.'

'But you've only got a few more things to do – right?' he said. 'You'll be done by ten-thirty at the latest and then we could go out somewhere.'

'We could go to Guiting Power again,' she suggested. 'We didn't really look at the village green properly, and we could try the other pub. Or do you want to go further afield?'

'Guiting Power is remarkably beautiful,' he agreed. 'And it's unusual in that it actually has people living there full time. Plus children and dogs.'

'It's more beautiful than Temple Guiting, that's for sure,' she said carelessly.

'Hush!' he admonished. 'You can't say that. It's axiomatic that *all* Cotswold villages are beautiful. Surely you know that. Besides, that manor house is pretty much as good as it gets, if you ask me.'

She looked blank. 'Which manor house?'

'Come on. In the middle of the village. Opposite the church, more or less. You must have seen it. I was wondering who lived there – I assume it's not one of the Temples or Pritchetts. It looks as if it's worth a couple of million at least.'

She frowned. 'I've hardly looked at the village,' she realised. 'Although I did notice those peculiar black-painted houses near the shop. I can't even

147

remember where the church is.'

He was about to tell her when he caught a movement through the window. 'There's somebody else here now,' he said. 'I didn't hear a car, did you?'

It was a person they had not encountered before, standing outside the front door as if unable to find the courage to knock. Phil watched as Thea went out and spoke to the young wispy-looking woman. The spaniel jumped up at her, wagging violently, causing the visitor some obvious irritation. He found himself wishing Thea could have trained the dog better. His own Claude and Baxter would never have dreamt of approaching a stranger so uninhibitedly.

He opened the casement window wider, making his presence obvious to the stranger. He heard her say something about Miss Deacon and the word 'horses'. For very different reasons, Phil entertained doubts as to whether this person was any more of a rider than big Janey Holmes could have been. Anybody scared of a cocker spaniel was surely not going to have much confidence with a horse.

But Thea's reaction made it clear that the girl had not come for a ride. She threw out her arms in a gesture of wild panic, and turned to call to Phil. 'They've got out! The horses are up in the road. We'll have to go and get them back.' Then she remembered. 'Or *I* will,' she amended.

He didn't pause to think. 'I'll come as well,' he said, already heading for the passageway and the front door. 'I can block up a gap, at the very least.'

The newcomer looked from one to the other in some confusion. 'No, it's all right,' she said. 'My Dad has got them tied up by now. They're very quiet, he says. He'll put them back in the paddock for you – but there's a gap in the corner of the field. He won't have time to fix it. It only needs a couple of stakes knocking in and a strand of wire – or something.'

Thea's panic subsided, but she still looked pale and worried. 'I'll have to come up and see where you mean.' She glanced at Phil. 'Can you walk?'

'Absolutely,' he assured her. 'It's a lot better today. I hurt my back at the weekend,' he explained to the girl, who looked younger the closer he got to her. 'Can you show us the gap?'

It all turned out to be a very minor difficulty. The girl, who belatedly introduced herself as Soraya, led the way to a point where the horses' field met the road a short distance from the spot where the beech tree had fallen. It seemed likely to Phil that one of the police team – which had all packed up and gone by this time – had damaged the fence in the process of examining the site after the skeleton had been discovered. Hopping over for a quick pee behind the hedge, in all probability.

Soraya's father turned out to be as fair-skinned and slight as his daughter. His shoulders were bony and sloping, in the skimpy black singlet he wore. When Hepzibah jumped up at him he swiped her away with a careless blow that made the animal yelp.

'Thank you so much,' Thea gushed at him, as she inspected the errant horses, having failed to

149

observe the unkindness to her dog. 'Are they all right? How far did they get?'

'They're fine,' he assured her. 'They hadn't gone any distance. They just fancied some of this fresh grass on the verge.' He pointed at a few clumps of slightly dusty grass, which to Phil's eye looked rather less tempting than that in the field.

'This is where they found those bones, then,' he said, his head cocked to one side, as if pointing towards the beech tree. His gaze never left Phil's face, as he spoke.

Phil merely nodded.

'You're a police detective, that right?'

Phil nodded again, adding, 'Off duty this week. Damaged my back.' The walk up to the road had gone easily enough, he was relieved to note. He began to think it could be possible to get back to work by the following Monday. After all, it couldn't be said that there were many physical demands on him these days. No lifting or bending or twisting for the average detective superintendent.

'But you saw them – the bones? Wasn't it you that found them?'

Thea had been tinkering with the fence, pulling at the wire, and dragging a piece of dead wood she had found into position across the gap made by the escaping animals. 'Will that do for the time being?' she asked. 'Or should I move them to the other paddock? Miss Deacon's got two, hasn't she? Have I got that right?'

The man shrugged, but Soraya spoke up. 'Best leave them where they are,' she said. 'They won't try to get out again – not if you give them a treat down by the house.' She glanced at her father as if to check that she had not spoken out of turn.

The man was still fixed on Phil's face, ignoring Soraya. 'Those bones,' he muttered, 'did you see them? Was there anything–? I mean, could you tell–?'

Phil sighed. Morbid curiosity was as annoying as it was understandable. 'You live round here, do you?' he countered.

'Not far, aye. Thing is, there's a fair bit of talk about it, and I was wondering... You never know what to believe, do you?' His expression turned to one of supplication. 'And you're a detective, they say. Must have been here when they took it all away.'

'I'm on sick leave,' Phil repeated, with a sense of going round in circles. 'What is it you're trying to ask me?'

'What it is, see,' the man glanced swiftly around, 'I might have an idea who it could have been. It came back to me, in the night – Christmas two, three years ago, there were a spot of trouble with an old chap living rough. Got the Council to come and shift him.' He grinned humourlessly. 'Not the sort of area for that kind of thing. Lets the place down, like.'

Phil made every effort to listen patiently, disregarding the flaring pain in his back as he stood unsupported, sending the optimism of a few minutes before flying right off into the blue yonder. Thea was engrossed in her fence repairs, as far as he could tell. Certainly she was offering him no assistance. 'A vagrant, you mean?'

The man nodded. 'Yeah. Homeless bloke. There

were folks dead against him, might have got a bit sharp with him.' He shifted from foot to foot.

'You think some of the locals killed him and buried the body under that tree?' Phil had no compunction about cutting through to the main point.

The man shivered in the burning sun. 'No, no, I ain't saying that,' he blustered. 'But seems like it's the same bloke. He maybe just froze after he'd tried to dig himself in under the tree to get warm.' The pleading look returned. 'That could happen, eh?'

'Dad,' came Soraya's soft voice. 'Leave it. We got the horses back. You don't know anything for sure, after all. Just leave it.'

Phil straightened his suffering back. 'Thank you for the information,' he said formally. 'And for rounding up the horses. It's much appreciated. Isn't it, Thea?' he added more loudly.

'Oh! Yes, of course. I hate to think what might have happened. But look – I've patched it up again quite well, haven't I? It only needed a few things straightening.' She wrinkled her nose and narrowed her eyes. 'I might almost think somebody had made the gap on purpose. That post in the middle had been pushed sideways, and some of the fence wire trodden right down low.'

'The horses must have done it,' said Soraya's father, with reddened cheeks.

Phil might have said something if he'd been on duty, if his back hadn't been flaming in all directions, if Thea had given him some encouragement. He knew a lie when he saw one after decades of questioning amateur criminals and pathetic fantasists. 'Well, everything's fine now,' he said. 'Can we go?'

Thea nodded and went to his side. 'Are you still all right for walking?' she asked.

'Have to be, won't I,' he panted. 'This is ridiculous. It's four days now – it ought to be better than this. It *swamps* me,' he complained. 'So I can't think straight.'

'Thanks again,' Thea said to the man and his daughter, who'd started to move away. 'It's nice to have met you. Apart from you, we've only met Janey Holmes and a chap called Rupert Temple-Pritchett. Do you know them?'

Phil was impatient to leave, but he knew how much Thea enjoyed pronouncing the man's name, and forced himself to allow her a few moments' chat.

'Yeah, we know them,' said the man, with a glance at his daughter. 'We see Rupert around quite a bit, even though he doesn't live local. Bit of a waste of space, if you want the truth.'

'Dad!' Soraya reproached him. 'We should go.'

The man and his daughter walked off towards a battered pick-up truck parked on the verge with a single backward glance. His hand was on her shoulder in a gesture of automatic control. Phil watched frowningly, remembering the way the girl had checked everything she said, and acted as if under orders throughout the encounter. Then he turned to face the bumpy sloping track down to the house. It could have been the north face of the Eiger.

An hour later, assisted by two painkillers, he was

slowly recovering. Thea was hovering restlessly, having remembered to go out and open the window of the snake's shed, and thrown the horses a few carrots to persuade them they were better off staying where they were.

'I think that bloke deliberately let them out,' said Phil. 'It was all a devious plot to get to talk to me about the dead body, and feed me that nonsense about a vagrant. And the girl was his accomplice. She was doing exactly what he'd told her to. You could tell at a glance he wasn't genuine.'

Thea blinked. 'I thought he was all right. Isn't that a bit convoluted? Why not just come down to the house if he wanted to say something to you?'

'Not his style. You didn't see him cuffing Hepzie, did you? You'd agree with me if you had.'

'He didn't, did he? I heard her yelp, now I think about it. What exactly did he do?'

Phil recounted the scene, exaggerating slightly. 'He's not a nice man,' he concluded. 'And I don't feel easy about that girl of his. He had her right under his thumb.'

Thea gave a long sigh. 'It must be awful to be you,' she said. 'Always suspecting the worst of people. You must see the world as such a dark and wicked place.'

'Don't start that again,' he begged her. 'Let's just stick to the reality in front of us, shall we?'

'OK.' She gave in readily, with a smile. 'And what are those facts, then?'

'You know as well as I do. We've unearthed an old crime, which has stirred things up for the locals, and they're panicking. Or some of them are. Something like this raises a lot of old fears

154

and secrets – even perfectly innocent people remember something they feel guilty about from years ago, and wonder if somehow this could lead to them being found out. Guilt lurks in all of us, just waiting to be activated. This is the very thing to get it going.'

'But–' she thought hard before going on, 'can that really be true? If I'd run over somebody's cat, for example, and left it in a ditch to die – would I think this would betray my guilty secret?' She didn't wait for him to reply. 'I suppose I might. But if I'd stolen some money from my neighbour, or written an anonymous letter to the Council about a farmer leaving dead sheep around – well, yes, maybe.' She rubbed her chin and gazed across the garden. 'Not the money, maybe, but anything to do with dead things. What if that vagrant had been living illegally in somebody's barn, and a local group of upright residents drove him out? They *would* feel guilty, wouldn't they?'

Phil laughed at her stream of consciousness, and nodded happily. 'See what I mean? There's always something. But it doesn't make my job any easier. That bloke just now – he was almost certainly trying to divert my attention, telling some story about a vagrant, when all the time he's got something else on his mind altogether.'

'At least he didn't look as if he'd claim descent from one of the Templars. I still think that's a major preoccupation around here. Listen – if you're too knackered to go out, I wouldn't mind spending the day browsing through some of Miss Deacon's magazines. You've persuaded me they're worth a look.'

'I thought you said we shouldn't touch them. You'll be in trouble if you get them dirty or torn.' He spoke idly, accustomed to her erratic approach to edicts from the owners of the houses she minded.

'So, I'll be careful. It's too hot for any more exploring, anyway.'

He knew she was making the best of things; that she would much rather be walking through shady woodlands or tracing the meanderings of the little River Windrush. He surreptitiously inspected the state of his back, and ventured a suggestion he thought he could tolerate: 'Wouldn't it be nice to try another local pub for lunch, rather than just going to Guiting Power? We're running out of days at this rate.'

It felt like a small martyrdom compared to what he knew she'd have preferred.

They ended up at The Butcher's Arms in Oak-ridge Lynch, where Thea had been the previous year, on her very first house-sitting assignment. The garden had a peculiar hedge running down the middle, dividing the area into two distinct parts. 'Better check there's nobody we know on the other side,' said Thea with a grin. 'It's a perfect place for eavesdropping.' She casually walked around for a quick look, and reported it all clear. 'Just an elderly couple with a labrador, sitting in the sun and smoking.' The midday heat was such that most of the lunchtime drinkers had remained in the bar. Phil would have quite liked to do the same, but Thea led him to a table with at least some shade from a nearby tree.

They found themselves talking about the Templars, although Thea had made little progress in her Internet research on the subject. 'I did see somewhere that they were mostly celibate,' she noted. 'Which makes it a bit odd that people seem so keen to claim them as ancestors. They were massacred in large numbers and wiped out more or less overnight. Somebody called them "warrior-monks", which sounds rather nice, don't you think?'

Phil did his best to pay attention. 'Isn't it mostly myth?' he said. 'After all, it's a very long time ago.'

'Eight hundred years,' she nodded. 'That just makes it more intriguing. They were fabulously rich and powerful for a while. That's probably why people turned against them and exterminated them. There's still a big mystery around why it all happened so suddenly.'

'Like the Jews in Germany,' he said with a nod.

'I suppose so,' she agreed, with the frozen look that often came over people when the Holocaust was mentioned. 'Although the Jews were never warriors.'

'Hmm,' he said, thinking of the hawkish behaviour of modern-day Israelis, and deciding there was no sense in getting into that. 'Stephen Pritchett seems to know quite a bit about the whole Templar thing. He said his father got Giles interested.'

'You can see how people might get obsessed with proving they're descended from one of the Knights Templar.'

'Enough to make them commit murder? Surely not!'

'You'd know more about that than me,' she smiled. 'I never manage to believe all the convoluted motives that make a person kill another human being. Mostly I think they must be mad.'

'You know that isn't true,' he said, looking down his nose at her. 'They do it because they think it's the only answer to a huge problem, or because they're so furiously angry they can't stop themselves.'

Their lunch was brought quickly, and they'd finished by half past one. Phil felt restless and hot, and began to think fondly of the comfortable garden lounger back at Hector's Nook. 'Can we go now?' he said, as the conversation lapsed.

The car, parked in full sun, seemed to shimmer in the heat. 'It's going to be baking in there,' Phil groaned. 'And no air conditioning, of course.'

'Of course,' she agreed. 'I'll have to drive nice and fast with all the windows open. That's much nicer, anyway. Carl used to love it, and Hepzie likes to put her head out and get her ears blown about.'

Phil did not exactly wince at the mention of Thea's dead husband, but he felt it as a sharp cold poke in the ribs, all the same. He had never met the man, but knew that if he had, he would have liked him. How could he not like someone who had valued Thea and played his part in a marriage that sounded to have been as good as it gets?

She drove back to Temple Guiting, the sun high in the afternoon sky. They met perhaps a dozen other cars on the way, which almost felt like a rush. 'Rather early for fetching kids from school,' said Thea. 'That doesn't start till half past three or so. They drive me mad, where I live. All those short unnecessary journeys that shouldn't be allowed.'

Phil remembered that he was a policeman. 'Let's not ban anything else,' he pleaded. 'The smoking thing's bad enough, without trying to force kids to walk to school. I can see it now – all the county's PCs stopping every second car to see if it contained a mum and her five-year-old who's too tired to walk half a mile home after school.'

'You're right,' she said. 'Far too many things are banned as it is. I still think the smoking ban is a wicked absurdity.'

He already knew what she thought. Initially he had been surprised at the strength of her feelings on the subject, considering she had never smoked in her life. But her passion for civil rights and individual freedoms greatly outweighed any arguments about health hazards. 'I don't believe secondary smoking matters at all,' she said sweepingly. 'And people should be allowed their addictions, if that's what they want.'

As an ex-smoker, Phil had a rather more ambivalent attitude to the whole business, but he mainly refrained from arguing with her about it.

The mood inside the car was slipping away into something quite oppressive. Phil tried to persuade himself it was due to the heat, and the returning ache in his back. Then he realised it was brought about by the fact of returning to the house, which was not theirs and which held mysteries that he had refused to confront. Not

159

just the snake, but the stacks of old magazines, and the proximity of a fallen tree where a dead man had been buried, with a hole in the side of his head.

But they found nothing sinister awaiting them and soon settled down on the lawn, as was their habit. Thea brought a small pile of journals out onto the lawn, placing them carefully on the garden table, weighed down with a pebble that she'd found beside the front door. Phil picked it up and turned it over in his hands. 'This must be a souvenir of some kind,' he noted. 'It's certainly not Cotswold stone.' It was dark grey, very smooth and shaped in a flat oval. 'Don't forget to put it back where you found it.'

'I won't,' Thea nodded absently. 'There are a lot of others as well. Must be some sort of collection. This is the nicest one.'

He would have liked to get up and go over to see, but his back urged him to stay where he was. He had collected stones himself in his youth; had even considered geology as his major subject at university for a short time. As it was, he'd taken geography and physics, which had never been more than mildly interesting, his results per-petually hovering around the minimal pass mark.

Thea turned the pages of the old periodicals carefully and frequently. They dated mainly from the 1920s and were part of a set of *The International Good Templar,* which had been published in Glasgow.

'It was a sort-of teetotal Freemasonry,' Thea observed, after a protracted examination of the contents. 'They gave women equal footing, and had a lot of activities for children. All terribly worthy – and nothing to do with the Knights Templar at all, as far as I can see.' She sat back in disappointment.

Phil, a one-time Freemason himself, pulled one of the magazines across the table for a closer look. 'They had processions, look,' he pointed to a photograph. 'And here's something about Rosslyn Chapel. Isn't that the Dan Brown place?'

'Let's see.' She got up and looked over his shoulder. 'It must be, I suppose. It's all a bit confusing. But I haven't found anything about Temple Guiting, and can't believe I'm likely to. Mind you, this is a wonderful collection. Must be worth quite a bit, and she's left them just sitting there for anybody to help themselves to.'

'Except she did ask you not to touch them.'

'Oh, pooh,' Thea said airily. 'It's far too tempting to resist.'

'Thea!' He reproached her in tones more like a father than a policeman and she responded girlishly.

'Sorry,' she lisped. 'I'll put them all back again, shall I? At least we've learnt something. I had never heard of the International Good Templars until now. They do seem rather sweet.' She had a thought. 'And I bet Miss Deacon's teetotal. There's no sign of any booze in the house.'

'Deacon is a Scottish name, isn't it? Maybe her father belonged to this outfit, and the magazines were his.'

'Or mother. They had women as well, remember.'

161

'So they did. Very enlightened.' He gave her a knowing look, which reminded them both of events in Cold Aston the year before – a shared history that was not entirely comfortable.

'I assume they're defunct now?' he said after a few moments of silence.

'Probably – the magazines only go up to 1930 or thereabouts. I could Google them on the lap-top to see. Remind me this evening.'

'Why bother? You'll have got your teeth into something else by then.'

'Yes, I might,' she agreed. 'There are loads of other magazines in that room, I only brought these out because they had the word *Templar* on the cover. I ought to ask Janey more about the local involvement, I suppose. I can't get a handle on how it all connects. The saints and the Knights and this Scottish stuff.'

'How do you know it does connect? They might be quite separate interests. If you're looking for clues about the buried body, I have to say it looks more like a random set of snippets you've picked up than anything that explains who and how and why.'

'Yes, I know. But one of those snippets might be the answer. And if you're not going to get down to any proper investigating, I might as well unearth what I can on your behalf.'

He shook his head at her, smiling broadly. 'Thea, my sweet girl – you know it doesn't work like that. You've been around police operations enough to realise I wouldn't be able to do any investigating like this, even if I wanted to. The best thing I can do is keep out of the way and let

Gladwin have a clear run at it. She'll come to me like she did this morning if she wants any specific advice, but I think she'll manage well enough on her own. All I want is to get this back fixed and be at my desk again as soon as maybe.'

She returned his smile, with her own hint of patronage. 'You have your methods and I have mine,' she said airily. 'If this is an old murder, there are precious few actual clues to what happened. I'm as likely as anybody to unearth something important. Aren't I?'

He sighed defeatedly. 'Probably,' he said. 'But you're on your own. I'm going to read a book, if I can find one.'

The limitations of his luggage had already become apparent, as his stay extended further and further beyond the original plan. He had not brought anything that might be classed as 'amusement', and minimal changes of clothes. Thanks to the quick-dry weather, this had not been problematic, but now he wished he'd brought the big fat thriller he'd started the previous week.

'There's a bookcase in the living room,' Thea reminded him. 'You could borrow something from that.'

He knew he should keep moving, that remaining in the garden all day was not likely to improve the state of his back, but having got comfortable there was every incentive to stay where he was. 'Do you remember what sort of books they are?' he asked.

She shrugged. 'Not really. Hardbacks mostly. Probably from a book club.' She sucked in one

163

cheek for a quiet moment. 'Do you want me to go and find something for you?'

He struggled valiantly and finally conquered his own idle inclinations. 'No, no,' he said. 'I'll go and have a look for myself.'

The bookcase was an elegant glass-fronted affair with three shelves, mounted on top of a matching bureau. He felt a strong sense of intrusion as he opened the doors and perused the book spines. Thea had been right that many of them were book club editions, in pristine dust wrappers, showing no signs of ever having been read. They dated from the 1980s in the main, and failed utterly to attract his interest, being novels by people such as Joanna Trollope and Maeve Binchy. But the top shelf proved to be a lot more interesting. These were faded volumes from the early twentieth century: the lettering hard to read, and the pages, when he pulled one out, dusty along the tops. They all seemed to be about the English countryside. It took him a few minutes to understand that Miss Deacon's interests lay very much in that which had been secret or hidden. Holy wells, tiny chapels, forgotten follies and lost gardens. Histories of eccentric architects or rich men intent on leaving a permanent mark, churchmen who had created bizarre graveyards, engineers who had found new ways of harnessing waterways, and ancient dolmens or cistvaens built by people whose motives were no longer comprehensible.

Despite his decision to lose himself in a fast-moving adventure story, he quickly found himself tucking three of Miss Deacon's more intriguing tomes under his arm and returning to the garden. Thea's spaniel was sitting in his chair, curled on the cushion he'd used to pad his back, panting gently in the warm sunshine. 'Off!' he ordered, never doubting that he would be obeyed. But Hepzie merely cocked a half-open eye at him and stayed where she was.

'She's keeping it warm for you,' said Thea.

'And I'm very grateful. Now can she let me have it back, please?'

'Off you get, Heps,' said Thea, with a flick of a hand. The dog uncoiled and jumped to the ground, the top-heavy body landing gracelessly. Without any sign of resentment, she recoiled herself under her mistress's chair.

'Why wouldn't she do it for me?' he complained.

'Because she loves me more. Obviously.' Thea was engrossed in one of the magazines she had stacked on the rickety iron table beside her and gave Phil only the slightest attention. 'This is fascinating,' she said. 'But nothing to do with your – our – murder.'

'Thank goodness for that,' he said, and lowered himself onto the excessively warm cushion, trying to push it into the right part of his aching back. 'I found some unusual-looking books. I'm going to read about holy wells until suppertime.'

'Mmm,' said Thea. She sounded lazy and somnolent, but Phil knew differently. Thea never really did nothing. Even when playing Scrabble on her computer, she was not being idle. For a woman with no regular employment, and little to impress in her past work record, she was unusually industrious. She employed her brain in seeking out new areas of history to explore, or in developing well-considered opinions. She read the more serious newspapers and journals, and would not let arrant nonsense pass as genuine argument. She was an attentive mother, sister and daughter and a courageous widow.

'You're happy to stay here for the rest of the day, then?' he asked.

'Absolutely,' she said. 'I like it here.'

He met her eye and tried to convey his admiration and gratitude and understanding in a single long glance.

'Besides,' she added, 'I'm being paid to watch over the place, so that's what I'd better do. I need to keep an eye on those horses, remember. They might decide to escape again.' The two beasts were standing idly under a tree, ears and tails flicking away flies every now and then, heads down in reverie. 'Not that they look very much inclined to go anywhere,' she added.

'I bet that bloke had real trouble getting them back through that gap,' said Phil. Then he had a thought. 'In fact I bet they never even *went* through it at all. They were in the field when we got there – who's to say they ever left it?'

'Too devious for me,' she said. 'What if we'd driven up there and caught him out?'

'He could still say he'd put them back for us while the girl was coming down here to call us.'

'Oh, well,' she shrugged. 'I'm not going to worry about it.'

'No, no. You leave all the worrying to me,' he said with a small chill in his voice.

166

'I will,' she said comfortably. 'I know how much you like to worry.'

Which he could not help feeling was distinctly unfair of her.

CHAPTER ELEVEN

Rupert Temple-Pritchett was as shockingly handsome at second sight as he had been the first time. '*So* sorry to intrude again,' he murmured, stepping onto the lawn so quietly that Hepzie quite failed to notice him. Thea turned her head, with no sense of alarm, soothed by the easy tones and the slow still afternoon.

'Oh, hello,' she said.

Phil had been dozing, his mouth open and head back against the chair. His eyes snapped open when she spoke, and he looked around sharply. 'What?' he said.

'Only me,' said the visitor. 'I hate to disturb you, but there doesn't seem to be any alternative. I might have telephoned, of course, but that can be every bit as much of a nuisance as a personal call, don't you find?'

'What's the problem?' Phil asked, finding the man irritating in the extreme.

'Ructions, my friend, that's it in a nutshell. Finding body parts in the open countryside – never a good idea.' He directed a patrician gaze down at Phil for a few seconds. 'Poor old Stephen and Trudy. They'll be in a fine old tizz, after what you turned up, and who can blame them? They'll have thought it was their Giles.'

Phil dredged up the fact that Trudy was Mrs Pritchett. 'Really?' he said shortly.

'So?' Thea interrupted impatiently. 'What do you want us to do about it?'

'Call off the hounds, in a word,' came the reply. 'They'll be questioning every bally member of the village, from what I hear. I do find,' he added with a world-weary sigh, 'that *sense* seldom intrudes at a time like this. I wouldn't put it past them to even start pestering the people staying at the Manor.'

Phil was inwardly groaning at the use of words such as *bally* and *tizz*. It could only be affectation. The man couldn't have been born before the mid-Sixties, when such language had already been obsolete for years. Either that, or he had been recently involved in a Noel Coward production and couldn't get out of character.

'The Manor?' Thea echoed, with a glance at Phil.

'Big place, on the right as you leave the village centre,' offered Rupert. 'It's let out as a hideaway, self-catering sort of idea. Never know who's there, of course. Hardly ever see them. Last thing they need is to get involved in a murder hunt. Senseless,' he concluded with a searching look at Phil.

Phil felt besieged, as if they both wanted some reassuring words from him. The claim that the police were questioning everybody in Temple Guiting was a clear overstatement. There had been a general plea for information and probably

168

a handful of interviews, but so far there had been no door-to-door enquiries. More interesting was his need to discover the real reason for the man's visit. He met Temple-Pritchett's eyes, fancying he caught a flicker of evasion in their dark depths. After all, his mission was fundamentally aggressive, when you thought about it. Aggressive, familiar and futile, Phil added to himself.

'You're asking Phil to call off the police investigation?' Thea summarised, her voice full of challenge. 'Isn't that rather unreasonable?'

'No, no, I wouldn't *presume* to go as far as that,' said the man. 'But perhaps if they could just avoid some of the more spectacular nonsenses that always seem to accompany the forces of the law. That's all we can ask these days, of course. These days of vice and folly and so forth.' He chuckled briefly. 'In particular, I might draw your attention to my beloved relative, who I fancy you met at the weekend, as well as subsequently, if my sources are correct.'

'Janey,' Thea supplied. 'She's your sister, I understand.' The utter unlikelihood of the relationship struck Phil all over again, and he waited to hear it denied.

'Indeed she is. The dear girl. At least in a sort of a way.'

Phil observed his own prejudices working hard. Obese people were never from the upper classes. They did not have drawling languid brothers displaced from the 1930s. 'You mean she and you do not share the same two parents?' he queried.

Temple-Pritchett drew in his shapely chin, and looked down his perfectly straight nose. 'Is that an official enquiry?' he asked.

Phil forced himself to remain relaxed. 'You wanted to talk about her,' he said. 'To *draw our attention* to her.'

'I did,' the man nodded. 'So let me explain. Janey and I do share a mother.' He tightened his lips in a grimace that seemed to Phil to include reluctance, resignation, and a foreknowledge of how his tale would be received. Again, thoughts of acting came to him, rehearsed speeches and careful timing. 'We were, in fact, born on the same day.'

'Twins,' said Thea, as if making a triumphant discovery.

'Yes and no,' said Rupert Temple-Pritchett. 'It turned out we have different fathers.'

'Blimey!' said Thea, who reserved this expletive for moments of severe surprise. Her mind was obviously computing the scenario with some relish. 'Blimey O'Reilly.'

'Not good for dear Mummy's reputation, obviously. Painfully complicated for the whole family. An open secret across the land, thanks to pioneering laboratory involvement. Little suprise that they decamped to sunny Tuscany and have scarcely been seen around here since.' Bitterness threaded his words, but Phil detected a different emotion in the voice that uttered them. Something closer to sadness, he thought.

'How long have you known?' asked Phil.

'Five or six years for sure, although it was talked about for much of our lives, how different we were, how closely I resembled a certain individual who was not married to my mother.

My darling sister took the biscuit, so to speak, in the gene war.'

This overturned Phil's newly fledged assumption completely. Who could have doubted that of the two, only Rupert could be of the blue blood, the rightful heir? 'But you kept the name?' he said.

'Of course I kept the name. What would you expect? The case continues, as we speak.'

'Case?'

'The old man has his legal people seeking to eliminate me from the Pritchett bloodline. A bit rich, you might think, when it's Mamma who carries the true Temple inheritance. But you can see his point, from a husbandly stand. The ghastly truth can only be that she hopped from bed to bed without pausing long enough to give the prime progenitor time to implant his seed and raise the barricades against further incursion. Not that we can ever know which that was. She says she can't remember the precise sequence of events.' Again a speech delivered with perfect nuance – the dash of wry humour, the awareness of being at the centre of a very peculiar story.

Phil scratched his hairline in an effort to imagine the scenario, mild embarrassment hindering him from asking for further details.

'It isn't quite as bizarre as you think,' Rupert said. 'They were all very young and feckless. Too much money, a dash of recreational whatnots, no thought for the morrow. The surprise, when you think about it, is that it doesn't happen more often.'

'I have heard of it happening,' said Thea. 'My

171

brother had a dog – it had three puppies by a Jack Russell and one by a labrador, all in the same litter.'

'My mother was a bit of a dog,' agreed Rupert with such a straight face that Thea giggled.

'So who was – is – your father?' Phil asked.

'Off the scene,' said Rupert shortly. 'Out of the picture. Gone and forgotten.' He pinched his own nose tightly, as if to stem an inconvenient emotion, and then brushed at an invisible speck on his immaculate trousers. His mouth appeared to need tight control.

'I bet the lawyers are ecstatic,' said Phil. 'There can't be any precedents for something like this.'

'Seemingly not,' Rupert nodded.

'And Janey? What does she think about it?'

The grimace returned, deeper this time. 'Janey chooses not to think about it at all. She has far greater calls on her attention. You will have noticed her size? There's a reason for it.' He met each pair of eyes in turn, with a challenge to avoid flippancy.

'Oh?' said Thea, with a perfect mix of interest and sympathy.

'She had a tragedy not so very long ago, and resorted to sugar for consolation. She doubled her body weight in six months. And then doubled it again, very nearly, in the next two years. Not a pretty sight, not something her nearest and dearest wished to see. But there was no stopping her.' He sighed.

Phil was doing sums in his head. If the woman had been seven stone to start with, the claim was just about possible, but he made allowance for exaggeration. 'Poor woman,' he said, realising for the first time that Janey must be nearly ten years older than his original guess. Her twin brother was certainly in his mid-forties at least. 'She looks younger than you,' he added.

'That's her size,' Rupert agreed. 'It does that. Keeps the skin smooth, I assume. But the fact is, she's forty-one, the same as me.'

Phil had to stop himself from remarking that Temple-Pritchett looked rather more than that. 'Well, it's a pity,' he said feebly.

'It is, but she gets by. She's everybody's darling, is Janey, with her societies and good works and so forth. Her attitude to life is exemplary. She works for the beleaguered farmers, filling in those devilish forms for them, hardly taking a penny in return. She's got a good brain in there. But obviously she isn't happy,' he concluded with a regretful little shake of his head. 'Not happy at all. And an unhappy Janey Holmes has never been anybody's cup of tea. A lot of humouring and tiptoeing and so forth get called into play. Exhausting, I might tell you.'

Phil recognised his own reaction as similar to that of the day before, when speaking to Pritchett. Once again, it was as if he was being subtly hypnotised or manipulated. 'I appreciate you telling us all this,' he said. 'But–'

'What does this have to do with my asking you to call off your investigators?' Rupert supplied. 'Basically, it's to protect my poor sad Janey. This sort of thing doesn't do her any good. It's sure to remind her, you see.' His gaze drifted over the shrubs, and his arms seemed to clamp to his sides as if to quell a sudden pain. 'To be honest, it's reminding all of us.'

'What of?' asked Thea.

Rupert sighed. 'I may as well tell you. Don't you find, though—' he looked across the lawn at nothing, diverting swiftly into a parenthetical observation, 'that in a village there are always a hundred little stories, all woven in and out of the people's lives, going back centuries, explaining a few current facts, but chiefly providing no more than background noise? Even now, when there are so many newcomers, and the farms are all gone and the second homes brigade have wreaked devastation, there's still so much we carry on our shoulders. It makes your job impossible, I would think.'

'Just what I keep saying,' Thea endorsed. 'There's so much *history*.'

'Right.' He gave her an approving glance.

'Janey's tragedy,' Phil prompted.

'Ah, yes.' Again the pinched nose. 'The fact is, she had a baby, you see. A lovely little girl, the fairest hair you ever saw, beautiful long fingers. She died one night. Cot death, they said, in the end. After the police and coroner and shrinks had probed every fibre of her mother's life and shaken her all to pieces. She never got over it. She was never the same person again.' There was a fierceness in his eyes that Phil interpreted as grief imperfectly concealed.

'Nobody ever does get over it,' said Thea quietly. 'Poor Janey. How old was the baby?'

'Five weeks. Funny the way she changed everything in that brief little life. A blink of the

174

eye, but she'd been ours, our little hope and joy. She was called Alethea – lovely name.'

'Alethea?' Phil looked at his girlfriend. 'Didn't Janey react when you told her your name?'

'Not that I noticed. She didn't make any comment.'

'She thinks you're here for a reason,' said Rupert sadly. 'That it's *meant* in some way.'

Phil and Thea both remained silent. Rupert went on, 'She isn't altogether *right*, you see. That's why – now do you understand my reasons for coming to talk to you? Janey can't take pressure or any hint of accusation. She lives in a pink-tinted world where nothing touches her. She has a fragile hold on present-day realities. You can't always credit what she tells you. Do you see?' he finished, with a new tone of urgency.

'Yes,' said Phil gloomily. 'I see. But there's no way I can agree to what you ask.' He remembered the message from Gladwin. 'By the way, could you let me have your address? Apparently they've had some difficulty locating you.'

'Oh dear.' Rupert sighed theatrically. 'That's always a problem. The thing is, I've been working away, and gave up my house accordingly. I can give you the place I'm lodging. It's in Warwick.' He rattled off a street name and number, which Phil quickly noted down on the pad he kept in his pocket.

There were more questions in his mind, but he limited himself to finding out how long ago all this had happened. 'Five years,' said the man. 'Our little girl would be five now. Like a princess in a fairytale, with all the godparents gathering to give her their blessings. Instead she's just one tiny little lost soul.'

Rupert left as quietly as he'd come, saying his car was parked some distance away. 'Fancied a little walk,' he said. They watched him go, saying nothing until he was out of sight.

'Sounds as if that baby meant a lot to him,' said Thea. 'What a doting uncle.'

'Must be the twin thing,' Phil said. 'Makes for a closer bond. That's a pretty weird story, though – about the mother.'

'They're the ones in Italy, aren't they? I'm losing track.'

'Right,' he confirmed. 'Who can blame them for leaving the country? If there's a case ongoing that centres on her sexual activities, it would be humiliating to know people are talking about it.'

'Yet they're still together. You'd think it would be enough to break a marriage up.'

'If they only got the official word five years ago, there's a lot of joint history to hold them together,' said Phil.

'She sounds a character. Perhaps he loves her, even now.'

'Perhaps he does,' said Phil, trying to meet her eye or catch hold of her hand and convey that Mr Temple-Pritchett was not the only middle-aged man in love.

But she missed both hand and eye, getting up to check where her dog had got to, and then going into the house.

Phil was feeling a distinct benefit from the hour spent in the comfortable garden chair with the cushion placed strategically in the small of his back. He got up and walked gently around the house, testing the muscles for strain, and feeling the damaged spot with tentative fingertips. 'I really think it's getting better,' he told Thea, who had not asked. 'I might be driving again by the weekend.'

'Desperate to escape from me?' she asked. It struck him like a slap. She was annoyed about something.

'What's the matter?'

Where almost anyone else would have said *Nothing*, Thea prepared an honest answer. 'It isn't really your fault, I know,' she began. 'But I don't like the way we're seen as the centre of this investigation, even with you out of action and me not being involved at all. That farmer, letting the horses out – if he did. That was infuriating – the more so every time I think of it. And Janey not telling me anything important about herself – just rambling on about her martyrs and saints. And that Stephen man, begging you to find his son for him. I don't like any of it. I wanted a nice simple holiday,' she shouted.

'But most of all you're cross about my back,' he said softly. 'And so am I, darling. Believe me, so am I.' He reached out for her hand, pulling her towards him. She didn't resist, but knelt on the grass beside him, resting her head on his legs. He stroked her hair. 'The frustration is excruciating,' he said. 'After such high hopes. And yet, you know, we did have a fantastic day on Sunday, didn't we? That was as good as anything ever gets, and we ought not to let anything else overshadow it. I think I realised, even at the time, that we'd reached some sort of peak.'

'Mmm,' came her muffled voice. 'Not much comfort, really.'

He sighed, sensing a grey shadow creeping towards them, that might never entirely go away. Life was like this most of the time, after all. Even in glorious sunshine, with birds singing and flowers blooming, there were always fears and worries and people intruding with their calamities. 'At least it's other people's problems we're being bothered with,' he tried. '*We're* all right, aren't we?'

'Apart from your back,' she reminded him, her face turned away. He had a nasty feeling that she might be silently weeping, that things might be worse than he supposed.

'Thea?' he said. 'Look at me.'

Slowly she obeyed. There were no traces of tears on her cheeks, but her eyes looked blurry. He gripped her shoulders and lifted her face to his. The kiss was slow and rich and deep. It united them completely, sealing them together, erasing annoyances and anxieties. At least, it did for Phil. He could not be sure how it was for her. You could never be sure how it was for the other person.

As he had known was likely, DS Gladwin put in another appearance just as he and Thea were wondering about an evening meal. 'I could have phoned,' she admitted, 'but somehow I wanted this to be face-to-face.' She eyed Thea carefully. 'I hope you're getting enough peace and quiet to compensate for all this disruption?'

Thea smiled dryly at this repeat demonstration of empathy. It was beginning to seem more like a device for disarming animosity than something entirely genuine. 'I am meant to be working,' she said. 'I have to remind myself of that every now and then. It isn't a holiday for either of us.'

'But it must feel like it, with this amazing weather. If all this hadn't happened, you'd be off exploring, I'll bet.'

'Depends what you mean by *all this*. If it's the bones, then yes, in theory. But Phil's back has blighted everything, anyway. What you might call a double whammy, I suppose.'

'If I hadn't been here on Tuesday, instead of reporting for work, the bones might never have been found,' Phil summarised.

'They would, though,' Gladwin argued. 'Of course they would. Somebody else would have spotted them, probably that same morning. They weren't hard to see.'

Phil smiled and shrugged, as if might-have-beens were quite beside the point. He waited for his new colleague to explain her reason for the visit. In the pause, Thea got up and made her excuses. 'Don't worry,' she said. 'I'm not going off in a huff. I have to see to a few things in the house.'

Gladwin watched her go into the house before speaking. 'The skeleton has almost been assembled now,' she reported. 'A couple of ribs and some of the smaller bones missing, that's all. And the lab people say the hole in the skull was the cause of death. At least, he was alive when it

179

happened.' She paused, watching his face. 'We're really not much further forward than before, to put it in a nutshell. I don't suppose you've gleaned anything that might be useful?'

Phil thought about the emotionally fragile Janey and wondered whether to say anything. Gladwin noticed the hesitation. 'What?' she said.

'We had another visitor earlier today. Rupert Temple-Pritchett. He came to ask me to call your dogs off, because they're upsetting the locals.'

'Dogs? Oh, I see what you mean. What a bloody cheek.'

'I got the impression he's quite involved with what's going on. Did you know his sister had a baby, five years ago? It died and she hasn't been right since.'

Gladwin shook her head. 'All I know is that Mr T-P is the twin brother of Janey Holmes. And we couldn't find an address for him, just some credit card records.'

'I can help you there, at least.' Phil produced the Warwick address, which Gladwin copied onto her digital notebook. She looked up. 'It's not easy to know where to stop questioning,' she admitted. 'Without an identity for the victim, it's all smoke and mirrors. Nobody from the village seems to be missing, and yet the way they're behaving, you at least have to start with the assumption it's got something to do with the Pritchetts and Temples.'

'That's not evidence, of course,' he reminded her gently. 'It's still just as logical to think the body and its killer were total strangers to the village.'

'But you don't think so?'

'No,' he said slowly. 'It all feels a bit too deliberate and planned for that – don't you think?'

'I do,' she agreed. 'It might be different if we were talking about a young girl, with her killer driving across the country to evade the hue and cry. This one isn't like that at all. The man was properly buried, as if that was all part of the process.'

Phil was impressed, and then embarrassed at himself for assuming Gladwin would not be capable of such clear thinking.

She showed no sign of noticing his thought processes. 'I've ordered up DNA tests,' she went on, 'to compare as many as possible of the locals with the body. It didn't go down too well with some of them.'

'Which ones have you asked? I mean, where do you stop?'

'I decided the two families – Pritchetts and Temple-Pritchetts had got themselves in the spotlight, for a start. If we can eliminate them, then I'll widen it out to everybody who's lived in the village for five years or more.'

'Expensive,' said Phil. 'Doesn't it feel a bit over the top to you? Especially given that nobody except Giles Pritchett has been reported missing.'

'And not even him, officially.'

'Right. But I can see there's not much else you can do.'

'It's clutching at straws, I know that. But without an identity we're completely stuck. You know as well as I do – better, probably – that even if there was no question of homicide, we'd have to do everything in our power to find a name for the

181

deceased. It's natural human dignity, as well as getting everything tidy.'

'That's true, of course. And it would obviously be a big help to know whether the dead man shared some genetic material with long-term residents of the village.'

'And besides all that,' she smiled ruefully, 'we're meant to grab any excuse to augment the database – isn't that right?'

Phil mirrored her grimace. The DNA database was on target to capture samples from every single UK citizen, an aim which many police officers believed would be counter-productive. Phil already knew of several mistakes that had been made in acquiring and analysing samples. 'But they're not cooperating? Is that what you mean?'

Gladwin nodded. 'Mrs Holmes flatly refused. Mr Pritchett was OK about it, though. The Temple-Pritchetts are in Italy, so we've set them to one side for the moment.'

'I've got some strands of Giles Pritchett's hair,' Phil remembered. 'You're welcome to take that. His father gave it to me quite willingly.' Only then did he remember that once Pritchett had been assured the dead man was not his son, he could well have changed his mind about volunteering a sample. 'Assuming I can find them,' he added.

Gladwin gave a conspiratorial smile. 'Actually, we can get hold of Mrs Holmes's and her brother's, if we want to. There's a legal case going on, to establish their paternity, and decide what the implications are for the estate. Samples of DNA already exist as central pieces of evidence.

182

We can ask for read-outs of their profiles.'

Phil nodded, feeling slightly grubby, knowing what Thea would say if she could hear them. 'Go on then,' he advised. 'It can't do any harm, after all.'

After she'd gone, Phil realised he had no idea what became of Holmes, who had presumably married Janey and fathered the doomed Alethea. One of those fleeting husbands that the world seemed full of, he supposed.

Thea was giving the plants a final bedtime drink, humming contentedly to herself. Phil wrestled with a fleeting sense of guilt at being so uninvolved in the police investigations. The sky was still a daytime blue, and a glance at his watch revealed that it was only half past seven. Would it be excessive, he wondered to himself, to suggest they go out again to eat. Thea had showed no sign of wanting to cook anything, and he knew how much she liked to explore the countryside.

CHAPTER TWELVE

'So what did she say about the way he died?' Thea was curious to know.

Phil shook his head. 'Nothing unusual. A powerful blow to the head with something pointed, like your Bible woman and her tent peg.'

'Oh.'

'You sound disappointed.'

'No. Only that I was sort of hoping there'd be something a bit more ritualistic. Something out of one of Janey's saint stories. Take no notice. I'm just being fanciful.'

'You don't like Gladwin so much now, do you?' he noted. 'And after she tried so hard, poor lass.'

'Too hard. That's the problem. She's not genuine. The first time, I fell for it completely. But now she just trots out the same spurious sympathy for me having to put up with you being so distracted. She doesn't really mean it at all. It's something she's taught herself to do.'

'I really don't think that's right. I'm much more inclined to think it's more that she's under a lot of strain. She might simply be following the training, because she's too nervous to be herself.'

'What training? The bit that teaches you how to gain the public's confidence by showing them you understand how they feel? I don't think Jess has done that module yet.' Thea had been conscientious in keeping up with her daughter's police training, as well as unable to resist arguing with much of it.

He closed his eyes briefly. 'If she had, I doubt if she'd tell you... She'd know what your reaction would be. It's only common sense, after all. Gladwin's going to be keen to keep me sweet, since we're sure to be working together a fair bit. I vote we give her the benefit of the doubt for a while longer.'

'Well I abstain from voting at all. The election's rigged, if you ask me.'

'Very funny.'

'We could go out for supper?' he offered, a few

184

minutes later. 'Somewhere a bit swanky. So long as their chairs aren't too low, I think my back could cope.'

'Do you have somewhere in mind?'

'Well, there's Winchcombe not far away. We could see if there's a place there.'

Thea went to her car and extracted a map. As she turned it to the right section, she sighed. 'Look at all these woods and footpaths and ruins. Hailes Abbey. Breakheart Plantation. Sudeley Castle. Even a Roman villa in Spoonley Wood. A person could spend months just exploring all this.'

'Breakheart Plantation? Sounds like Brokeback Mountain. Show me.'

She pointed out a patch of green to the south west of Winchcombe. It had quarries on every side, with steep contours rising and falling crazily all around. 'Looks dramatic,' he agreed. 'We'll go there one day, I promise. There's plenty of summer left for jaunts like that.'

'Yes, but I'm here *now*,' she complained in frustration. 'At least, for another two days.'

'Two days?' He looked at her in alarm. 'Is that all it is? I thought you were having two weekends.'

'Tomorrow and Saturday. Archie arrives on Sunday. I'll have to be out of his way sometime during the afternoon. He'll be wanting my bed.'

Phil shook his head. 'Where did the week go?' he mourned. 'No wonder you're feeling so frustrated.'

'So, we'll go for a drive,' she said, suddenly invigorated by the prospect. 'We can head for Winchcombe and see if we see a likely place to eat. Somewhere with a west-facing garden,' she added, with a glance at the sun, shortly to vanish behind the trees of Temple Guiting.

They shut Hepzie in the house, changed into fresh clothes and set out in Thea's car. 'Oh drat,' she said, as she was turning on the gravel. 'I forgot to shut Shasti's window.'

'It can wait,' said Phil, who was still trying to convince himself that the car seat was not jeopardising his back. 'It isn't going to get cold until the small hours, and even then it won't be enough to matter.'

'OK,' said Thea slowly. 'I suppose it'll keep. It's just – Miss Deacon *did* say I should keep her firmly shut in.'

'She's in the cage,' Phil said. 'Stop worrying.'

Driving to Winchcombe was less pleasant than anticipated, thanks to the sun shining right into Thea's eyes. She pulled down the visor, but there were moments when she was completely blinded. 'I can't see if anything's coming,' she said on one bend. 'Can you?'

'It's OK,' he said tightly. 'I find it helps to keep the windscreen clean.'

Without a word, Thea activated her screen washer, which effectively blotted out all residual visibility as the dry wipers smeared dead flies and country dust across the glass. 'Bloody hell!' she said, squirting more fluid and setting the wipers at full speed. 'This is ridiculous.'

'Watch out!' cried Phil, pressing a phantom brake with all his strength. When the car stopped as if he had indeed managed to control it by magic, the panic did not abate; indeed it almost consumed him. 'You've hit somebody,' he gasped, entirely superfluously. Not until he reached for his door handle and seat belt catch did he realise the consequences of the impact on his delicate spine. 'Aaghh!' he groaned.

'Shut up, shut up,' Thea muttered, as she opened her door and left the car in a single movement. 'I couldn't see, could I?' she flared back at him. 'You know I couldn't.'

All that Phil could see was Thea's white face, and great tragic eyes like a melting waxwork. Voices screamed at him inside his head: *Take charge, you idiot, you're a policeman. If you hadn't said what you did about the windscreen, this would never have happened. If somebody's dead, Thea could be charged with manslaughter. Careless driving, at the very least. Jesus, my back hurts.*

He finally thrust open his door, and rolled out of the seat. Clinging desperately to the door frame he tried to see what they had hit. Initially there was only a piece of yellow cotton visible on the other side of the car. Standing taller, he managed to locate a fair head and a bare arm.

'It's that girl, Soraya,' said Thea, in an oddly normal voice. 'She doesn't look too badly damaged. Oh dear, I am *so* sorry,' she said more loudly. 'What on earth have I done to you?'

Never admit fault, the voice in Phil's head insisted, forgetting his police role in his instinct to protect Thea.

There was no reply, and Phil inched agonisingly around the front of the car for a better view. The girl was pushed into the grassy verge, the car's front wheel still touching her leg. He

187

remembered how very abruptly Thea had stopped, how violently he had lurched against his seat belt as a result. Even so, the car must have carried its victim several yards.

'My leg,' came a small voice. 'It hurts.' Soraya's little face looked at Thea. 'I was trying to get out of your way, but you came right at me. Were you deliberately trying to kill me?'

'Of course not! I couldn't see you. The sun was in my eyes. I couldn't see a thing. At least I was going slowly. You don't look too badly hurt. I'll call for an ambulance.'

'Oh no,' the girl dissolved into sudden childish tears. 'Dad's going to be furious if you do that.'

'Well, that's his problem. Isn't it, Phil?' For the first time Thea sought out her companion. When she understood his plight, she frowned fiercely. 'Oh, God almighty – I've hurt you as well, have I? This is bloody ridiculous.'

The expletives left him in no doubt as to her stress level. He was being asked for support, assistance, reassurance, and all he could do was to remain in an upright position without fainting or vomiting. The pain was as bad as it had been on Monday morning, thanks to the jerk of Thea's braking and his own efforts with the phantom pedal.

'I've got a phone,' he said, wondering who he should call. An ambulance was almost certainly going to be required, but first he ought to assess Soraya's injuries. If she was only bruised, it might turn out to be embarrassing. On the other hand, the thought of calling aid for himself, summoning strong hands and warm red blankets trussing

188

him tightly onto a purpose-built back board, was very sweet. The flaming punches that his muscles were throwing at him every time he moved were sapping not only strength but logical thought.

'How badly hurt is she?' he managed to ask.

Thea looked at the girl, still huddled in the long grass, white flowers appearing to crown her fair hair. A nymph, thought Phil wildly. A hedgerow nymph, weeping for the sorrows of the world.

'Can you stand up?' Thea asked, holding out an encouraging hand. There was very little space to move between the hedge and the car. As Soraya began to gather herself, they all heard an approaching engine.

'There's room for it to pass,' said Phil. The lane was narrow, but not quite single vehicle width. Besides, Thea's car was mostly on the verge.

'It'll stop to see what's happening, though,' said Thea. 'Anybody would.'

Soraya squawked at that. 'Dad's going to be so cross,' she whined. 'I should have been home by now.'

Phil forced his mind to function. He tried to assess how far they had come from Hector's Nook – he thought not more than two or three miles. Probably less, given the small roads. 'Do you live close by?' he asked.

The new car had come into view, travelling slowly. 'He can't see, either,' Thea realised. 'I hope he doesn't hit us.'

The *he* was a she, who stopped alongside the fracas and wound down her window. 'Gosh – what happened?' Phil thought he had heard the voice before.

'The sun was in my eyes, and I hit Soraya,' said Thea succinctly. 'Do you know her?'

'Of course. She lives just up the road. Hi, Sory. Are you badly damaged?'

'Huh, Fiona,' came the indifferent reply. 'I'm just trying to stand up. I think I'm all right. She pushed me into the hedge so I'm a bit scratched.'

Fiona – Janey's friend. The historian who liked saints as much as Janey did. 'She doesn't seem too badly wounded,' came the quick assessment. 'But you two look rather shell shocked.'

Phil tried to smile at her. 'We are rather,' he admitted. 'These things always come like a bolt from the blue, don't they.' It was a dopey thing to say, weak and unprofessional. He tried to gather himself. 'The sun was in Thea's eyes.' He remembered that Thea had already said that.

'Tell me about it. You'd think they could invent better shields against it, wouldn't you?' Fiona's tone was in no way accusing, which was something to be thankful for.

'You don't appear to be at all well,' she observed. 'In fact you look worse than Soraya, if anything. Poor old you,' she addressed Thea. 'Surrounded by crocks. Lucky I came along. I can take Soraya home, if you like. Her dad doesn't like her to be out for long.'

Phil had heard such remarks a thousand times, but in a very different context. Asian families kept a tight rein on their daughters, fathers worrying themselves into acute anxiety states at the hazards a girl faced in this wicked society. But Soraya – despite her exotic name – was no Asian. She was as pink-skinned as the purest Saxon, and her father likewise.

'It isn't that simple, I'm afraid,' he said. 'She might press charges against Thea.' He gave his girlfriend an apologetic glance, which she ignored.

'Oh, I wouldn't worry about that. She's tougher than she looks – aren't you, pet?'

Soraya managed a grin. She was standing upright by this time, swiping a hand down the front of her yellow dress, and brushing at her bare knees. Phil noted how old-fashioned and childish she looked, dressed like that. He couldn't recall when he'd last seen a girl her age in a frock.

'Where were you going?' Thea asked, apparently noticing the same thing. 'You seem to be dressed up for something special.'

'Oh! No, not really. I've been taking the cows back after milking, that's all.' Soraya paused, sucking in her lips. Then she added, 'I thought I'd have a look at the house martins at Fairoaks. The people aren't there, so I can stay and watch them for a bit.'

'Milking?' Thea stared around as if looking for cows. 'I didn't think there were any dairy farms left here.'

'We're organic,' said the girl, as if that explained everything.

'They've got a hundred shorthorns,' added Fiona. 'As you can see.' She pointed a short way down the road behind them, where two field gates stood opposite each other. The road was splattered with manure. 'She crosses them over after milking.'

'Gosh! Lucky I didn't turn up when they were crossing,' groaned Thea. 'I might have ploughed

191

right into them.'

'Well you didn't,' said Fiona. Something about the look she gave Thea, combined with the managerial way she had taken charge of Soraya, sowed a flickering idea in Phil's mind. He watched her more closely as she ushered the girl to her own car.

'Don't worry,' Soraya said, turning to address Thea. 'I'm really not hurt. But I will have to tell Dad about it – he'll notice the scratches.'

'Well, tell him I'm awfully sorry,' said Thea. 'And thanks, Fiona, for taking her home. You've been very helpful.'

As a distraction from his worries, Phil was entertaining nostalgic thoughts of farm girls on a summer evening, slow-swaying cows, flittering house martins and perhaps a barn owl for good measure. *Stop it,* he told himself. *You're getting delirious.*

The atmosphere was definitely lighter, though. Thea was recovering her spirits, and soon he would have to get back in the car and confess his renewed disablement. No way could he manage a meal in a formal setting, or any sort of meal, come to that. She would have to take him home and fetch his painkillers and abandon the plan for him to sleep upstairs with her. It was so disheartening that he moaned aloud.

'So – no ambulance for Soraya then?' Thea said.

'But she isn't the only invalid, is she?' said Fiona, looking probingly at Phil. 'Your bloke looks in a bad way to me.'

'Well, he's not having an ambulance,' said Thea decisively. 'We know the only treatment is rest and

192

time.' She sighed. 'I braked too hard,' she said regretfully. 'It can't have done him any good.'

The three women all contemplated the helpless man for a long moment. He could read some of their thoughts and felt the shame and humiliation of the failed hunter, the useless defender. 'Just leave me on the hillside to die,' he said.

'Fiona's nice, isn't she,' said Thea, absently. They were eating scrambled eggs in Miss Deacon's living room, Phil slumped on the sofa, surrounded by cushions. The plate was balanced on his knees. Thea was sitting beside him, crowded into a corner.

'A bit dykey,' he said carelessly. 'But normal enough otherwise.'

'What? Dykey? Just because she took Soraya home?' She stared at him and he realised too late that he'd said the wrong thing. Would *butch* have been better? He doubted it.

'And the look she gave you. You won't have noticed.' He smiled, hoping to get her back on his side – a man's woman, who never even registered lustful glances from another woman.

'I suppose you think she's in a relationship with Janey, as well?' she said, her voice full of angry accusation.

'It never crossed my mind,' he said, with perfect truth. The lurking images were too much to bear.

Mercifully, Thea seemed to catch a glimpse of them herself and a smile tweaked the corners of her mouth. 'Well, just stop it,' she said. 'It's not worthy of you.'

'I don't see what's wrong with making an

observation,' he persisted. 'And I just bet I'm right, as well.'

'I don't care if you are. It's got nothing to do with anything. Besides, I like Fiona. To me she seems perfectly nice and normal.'

'She can't be entirely normal, though,' said Phil. 'She belongs to Janey's saints thingy, after all.'

Thea heaved a sigh. 'I still wish I'd gone with them that morning, just to see what they do. Every time it's mentioned I get the impression it would have been something quite special.'

'You could have gone. Why didn't you?'

'I told you before – I was too flummoxed, having you to deal with. And I was tired. And a bit cross.'

'I guess I rather spoilt things,' he admitted.

'Don't start that again,' she said. 'Do you want some ice cream?'

CHAPTER THIRTEEN

Phil's prime emotion since the accident in the narrow lane was guilt. He had suggested cleaning the windscreen at the exact wrong moment. He had braced himself all wrong on impact, sending his back into regression on an epic scale. He had effectively wrecked all hope of Thea enjoying a final two days of outings and explorings, which was what she enjoyed most of all. Born of some vague sense of expiation, he focussed his mind on the police investigations centred on the village. If they couldn't go out together, they would stay in and discuss murder and strange village cults. Thea could Google Templars and saints and large dignified manor houses, and perhaps locate a pattern. The fact that a team of dedicated police officers would be doing much the same thing at the station was neither here nor there.

'I ought to make sure Soraya's all right,' Thea worried. 'What if she's got internal bleeding or something?'

Phil had been similarly concerned, fully aware that there were procedures they had ignored. The girl had been taken home by Fiona, after an assurance that she had no sign of any broken bones or concussion. 'I promise you, it's the best thing,' Fiona had insisted. 'Robin doesn't like her to be away for long.' Soraya had settled into the passenger seat of Fiona's car and waited restlessly while Phil and Fiona exchanged a few further words.

Before getting back into his own car, Phil must have indicated surprise bordering on suspicion at the girl's anxiety to get home. Fiona paused, and stood facing him. 'Oh, it isn't what you think,' she said in a hushed voice, which neither Soraya nor Thea could possibly have heard. 'He's not an abusive father in any sense. Actually, he's completely dependent on her. He's not well – one of those nervous system things – and needs her to do most of the farm work.'

And that's not abusive? Phil thought to himself. 'How old is she?' he asked.

'Twenty. Her mother went off years ago, and it's been really hard for them.'

'Just the two of them, there alone?' He couldn't

help it – the scenario screamed alarm bells at him.

'Yes, but Janey Holmes keeps an eye on them, helps out a bit. A few of us do, in fact. We still have a few vestiges of community spirit, you know.'

'And does Soraya go with you on your saints' festivals?'

Fiona grinned. 'Sometimes. But it's Robin who's most interested. He's a founder member, in fact, with Polly and Jasper. You don't know Jasper, he lives in Italy.'

'Janey's father?'

Fiona blinked, before expelling a short laugh. 'No, gosh no. He's called Bernard. Jasper's no relation. He lived here for a while, but he's not really a local. He's just – well, he's just Jasper. Something of a Flying Dutchman, I suppose. We haven't seen him for two or three years now.'

Phil held himself tightly as his back raged for a few moments. 'Same as Giles Pritchett,' he noted. 'Did they know each other, by any chance?'

'Vaguely, I suppose,' she said absently.

'And Rupert Temple-Pritchett? You all know him as well, I assume?'

The reaction was violent and entirely unpremeditated. 'That bastard? We certainly *did* know him, before–' Then she caught herself up, reminding Phil suddenly of the way Soraya had checked herself a few minutes earlier, as she spoke of going to see the house martins. 'Why?' Fiona asked him, with a penetrating gaze. 'What have you heard about him?'

'He's been to see us at Miss Deacon's. Twice. He appears to have a lot he wants to tell us.'

The woman's eyes widened, and her gaze

flittered from one patch of hedgerow to another as her thoughts visibly whirled. 'I see,' she said eventually. 'Oh well – he's not really such a bad bloke. What was it you wanted to know about him?' She glanced at where Soraya was sitting in her car, starting to peer around to see where her driver had got to. 'Actually, I'll have to go,' she said. 'Maybe we can talk about it another time.'

'Thanks for taking her home,' he said. 'Thea and I have enough to cope with already.'

And they had parted company. The proposed evening out had been abandoned and Thea had slammed together some scrambled eggs and bacon with shaking hands. 'I can't believe I hit that girl,' she said, more than once. 'I ought to have stopped when I realised I couldn't see anything. Why doesn't she sue me for dangerous driving?'

'Because she wasn't hurt and she doesn't want a fuss,' he said patiently. 'She's got her own reasons for keeping things simple, I expect. Most people have. Although her father might yet persuade her to change her mind. You can't be sure you're out of the woods just yet.'

Thea groaned. 'If the story gets out, you know what they'll say, don't you? That you exerted undue pressure on her, pulling rank as a senior police officer. Have you thought of that?'

He sighed. 'Yes, I have. And it's a risk I'll have to take, isn't it? I doubt very much if anything's going to come of it. After all, the locals have got more interesting matters to gossip about just at the moment, don't you think?'

'Hmm,' was all she said to that. But a few minutes later, she spoke again with a characteristic shift of subject. 'Do you think Giles Pritchett was in the Saints and Martyrs Club?'

'I have absolutely no idea.' He looked at her. 'Why?'

'Oh, something about Janey's reaction when you mentioned him yesterday. Saying he's not lost. And she was so quick to change the subject when I mentioned Rupert. Not a word about him being her brother. Didn't you think she was acting oddly?'

'Definitely,' he agreed. 'But I've thought her odd from the start. Now we know about her personal tragedy, that isn't so surprising, is it? Did I tell you what Pritchett said about the trust?' He forced himself to concentrate on Janey, hoping to keep Thea's mind off the road accident.

'Yes, you did,' she replied. 'If you mean the trust that owns her fabulous house.' She sighed. 'Gosh, though – wouldn't you love to live there? She's got it so beautifully done out, and clean and tidy. It's like a palace.'

'Probably has a cleaning woman,' he said. 'And I guess most of the houses around here are like that inside. We ought to try and get a peep inside Temple Guiting Manor. I bet that's just as good.'

Thea wasn't drawn. 'Yes, but don't you think Janey's got reason to defend her lifestyle, if she thought there was a threat to it? I mean, something like that could provide a motive for murder, couldn't it? What if there's something in the trust to say she can only have it until she's forty-five? Or provided she produce a son and heir to take it on after her? Or that she climbs Mount Everest before midnight on January 1st 2010?'

'Stop, stop!' Phil held up a trembling hand. 'Please don't make me laugh. It hurts.'

'No, but seriously,' Thea gazed hard at him. 'It's possible, isn't it?'

'Anything's possible,' he said weakly. 'But I don't think any of those ideas are very likely. Apart from anything else, the law wouldn't uphold conditions like that, these days.'

'But she might not know that.'

His ruse had succeeded better than he could have imagined. Thea was in full spate, brainstorming reasons why Janey might have felt driven to kill by a threat to her home. And gradually he found himself believing that she could have a point. After all, the facts of Janey's birth were sufficiently bizarre in themselves for any theories to sound almost convincing.

'But she reported the fallen tree,' he remembered. 'She'd never have done that if she knew a dead body had been buried under it.'

'She might, because Fiona was there. She wouldn't have had any choice.'

He reached out a hand to her, holding her forearm. 'You're so good at this,' he sighed. 'I feel I should resign instantly and let you take my job.'

'No thanks,' she laughed.

'But what about the Templars?' he remembered, a few moments later. 'We mustn't forget the Templars. After all, Fiona did say Janey had Templar blood. As does Giles, apparently.'

'Ah! I was coming to that,' she said, holding up a didactic finger. 'I did a bit more Googling earlier today, when you were in the garden. Temple Guiting was a preceptory – which sounds a bit like a monastery or a hospital – but there's no physical trace of it left, as far as I can work out. There's a very tenuous sort of link with Janey's saints. Thomas à Becket was a martyr who got canonised, right? Well, the knights who killed him had to hand over all their properties to the Templars, which seems to have been a serious punishment. Maybe there's some sort of revenge still at work.'

'Utterly tenuous,' Phil confirmed.

'I know,' she admitted. 'But there's definitely something about the name Temple that we haven't got to the bottom of.'

Suddenly he felt weary of the whole arcane discussion. 'The fact is, we still have an unidentified murder victim,' he said. 'With all the usual questions and examinations that go with that.'

'And a missing son and heir,' Thea reminded him. 'We shouldn't ignore Giles Pritchett. He might easily be the key to the whole thing.'

'It is strange the way his parents are behaving,' he agreed. 'All I can think is that they panicked when they heard about the body under the tree, and even though they don't seriously believe he's dead, they had to make sure – especially Trudy. That was why Stephen came over to see me the way he did, trying to keep it unofficial.'

Thea looked dubious. 'I think there's more to it than that,' she insisted. 'What if *he* – I mean Stephen – insisted they keep quiet about it, while *she* was convinced the lad was gone forever – and that's why she has to drug herself into the twilight zone?'

'That would be too cruel. Pritchett isn't cruel.'

'He might think he's doing it for the best. But the poor woman, in any case. It must be awful for her.'

From some indirect mental association, Phil found himself permitting the memory of his daughter to filter carefully into the forefront of his mind, linked to the mysterious absence of Giles and the effect on his mother. Yes, he knew for sure that Emily was dead, and yes, he had a son as well, to cushion the loss at least slightly. And still his foundations had been shaken, his assumptions cracked and broken, his confidence in a stable, reliable universe rocked. To lose a child was truly terrible, and it took years to start picking through the wreckage for the core essentials that might just still be surviving.

'Poor old Trudy,' he muttered quietly. Thea didn't hear him.

He couldn't manage the stairs that night, either. Thea put him to bed like a child, bringing him a glass of water and another painkiller, kissing him goodnight. 'I'm sorry,' she murmured into his ear. 'Really sorry. If it's still bad in the morning, we probably ought to find you a doctor.'

'No, no,' he argued bravely. 'There's no point. When I get home, I'll go to my usual GP. He'll have had a note from the hospital and know what's happened. I'll need him to sign me off work, in any case. I can't see me going back for another week or two yet.'

'Well, we have to leave here on Sunday,' she reminded him. 'Although I thought I'd have heard from Archie by now.'

'What if he doesn't show?' Phil wondered. 'Will that mean we can stay here?'

She smiled at him. 'Would you like to?'

He rolled his eyes. 'Just at the moment, all I can think of is never again getting out of this bed. Ask me again tomorrow.'

'Well, you won't be too hot in the night. I've left the front window open at the top. And you must have got used to the fish tanks by now. Sleep tight, and I'll see you in the morning.'

His dreams, when they came, were pleasurably erotic – at least at first. A cool body was pressing against his, seductive and sensuous. His partner – a faceless woman heavier than Thea – wound herself around him, weighing him down even as she stimulated him. Her arms and legs were everywhere: on his chest and thighs, moving in small waves. There was something oddly persistent and inhuman about it, which steadily changed the pleasure to something closer to panic. Only when something touched his face did he awake with a jolt, his eyes flying open.

There was a faint grey light coming through the window, but not enough to see properly by. Instead, he was forced to use his hands, bringing them up to the peculiar sensation at his neck. His fingers encountered a solid dry substance that moved at his touch. Fumbling, he tried to lift it away, dimly aware that there was also something on his belly and beyond. Logic failed him, as he struggled to name the thing he was touching. The very strangeness of it was terrifying, even though he felt no pain and could not identify any actual threat.

Finally, after perhaps ten seconds of pure bewilderment, he screamed and contorted his body in an effort to escape what he had belatedly understood. The snake! It was Shasti the python, draped on top of him, her head tucked into the crevice below his jaw, and her other end flicking provocatively at his genitals.

'Thea!' he screamed at full decibels. 'For God's sake, Thea!'

Shasti, annoyed by the noise and the writhings of her new friend, slithered down from the bed and across the floor, and was gone from sight long before Thea could get up and stumble down the stairs to the rescue.

'But why didn't you hold onto her?' Thea wailed again, having searched the house in vain for the third time. The back door had a cat flap, despite the absence of any feline inhabitants, and it was increasingly obvious that the python had dived through it moments after abandoning Phil.

He made no attempt to reply, having given his answer to the question some time earlier, and finding no useful elaboration to make. Thea's total lack of sympathy had reached epic new proportions, once she understood what had happened. Initially blaming herself for forgetting to close the shed window, she had transferred her reproaches to Phil for his spineless reaction to finding himself in bed with an amorous snake. 'She wouldn't have hurt you,' Thea insisted. 'She's not strong enough to damage a fully grown man.'

Not a word about his back, he noticed. When he had tried to sit up and give a coherent account of himself, the muscles had spasmed excruciatingly. 'You can't imagine what it's like,' he whined. 'It was like being in a horror film.'

'Well, we'll have to find her. She's in terrible danger out there with idiot people reacting so stupidly. Someone's going to chop her in half with a spade, or she'll get run over.'

'Or she'll eat somebody's pet guinea pig, or scare someone out of their wits,' added Phil.

'But where do I start to look? How fast can they travel? Will she find a warm, dark place to curl up in?'

'Probably, yes, judging by the warm, dark place she headed for the moment she was free,' he said. 'How did she get in here, anyway?'

'The window was open.'

'Yes, but at the *top*. Can she slither up glass? They don't have suckers to hold on with, do they?'

'No, of course not. But she could have got onto the sill, and then up from there. Or maybe she came in through the cat flap, as well as going out that way.'

'Can't imagine why, though.' He frowned. 'What if somebody deliberately pushed her in through the window? Wanting to scare us?'

Thea was halfway out of the door, and paused only briefly. 'Don't be silly,' she said.

She was gone for over an hour, and came back hot and pink and worried. 'Not a sign of her,' she reported.

'Thea, it's barely half past five in the morning. Nobody's going to meet the thing at this hour. Put some of her favourite food in the shed, and she'll come back of her own accord, like as not.'

'I can't rely on that, though, can I?'

Phil was having to work hard to suppress his own rising concern. The prospect of informing the police of the escaped python was not appealing. Gladwin would get to hear about it and was not going to be at all impressed. He couldn't blame her, either. People really should not keep such creatures in captivity. It made no sense and caused havoc when they got loose.

Thea disappeared again for ten minutes. When she came back she had followed Phil's advice and left some dead mice in the snake's cage. 'She'd got the catch to the cage undone somehow,' she said. 'I can't have fastened it properly. And on top of that, I'd forgotten to close the window, after all the excitement last night, so it was easy for her to get out of the shed. I'm going to be in really awful trouble. I don't expect Miss Deacon will pay me after this.'

'What's the catch like?' His earlier suspicions had resurfaced with a vengeance.

'It's a hook, which snaps closed.' She operated her fingers to demonstrate. 'You push it through a little hole in an underneath bit,' she explained. 'To open it, you have to squeeze it hard to disconnect it.'

'And you think a snake could get that undone?'

'Well, somebody did. The door's standing wide open. It probably wouldn't have mattered if I hadn't left the window open as well.' She wrung her hands. 'I'm useless at this job, being so careless.'

'I don't think it's your fault at all. I think somebody deliberately fetched the beast and sent it in

205

through the living room window, as a piece of mischief.'

'What a horrible, stupid thing to do!' Thea cried. 'That poor snake. That's so cruel. Who would do such a thing? And what would be the point?'

'Revenge?' he hazarded. 'It's the kind of thing a person might do to get their own back. Unless they thought a python was poisonous, and they hoped it would kill us.'

'The only person who might want revenge is Soraya,' Thea said slowly. 'Or her father, more likely. And they *did* let the horses out – or so we think. It would be the same kind of act, using the animals against us. Getting us into trouble with Miss Deacon. But it still seems mad.'

'Maybe it's symbolic. The serpent in the Garden of Eden, something like that.'

Thea gave this more serious consideration than he had expected. 'Robin and Soraya do seem rather *intense*,' she nodded. 'Like people in some sort of sect or cult. But Fiona didn't say there was anything like that, did she?'

'No – but why would she?'

'Because if they are Mormons or Jehovah's Witnesses, that would be one of the first things she mentioned about them. It would be how the locals define them.'

'Unless they all belong to the same outfit. Then it would go without saying.'

'But they're not,' said Thea.

'Not as far as we know,' he said, thoughtfully. 'Unless you count this Saints and Martyrs malarky as a sect. Which disapproves of cohabiting couples who come here and stir everything

206

up the way we've done.'

'But we've got Miss Deacon's blessing. And it sounds as if anything Miss Deacon says goes.'

'*You've* got her blessing, but I haven't. I'm not supposed to be here. Janey came over the minute you got here, to check that out. It's me they don't like. And they know I'm sleeping here in the front room. They'd know the snake would make straight for me.' He shuddered reflexively. 'They must have known how horrific it would be. I'm going to have nightmares about it for the rest of my life.'

Thea clenched her small fists. 'Well they won't get away with it. I'm going out again to find that snake, and this time Hepzie can come and help me.' She had left the spaniel behind on her first search, worried that the dog would send the snake deeper into hiding. 'She's not much of a blood-hound, but she might be better than nothing.'

While she was gone, Phil lay back and let himself doze, having a growing hunch that the coming day would see little opportunity for rest. If he could persuade his back to relent enough to let him get up and dressed, that would be a good start. But first, just a few more minutes of sleep would be very restorative...

'Found her!' came Thea's triumphant cry, forty minutes later. 'Safe and well under the horses' trough. It was all thanks to Hepzie, clever little thing. And you know, she – Shasti, I mean – seemed quite glad to go back home. I think she was scared out there in the wide open spaces.' She was babbling in her relief, kicking off her shoes and ruffling the spaniel's long ears in congratulation.

'That's good,' mumbled Phil, only half awake. 'Did you put a padlock on the cage?'

'I would if I could find one,' Thea said wholeheartedly. 'Maybe they sell them in the local shop. What time does it open?'

But Phil gave no response. He was thinking about the string of uncomfortable awakenings he had had in Hector's Nook, and resolving that there would not be any more. Enough was enough – but he had no idea how he was going to convey his decision to Thea.

She produced a full English breakfast in the glow of her relief from snake anxiety and began to make plans for the day. It took Phil several minutes to break through her prattle and make her understand that he had undergone a change of heart. 'No,' he said, rather loudly. 'No, I don't want to go to an arboretum or a farm park or a holy well on top of a hill. Sorry – but I think this is as far as it goes. I can't pretend any longer that it's OK for me to have an unscheduled holiday while there's so much going on out there.'

She blinked at him in confusion. 'But you said–' she began.

'I know what I said, and I've changed my mind. A policeman is never really off duty, as you know full well, and I've spent too long as it is just pottering about down here. If somebody did send that snake in through the window, then they did me a favour. It was a wake-up call. Sorry, love, but I'm going back to the flat this afternoon, where at least I'll be close at hand if they need me.'

His flat was in Cirencester, a two-minute walk from the police station. He had a computer linked to the police network and a dedicated phone line. As long as he could manage to sit at the desk, he'd be able to help with some of the checks and analyses associated with any of the ongoing cases – as well as keeping abreast of developments. He said it all knowing perfectly well that it was untrue. His reasons for leaving Temple Guiting had little or nothing to do with his work. But Thea took it all at face value, at least initially.

'Can't you leave it one more day?' she asked. 'They can't be that desperate for your help if they haven't phoned all week. Besides – which case is it you think you're needed for? The ricin nonsense or the skeleton under the tree?'

'Both – or neither. I just feel I should be back in action. We're not getting anywhere here, are we?'

'Aren't we?' she said, in a hollow voice. 'I thought we were doing quite well, considering.'

'Oh, Thea,' he sighed. 'I didn't mean *us*. Although–' He gave her a probing look, remembering her lack of sympathy, her irritability and failure to enter into some of his moods. 'Well, I'm not sure we've been doing too well on that front either, have we?'

She seemed stunned. 'Haven't we? I've been really glad that you're here – somebody to talk to and eat with. I thought it was all quite good fun, in spite of your back and the bloody silly bones. I know I'm not particularly good at nursing – I did warn you about that. But haven't you enjoyed meeting Janey and Pritchett and the others?'

'Enjoyed?' he repeated. 'They're all suspects in

a murder enquiry. How could I *enjoy* meeting them?'

'Is that how you see them?'

'Perhaps not entirely, but I can't just forget that a man was unlawfully killed and buried only three hundred yards away. It's virtually certain that at least one of the people we've been socialising with knows something about it, even if they didn't personally slaughter him. And I've been pretending to be an ordinary guy – not taking notes or questioning them. How do you think that makes me feel?'

'I have no idea,' she said stiffly. 'I thought you were happy to leave it all to Gladwin. You said it was her case and she wouldn't appreciate you interfering.'

'I was wrong,' he snapped. 'I see that now.'

'Well, I don't understand what changed.'

'I had a wake-up call,' he repeated doggedly. 'No more or less than that. Put it down to having a snake in bed with me.'

She kept a quiet serious eye on him, saying nothing, as he drained the last of his coffee and heaved himself out of the chair. Miss Deacon's walking stick had been retrieved from its place beside the front door, and he leant on it with both hands, feeling like an old man in a children's picture book.

'You couldn't have taken notes or asked questions,' she said levelly. 'Not if you're not actively part of the team. I do know that much. Besides, you're way too senior for that sort of work.'

They both remembered, at the same moment, the first time they'd met. He had been asking questions then, interviewing Thea in a room at the station, his leg in a plaster cast. 'That isn't true,' he said. 'Nobody is ever as senior as that, in CID.'

'OK. So you're packing up and driving back home today – is that right?' She kinked an eyebrow at his efforts to stand up straight and move across the room, and he realised that she had begun to see through his excuses. 'And I can just get on with it here?'

'You'll be all right.' He had spent months trying to protect her, warn her when he knew she was in danger, rushing around the area searching for her and her precious dog, only to find that she had been quite capable of looking after herself. Even a Sir Galahad tired eventually, when he saw his efforts unappreciated. 'You just have to keep out of people's way until Sunday.'

'You won't be able to drive,' she said with crystal clear finality. 'And I'm not going to take you. I think you're being ridiculous. If you're fed up with me, I can understand that, but this guff about needing to get back to work doesn't convince me at all. If you really wanted to be involved, you could call Gladwin and ask her to give you a summary of where she's got to. Then you could perhaps follow a few things up for her, or give her some advice. Just like you have been doing,' she finished fiercely. 'Don't you think she'd use you if she needed to, having you right here on the doorstep?'

He turned gingerly, in the kitchen doorway and faced her, his mind in turmoil. He hadn't meant to say anything about their relationship, hadn't

211

even known there was anything *to* say, until she pressed the button. He felt trapped and thwarted, the constant nagging pain in his back acting as a low-level torture, preventing him from thinking properly. He didn't really want to go back to work, although his conscience was prodding him about it. He didn't want to separate from Thea with bad feeling and unintended hurts still raw between them. What he wanted was for the pain to stop, for everything to be all right, and the world to stop attacking him and his fellows. There was a connection in his mind between the people who made ricin in order to poison large crowds, and the person who sent a snake into his room in the night. And knowing that Thea would belittle and dismiss both dangers as almost entirely imaginary did nothing to console him. There was evil intent behind both acts, and that alone was enough to warrant concern and proper action.

'It isn't you,' he said. 'I'm just in a mood. I'm being pathetic.'

'A mood?' she echoed. 'All this is just a mood?'

'I've never been much good with physical pain,' he admitted. 'It addles my brain. I'm not much of a stoic.'

'You're a wimp,' she said, only fractionally more softly. 'Detective Superintendent Phil Hollis is a wimp. I should get posters printed and send them to all your colleagues.'

'Don't you dare.' He wanted to make an elaborate point about the way the increase in female police officers should have made it more acceptable to show one's weaker side, when in fact it had done the opposite. But he needed to sit down, his muscles losing the struggle to stand erect and manly.

'I think I've been making it harder for you,' she acknowledged. 'Not only am I a lousy nurse, but I jerked you about in the car last night and made it all ten times worse. Let's see if I can make up for it somehow.' She frowned thoughtfully for a moment. 'What's the most comfortable position for your back?'

'Sitting or half-lying,' he replied promptly. 'At an angle of around twenty-five degrees between me and the support.' He would have demonstrated with his hands, but he was still holding tightly to the stick. 'The garden lounger is just about perfect.'

'OK. Well, you'll have noticed the sun's shining again. I think we should put you out there with a pile of books or magazines, your phone, a drink of best lemonade and two more painkillers. I'd tuck a blanket round you as well, except you'd be too hot. Then I'll take my dog and get out of your way for the morning. Then I'll come back and make a delicious lunch, followed by a long lazy siesta to make up for the early start. We won't talk or think or argue or anything. Does that sound acceptable?'

He closed his eyes against the great wave of weakness that rushed through him. How had he become so pitiable, so out of control? Could it just be his damaged back, bringing with it a host of profound fears? Fear of disablement, death, loss of self-esteem? Fear of being left alone, because the only woman who was permanently attached to him was his sister Linda, and she had

213

plenty of her own problems. Thea would abandon him if he didn't come up to her expectations, and who could blame her?

'Thank you,' he said. 'I'll try and pull myself together by lunchtime. I'm sorry,' he added miserably.

'That's OK,' she said, much too coolly for his liking.

She and the dog drove off, taking bottled water and some fruit. The sky was as blue as ever, the heat already quite un-British. Phil was settled under the willows, where the full blast of the sun would be kept away until midday. The silence was broken only by a distant drone of some agricultural activity – probably haymaking, he concluded. It felt like being in a parallel reality, where nobody ventured and nothing ever happened. He wasn't interested in the books or magazines, but dozed fitfully, dreaming about his dogs, which were in his flat, chewing the cables of his computer, which abruptly turned into snakes that hissed in the animals' faces. But Baxter, the Gordon setter, merely grinned his goofy grin and sat down watching the snakes slither harmlessly across the floor. The nightmare had been conquered and Phil woke up gently, with a welcome sense of peace overlying the guilt and worry at the way he'd been earlier with Thea.

It took him several bleary seconds to focus on the object standing four or five feet away, in the bright sunlight. A very tall man was facing him, his expression desperate. In his hand was a small gun, directed right at Phil Hollis's heart.

CHAPTER FOURTEEN

'Giles Pritchett,' he breathed, some seconds later. 'You must be Giles Pritchett.' Not only the extraordinary height, but the features that so closely resembled those of Pritchett Senior, had served to identify him. 'What the hell do you think you're doing?'

Already he knew that a line had been crossed with utterly inevitable consequences for the gunman. It was not possible to point a pistol at a senior police detective and get away with it. In those first moments, Phil's concern was more for the other man than for himself. A murky picture of a succession of interviews, charges, trials, punishments flashed through his mind. Even if he put the gun down now and walked away, there would be repercussions.

It was a small weapon, in a large hand. It looked like a harmless toy, and Phil's fuddled brain had to remind itself that there was death contained within it. It was not an automatic association – the fear was a long time coming. When it did finally hit, it was with almost as much physical force as if the bullet had already struck his flesh. Sweat flooded from his armpits and hairline, and his guts filled with a thick dark cloud that roiled in strange waves. 'Put the gun down,' he said with as much authority as he could muster.

In twenty-three years as a police officer, this had never once happened to him. He knew people it had happened to, and had been present at their debriefing. He had trained and practised the correct procedure for when it did happen. You examined the situation calmly, kept control of yourself and, ideally, the gunman as well. You offered him respect and full attention. You tried to understand what it was he most wanted at this present moment. Compared to an ordinary untutored person, he was coping well. Only his skin and internal organs knew the truth.

'What do you want, Giles?' he asked, trying not to look at the steadily pointing gun. 'What are you doing here?'

'You know who I am.' It was not a question, but there was surprise in the words.

'I know your father. He told me you were missing. You look like him.' Phil aimed, with partial success, for a neutral, conversational tone. *Keep things normal.* 'What do you want?' he repeated.

'I want to kill you.' It was said with a calm conviction that Phil found terrifying. 'You've ruined everything, finding those bones.'

Don't argue, a voice insisted in Phil's ear. 'Have I?' he said.

The gun came closer, unwavering in its aim. How much noise would it make, he wondered? Would nobody hear it, his body lying undiscovered until Thea came back to find it in a glistening red pool, covered with flies? A long time seemed to pass, all thoughts suspended as both men waited for the promised moment.

A sound attracted their attention, at the top of

the drive. The sound of a car engine being turned off, and a car door slamming. Was somebody walking down to Hector's Nook? Giles Pritchett turned to look and Phil cursed his defective back which prevented him from launching himself valiantly from the lounger and knocking the gun to the ground. Cursed it, and secretly gave thanks for it, at the same time. Heroics only looked good if they succeeded. Giles could easily pull the trigger at the slightest hint of movement.

Nobody appeared, after a full minute, and Phil abandoned hope of rescue. It was probably a sightseer come to gawp at the fallen tree where the remains had been found. He tried to guess what time it was from the height of the sun, and estimated it to be around ten o'clock.

Already he was minimally less afraid of the gun, the small black hole of its muzzle growing almost familiar. The received wisdom was that the longer an attacker delayed in pulling the trigger, the less likely he was to do it. The necessary adrenalin and bloodlust dissipated quickly, making it harder for the fatal act to be accomplished. His own imagination would start to operate, images of the man before him flopping lifelessly to the ground, the blood and screams gaining reality minute by minute. Only a true psychopath, who relished these aspects of murder, would remain intent on his plan.

Giles did not seem to Phil like a psychopath. He was angry and frustrated, irrational too – but there was no cold glint of malicious insanity in his eyes. He seemed young and lost, but Phil suspected that was more in his own mind, knowing how Giles's parents had worried about his disappearance.

He wanted to ask a hundred questions. Where have you been? What do you know about the murdered man? How have I thwarted you? Why have you caused your poor mother such anguish? But none of them was possible. He wanted Giles to see him as a fellow human being, just another man, and certainly not as a policeman. 'We can talk about it,' he offered. 'If you'd only put the gun down.'

'I came to kill you,' he repeated as if trying to convince himself. 'When I saw your girlfriend leave, I knew you'd be here alone. And I knew the snake hadn't done what I'd wanted. You deserve to be killed, you know. Janey says so.'

'Janey? Does she know you're here?'

'Of course not. Don't be stupid.'

'Sorry,' muttered Phil. 'I don't understand.'

'You don't need to.'

Phil met the man's eyes, which were shadowed now by the willows, a halo of sunlight behind him. He could not read their expression clearly, but he thought he saw a softening, a desire to squat down on the grass and just explain everything. He thought he saw signs that he would not be shot after all, that the danger was all but past.

And then, behind Giles, he saw movement. A figure in black had stepped out from the hedge bordering the drive and was pointing a long-barrelled gun at Giles Pritchett's back. Before he could stop himself, Phil shouted, 'No!'

Pritchett spun round, waving his own gun wildly. Then a *crack!* rang out and the tall man jackknifed violently, his legs and shoulders shooting forwards, his midriff bending back. The bullet had hit him somewhere in the abdomen, causing him an agony that Phil knew he was never going to want to think about. There were screams and shouts.

People appeared then, scuttling over the garden like alien creatures, their faces pale and intent. Sonia Gladwin materialised and headed directly for Phil. He stared helplessly at her, marooned at the same twenty-five degrees he had been in from the start. 'What have you done?' he demanded. 'Is he dead?'

'He would have killed you.'

'No,' said Phil, with conviction. 'No, he wouldn't. How on earth did you get an armed response here so quickly?'

'He was seen an hour ago with the gun.'

Pritchett was being attended to, there on Miss Deacon's lawn, before medics came rattling down the drive to collect him. People spoke into phones and radios, and Phil half-expected a helicopter to join the action before long.

'Poor chap,' said Phil. 'What have you done to him?'

'What do you expect?' Gladwin spoke angrily. 'What else could we have done?'

'Left him to me,' muttered Phil, knowing he was talking nonsense. Hadn't he realised, from those first moments, what danger Pritchett had placed himself in? Hadn't much of his fear been for the other man, and not himself, throughout the encounter? Didn't everybody know, by now, that they couldn't mess with the police and firearms with impunity? For heaven's sake, even a man carrying a chair leg was blasted out of existence, just in case he was dangerous.

And Thea. What was Thea going to say?

Phil was still in the garden two hours later, when Thea returned. So were a dozen personnel with cameras, specimen bags, tape measures, note-books. Most of them wore white jumpsuits and face masks. She came running down the drive, having been unable to get her car past those belonging to the investigators. Hepzie lolloped after her, tail held horizontal behind her.

'Are you all right?' Thea cried, hurling herself at Phil. 'Nobody would tell me anything, except there'd been a shooting incident. Why didn't you phone me?'

'I wanted to keep you out of it for as long as I could,' he said, pulling her to him. He was sitting on a more upright chair, in one corner of the garden, watching the proceedings. He would have to produce a detailed report of what happened, answer a thousand questions, and eventually appear in court. The automatic attention of the Independent Police Complaints Commission would mean a prolonged and distracting investigation into every detail of what had taken place.

'And yes, I'm fine,' he assured her, when she asked again.

'So – who was shot? Where did the gun come from? *You* haven't got one, have you?' she demanded, eyes wide.

'No, of course I haven't. We can go inside and I'll explain it all. It's a miserable business, I warn you.'

When she finally had the whole story straight, she was every bit as outraged as he'd expected. 'That poor man! What if he dies? They'll have *murdered* him. God, it makes me sick.'

'There wasn't really any choice,' Phil insisted. 'What else could they do?'

'Not have been here in the first place,' she said mulishly. Phil raised one eyebrow at that piece of nonsense. Thea lifted her chin in defiance, but changed tack to less confrontational ground. 'Who told them about Giles being here? Have they said?'

'Not yet. But if he was marching down here with a gun in his hand, he must have looked as if he meant business. Anyone would have called the police.'

'But how could they get here so quickly? I thought it took ages to mobilise an armed response.'

'It takes twenty or thirty minutes. We think Giles must have been here watching me while I slept. He didn't want to kill me until I woke up.' He laughed ruefully. 'He didn't really want to kill me at all. He just wanted me to understand how angry he was. He wanted to frighten me and possibly make me apologise. He was just coming to the point when it happened. And it was my fault,' he added with a shudder. 'I shouted out and distracted him. That gave them their chance. They couldn't shoot while he had the gun trained on me. It might all have been defused if I hadn't been such a fool.'

'They'll think you did it deliberately to help them,' she said.

'Yes,' he agreed sadly.

They sat in the hot living room, closing the curtains against the relentless sun. Finally DS Gladwin came in, having left the scene some time earlier, and now returned. 'We need to interview you formally,' she said. 'And Mr Pritchett Senior wants to speak to you, not surprisingly.'

'How's Giles?' Thea asked.

Gladwin sighed. Her narrow face was drawn and pale. 'Still alive. His liver's been damaged and his guts are in a mess. He won't be right again, whatever happens. When will people realise...' she burst out, and then stopped, seeing Thea's expression. 'There was no choice,' she said firmly. 'None at all.'

'That's what Phil says,' Thea nodded. 'Excuse me if I don't entirely believe it.'

'Would you go and see Janey?' Phil suddenly asked Thea, the words erupting from an idea that he could scarcely grasp before it faded again, leaving him wondering at the odd deviation.

She stared at him in surprise. 'What on earth for?'

'I have a feeling Giles means quite a lot to her, and she'll be needing some comforting, that's all,' he floundered. 'I mean – she should know what's happened.' He recalled Giles saying Janey thought he, Phil, should be killed, and it forged a link between the two that he had not previously detected. 'But be careful,' he added. 'She's going to be very cross.'

'That's no problem,' said Thea. 'We can be cross together.'

'Hang on,' interrupted Gladwin. 'Is this something I ought to know about? I'm not sure you can just dash off and splurge restricted information to anybody you like.'

Thea bristled and opened her mouth to challenge the concept of *restricted information*.

Phil headed her off. 'It's OK,' he told Gladwin. 'You haven't missed anything important. Anyway, it'll all be in my report, including the bit about the snake.' Gladwin's nervous glance around the room confirmed his suspicion that she was afraid of the creatures, despite her efforts to pass off her earlier reaction as outrage at the exotic pet trade. 'Don't worry,' he said. 'She's safely in her cage again now.' He looked at Thea. 'Did you get that padlock?'

She nodded. 'I'll go out now and attach it.'

'Try not to let any of those bods outside see what you're doing. The snake might complicate things if you do.'

She gave him a wide-eyed look, checking the implications of what he had said, remembering the events that had begun their day far too soon. 'They wouldn't take her away, would they?' she asked.

Phil shrugged. 'I doubt it, but you never know.'

'Because it might have been Giles who–?' She glanced at Gladwin.

Phil nodded. 'Yes, it was him. He said so in no uncertain terms. He hoped Shasti would kill me.'

'What a mad thing to do.'

'So is sneaking down here and pointing a gun at me,' said Phil forcefully. 'I never did find out what exactly I'm meant to have done to upset him.'

223

'I think I know the answer to that,' offered Gladwin, calmly. 'You gave his parents renewed hope of finding him.'

'But how–?' Phil's mind began to whirr. 'Oh – Stephen was at Janey's on Wednesday. And Janey's close to Giles. She must have told him everything she'd gleaned about us. But that still doesn't really explain anything,' he finished with a sigh.

'Too soon for explanations, mate,' said Gladwin. 'All I can hope is that Giles P. confesses to killing the man under the tree, and makes as good a recovery as possible.'

'Only to be sent down for ten years or more,' said Phil dryly.

'How could it have been him, though?' Thea spoke quietly. 'If it was five years ago, he'd only have been fifteen. That doesn't sound very likely to me.'

'Plenty of fifteen-year-olds have killed people,' sighed Gladwin. 'But I admit it looks just a bit too tidy. I really just want to get this case off my desk. I can't pretend I'm enjoying it. It's all whispers and mirrors. I *really* don't like this business about saints and martyrs. It seems as if everyone we've spoken to's been involved in it in some way. Have you ever heard of St Melor?'

Thea and Phil both shook their heads.

'Well, you have now. And you'd probably be interested to know that his uncle cut off his right hand and left foot.'

Thea and Phil both stared blankly at her.

'Oh – did I forget to tell you? Our skeleton was missing just those pieces. And yes, we have questioned Mrs Holmes about it.'

Phil blinked at her. 'You said a few of the smaller bones had gone. Nothing about a hand and foot.'

She smiled unapologetically. 'So I'm telling you now, OK?'

'But that changes everything,' Phil realised. 'How did you find out about St Thingy anyway?'

'I'd like to pretend it was clever Googling, but in fact we did it the old-fashioned way and trawled through those saints books that Miss Holmes has in her library. January 3rd is his feast day. A British martyr, fifth century. A monk had the poor bloke's head cut off as well, just for good measure. It's more of a fable, really, according to the Baring-Gould chap. Quite a good story, for all that.'

'You think they enacted it on this unidentified bloke and got carried away? What does Janey say about it?'

'She's acting dumb – can't properly remember anything that happened five years ago, and says she was in and out of mental hospitals with depression. We checked that, and she actually only had two periods as an inmate, both of a few weeks. But she insists she's sure they never did re-enact St Melor. That woman's got more than her share of problems, I must say. I spent two hours with her yesterday and was practically ready to take her home with me at the end of it, poor cow.'

'The one thing she doesn't need is a new home,' said Thea. 'That house is a palace. And you can see she loves it.'

Gladwin waved this away impatiently. 'Whatever. The thing is we're just going round in stupid circles, no closer to finding out who the dead guy is, what exactly happened to him, how long he was under the tree. The forensics are a shambles, as well. Bits of sawdust and chips from the chainsaw are all over everything, plus footmarks from the man who operated it. And now this shooting, which is going to put everything on hold while it's investigated.' She glared aggressively at Phil. 'And you with your back,' she finished.

Phil laughed at that. 'Yes, me with my back,' he agreed. 'It all comes down to that, when you think about it. It's been getting me into every sort of trouble all week. But I'll tell you something – when you're nose-to-nose with a pistol, a bad back fades into insignificance. I hardly gave it a thought the whole time Giles was here, except to realise it would stop me performing any heroics.'

'I don't want to go and see Janey,' Thea said after a pause. 'Not on my own, anyway. I don't want to be an unpaid spy for the police, and I can't begin to understand what she knows or thinks about what's been going on. What would I say to her? I'm not her friend – I only met her a few days ago. She's got Fiona and presumably plenty of other people. And what if she's got a gun as well as Giles? Most people seem to have guns these days, just like in America.'

'Hardly,' said Gladwin tightly.

Phil recognised the same fed-up Thea of breakfast time. Events since then had done nothing at all to cheer her up – although he was satisfied that she was genuinely appalled at the idea that he, Phil, might have been shot. She had unconsciously touched and stroked him repeatedly, as if assuring herself he was still alive and available to her, even when reproaching him.

He had a growing sense of events receding from his control. He would be leaving Temple Guiting soon, returning to his flat where his back might take another few weeks to recover. Although in principle the dismembered victim of a decade-old murder would be accorded the same attention and urgency as any other murder case, it was inevitably not going to arouse the same degree of high-level activity that more recent and more emotive cases would. Although, he reminded himself, if the media got hold of the details of the severed hand and foot, that could change. It would conjure echoes of the mutilated black child found in London, and painstakingly traced to a gruesome African cult that did unspeakable things to youngsters. There would be plenty of scope for imaginative pathology to create theories around this latest set of remains. With Gladwin's discovery of the highly pertinent St Melor, there was still a clear line of enquiry to pursue.

'Are there no likely missing persons to try and match him up with?' Phil said. 'What's happening with the DNA?'

'Results due later today. Meanwhile, we've got a little list, but they're not very promising. There are really only two who could possibly fit the bill.' Gladwin produced her electronic notebook again. 'A bloke called Thomas Hitchins, from Painswick. Went missing nine years ago, with no warning. But there's a note in the file that says his daughter hinted that she knew he wasn't dead.

The interviewing officer had a strong feeling he'd gone off with a new woman and was secretly keeping the girl posted. We're trying to find her now, and ask whether she's heard from him. Plus, he was fifty-nine, and that's on the old side for our chap. The other one's more of a goer. Cedric Collins, thirty-eight, heavily in debt, usually drunk. Lived with his parents and just never came home one night. His mother insisted he must be dead, because there's no way in the world he'd have done such a thing to her.' She smiled tightly. 'But the reality is, it could have been any of a hundred drug addicts or illegals, scooped off the street in Gloucester or Bristol and never really missed. Certainly not reported. It's needle-in-a-haystack territory, this. If you wanted a body to play with, and weren't too squeamish about it, it's as easy now as it was in Victorian times. Easier, if anything, because the numbers are so much greater now. Scary, but true.'

'You can presumably eliminate these two, anyway, with DNA?' Thea said.

'Collins, yes. His mother's still got his hairbrushes and stuff, more or less untouched. But Hitchins has been wiped off the face of the earth. His wife married again the moment the five years was up and she could get a divorce without his consent, and moved away.' Gladwin seemed disheartened and weary. 'Besides, now we've got this business with Pritchett to distract us, the whole thing's going to be a lot more difficult.'

'Plus it's Friday,' said Thea with a knowing smile.

'So?' Gladwin shrugged. 'Weekends don't mean

a lot in this job, you know.'

It was a scratchy moment. Phil understood that Thea had been trying to convey that she was aware of the stresses of the working life, even if she wasn't personally involved. Gladwin's perception of her was probably as an idle, freeloading female, and it was unlikely they would ever find much common ground. 'My daughter's in the police,' Thea said calmly. 'So I do know something about it. What I meant, actually, was that I realise that Fridays and Saturdays are worse than any other days. There'll be more distractions and interruptions.'

'Oh, yeah, I see what you mean,' Gladwin sighed. 'Plus my kids always seem to think I should be around at the weekend.'

'How many have you got?'

'Two. Twin boys, seven and a half.' She sighed again.

'Twins!' Thea's eyes lighted with interest and a flicker of mischievous glee. 'I bet that came as a shock.'

'Right,' nodded Gladwin, looking ever more drained.

Phil made an incautious move, from some vague notion of rescuing his new colleague from further unprofessional diversions. His back brought him up short and he expelled an involuntary groan. Furious with himself, he overrode the pain with gritted teeth. He would not continue to let these women regard him as a useless wreck.

'Thea, if you're not going to Janey's it would probably help if you drove me to Cirencester soon, so I can give a full report of what happened this morning. Would that be OK?'

Thea nodded. 'Of course. I'd rather do that than offer myself as counsellor to Janey Holmes. If she's got something to do with you almost being killed, then I'm not sure I ever want to see her again.' She smiled ruefully. 'And it's nice to know you still trust me to drive, after last night.'

Gladwin heard this, and cocked her head. 'Did something happen last night? Is it anything I should know about?'

'Absolutely not,' said Thea quickly. 'We don't have to tell you every move we make, do we?'

Phil uttered another small groan, this time from a very different cause. 'Tell her,' he ordered.

Thea told the story in very few words, waving away any suggestion that it could be relevant to Gladwin's enquiries. 'They seem quite old-fashioned people,' she said of Robin and Soraya. 'A bit awkward in company.'

'Hmm,' was all the DS would say to that.

CHAPTER FIFTEEN

It took some minutes to transfer Phil to Thea's car and set out for Cirencester. There had been indecision as to what to do with Hepzie, given that they didn't know how long they'd be. 'I hate leaving her,' worried Thea. 'Who knows what might happen?'

'Bring her then,' said Phil.

'But it's too hot to leave her in the car. She'll have to be with me the whole time, and that might not be allowed. If you're ages, I'll want to go and get a drink and a sandwich somewhere.'

'You could go to Painswick and visit Linda and my boys,' he suggested. It felt like a sudden brainwave. He had been worrying about Claude and Baxter, abandoned for so much longer than usual. Even when he was working on a demanding case, he almost always made time to go and see them and take them for a quick walk every second or third day.

'Yes, I suppose I could,' said Thea without enthusiasm. She had met Linda twice, and found that they had almost nothing to say to each other. Phil's sister was divorced and childless and not very happy. She had lost a job she liked, five years before, and never found another one. 'She never will now,' Phil had predicted. 'She's lost her nerve. She finds the world altogether too alarming. She never was very brave.'

Letting her take care of the dogs was at least partly meant as a sort of therapy. Linda was a lost soul, he had long ago realised. She had been born out of her time, unsuited to the competition and corruption that mainly comprised the world of work. Diagnosed with a vague 'anxiety disorder', she received state benefits and lived in a small house partly financed by her brother. He regretted the fact that Thea had been slow to understand how much help she could be in the matter of Linda. 'She sees you as family,' he tried to explain. 'And the thing Linda loves best is family.'

'I know,' sighed Thea. 'It's just that I find her

231

such awfully hard work. She makes me feel I have to hide my own modest talents, for fear of making her feel intimidated.'

'Well, it's just a suggestion. Hepzie would like to have a romp with the boys.'

'All right,' said Thea. 'Now, let's get going, shall we?'

She drove steadily, the accident of the previous evening having made no discernible dent in her confidence. Phil did his best to relax the muscles of his back, surprised that they weren't more painful after the trauma that morning. But he knew better than to permit any real optimism to blossom. Anything other than slow upright walking was still to be avoided.

They passed the end of the road containing the village shop, and Phil glanced idly down it. 'There's Pritchett,' he noted. 'And a woman that's probably his wife. You'd expect them to be at the hospital, wouldn't you? At Giles's bedside. What are they doing here?'

'Maybe they've been thrown out while he has an operation or something. Do they live down there? I never worked out exactly which is their house.'

'Nor me. I suppose it is hereabouts. Oh, look at that! Isn't it magnificent!' He was staring ahead at Temple Guiting Manor, the façade of which looked down at the road they were on.

Thea slowed the car and peered up the gently rising driveway. 'Lovely,' she agreed. 'Like a mansion in a fairytale. Or a horror story, more like. It must have seen some adventures. What a comedown to be rented out to groups of tourists for their stag parties. Do you think the original furniture's still there?'

'I'm sure it is. It's not stag parties, but fat cat stockbrokers having a break. Or groups of awe-struck Americans who can't believe the plumbing. But I agree it's not what it was intended for.'

'Was it here at the time of the Templars, then?' she wondered aloud. 'Surely it can't be as old as that? Thirteenth century?'

'You know more than I do about dates, but no, I suppose it can't be earlier than the sixteenth.'

They left the Manor behind them and pressed on to Cirencester. Phil mentally relived the encounter with Giles, trying to make sense of the man's behaviour, wondering how he could possibly have warranted such rage simply by finding the scattered bones of a human skeleton. The obvious explanation was that the bones were those of a man killed by Giles himself, or by somebody Giles cared about. But it was wildly irrational to punish the messenger in such an extreme fashion, especially when it would so obviously bring such oceans of trouble down on his head. Presumably he had thought he could calmly shoot Phil and then disappear again, with nobody ever guessing who had done the deed. It was a fragile theory, demanding a level of stupidity or insanity that Giles had not mani-fested. His whole being had been consumed with a rage that transcended any that Phil had previously encountered. Rage, he mused, was very often born of frustration – the apoplectic tantrums of a thwarted toddler; the blind fury of a jilted lover; the vicious punishments handed out by an extreme control freak when disobeyed. None of these fitted what he had seen of Giles Pritchett, but the idea that he had somehow been frustrated still seemed to be viable. There had been a sense of being punished, he remembered. He had done something that put him beyond anything Giles found acceptable – deserving, in fact, of the death penalty.

'I wonder what it was I did,' he murmured aloud.

'Sorry? What did you say?' Thea had evidently been lost in her own thoughts.

'What was it I did to enrage him so badly?'

'Who knows? He's probably just bonkers.'

'I don't think so. I think he really believes I brought it all on myself, with something I did to rock his boat when I found the bones.'

'I thought we'd already decided all this?'

'Except it doesn't make sense,' he sighed. 'The more I think about it, the less sense there is.'

'It seems logical enough to me,' she said. 'You put the cat amongst the chickens, as my sister would say. And made Giles very cross in the process.'

'He was certainly that,' Phil agreed, with a feeling of giving up. Combined with that was a sense of free-floating guilt. He *had* done something, he must have done. And if it had been serious enough to make a man want to kill him, then he really wanted to know for sure what it was.

The session at the police station had a surreal edge to it. DS Phil Hollis was in the witness chair, at least metaphorically, while at the same time battering his brains to make sense of the whole tangled story that had been emerging since Tuesday morning. He reported everything he could remember of Giles Pritchett's words, while openly speculating on just how his actions connected with the murder investigation.

'It has to do with families and bloodlines,' he concluded. 'Stephen Pritchett effectively said as much.' He repeated all he could remember of Pritchett's words on his first visit to Hector's Nook. 'Then Janey Holmes is of the Temple line, as is her brother. But only she has Pritchett blood, according to Rupert. Do we know how her father is related to Stephen and Giles Pritchett, by the way? I assume there has to be a connection.'

DS Sonia Gladwin, looking very jaded, consulted a file on the table in front of her. 'They're first cousins. Janey's father is called Bernard, aged sixty-eight, married to Jacqueline. They spend most of their time in Tuscany, and have not been back to England since February last year. Stephen Pritchett is forty-nine, married to Gertrude, known as Trudy. She has nervous trouble and seldom leaves the house. They've all been questioned and insist they have no idea of the identity of the dead man, given that it is not Giles Pritchett, who went missing two and a half years ago after some family trouble. The disappearance was never reported, and he is not listed as a missing person.'

'Have you looked into their finances?' Phil asked. 'Is there anything about property inheritance, dependent on pure blood? Rupert said there was a case ongoing, to do with his paternity.'

'We've asked for sight of the trust documents, just in case – but we're on very shaky ground. Mrs Holmes already refused to let us have a DNA sample. She's quite within her rights to object to us investigating her at all. The only link between her and the body is that she reported the fallen tree. And that's no link at all when you look at it rationally. All I've been going on is guesswork. But now Giles has reappeared so dramatically, we've got more of a link.'

Phil frowned, trying to collect his thoughts through the blocking effects of his back and the painkillers. 'If only we had an identity for the dead man,' he said irritably. 'It would all make sense then. But the frustrating thing is that nobody from this group we're looking at seems to be missing. I keep running into that like a brick wall.'

'It might yet turn out to be a homeless vagrant, of course.'

'We'll have to hope there's a result with the DNA comparisons, then,' said Phil doggedly. 'I'm convinced there's something going on between the families that will explain the whole thing.'

'It's tempting to think so, I suppose,' she said. 'But I'm not sure it makes any real sense. If one of them had been killed, it could never have been kept quiet for so long.'

Phil blinked slowly. 'You're wrong,' he said. 'What if it *had* been Giles? Nobody ever reported him missing. If there was a collective agreement to keep quiet about his disappearance, then why not somebody else's as well? These people stick

236

together, don't you see? They all tell the same story, a story they've rehearsed for just this eventuality.'

Gladwin nibbled her lower lip. 'We can only guess until we get the first of the DNA reports. There's no actual *evidence* of anything.'

Phil put a hand to his fuddled head. 'I'm not being much use, I know. I can't think properly. Thea's doing a better detective job than I am.'

She treated him to a soothing smile. 'You've had quite a day, one way and another. Quite a *week*, in fact. Nobody could expect you to be operating at full capacity. But I agree with you about the main point.' She tapped the file in front of her. 'We won't get anywhere until we know who those bones belonged to. Which is why I've got all my hopes pinned on the DNA results.' She gave him a challenging stare. 'Even though I still think it's impossible that any of the local families could have lost somebody without the story getting out.'

'To lose one son might be careless, to lose two is beyond credibility – or whatever it was Oscar Wilde said.'

'Right. But it's all we've got. Besides, it might turn out to be the answer. We'd look very silly if it does turn out to be another Pritchett, wouldn't we?'

Phil had a thought. 'So the entire population of Temple Guiting's going to find itself on the DNA database permanently,' he said. 'Seems a bit like overkill, don't you think?'

'Not the entire population. Anybody currently under five is exempted, plus those who have

237

moved here during the past five years. And we are meant to be collecting as many individual samples as we can, remember.' They exchanged the usual long-suffering glance which police officers everywhere permitted themselves when the subject of the national DNA collection came up. The prospect of sixty million people all registered permanently on a gigantic computer system, susceptible to having their DNA compared with samples taken from crime scenes forever after, sounded a lot more seductive than they all knew it would be in practice. There would be mistakes, corrupt files, contaminated samples, endless appeals and challenges. Careless female police officers would face prosecution for violent rapes, because their own mitrochondria would have accidentally mixed with someone else's. Everyone knew it was one of those too-good-to-be-true Government ideas that would explode in the face of the police force before much longer.

Meanwhile, every DNA test cost money, often with no discernible benefit. 'Oh, well,' sighed Phil. 'I can see you didn't have much choice, once the dental records got you nowhere.'

'Meanwhile we have to hope young Pritchett pulls through and explains himself,' she corrected. 'Last I heard he was too groggy by far to be interviewed. Don't you hate it when your main witness is half-dead in hospital and you've got to keep a 24-hour guard on him?'

'Main witness?' Phil repeated. 'I hadn't thought of him like that, but I suppose he is.' He rubbed his head again. 'Giles must know the whole story, then.' Suddenly it seemed too easy. 'Maybe we

238

won't even need the DNA after all.'

Gladwin pursed her lips. 'Or maybe I'll let him think we already know exactly who the dead man is. That might just bounce him into splurging what he knows, don't you think?'

'That's up to you,' said Phil carefully. 'It might be better if I don't know what you're planning in that respect.' Lying to witnesses in order to convince them that they may as well reveal all was a time-honoured practice which had no overt prohibition on it, but Phil never liked to do it. It could rebound painfully, as he had discovered. But sometimes it could work, and he knew better than to try to teach Gladwin her job. 'Of course, the glaringly obvious answer is still that Giles is our man, even if he was only fifteen at the time.'

Again Gladwin manifested disagreement. 'I thought so at first, but it doesn't really work. If it was Giles, why didn't he simply stay missing presumed dead?'

'Good question,' smiled Phil, beginning to tire of the need to conciliate this woman. 'Now, if we're finished, I think I need to get back to my sick bed. This chair isn't doing me any good at all.'

He phoned Thea, who promised to be with him in twenty minutes. The time passed swiftly in a shuffling visit to the lavatory and a word with DI Jeremy Higgins, who was evidently fighting to hide his disappointment that his superintendent wasn't returning to work for some time to come. 'We're managing,' he said bravely, 'but it's never the same without you, guv.' The ricin drama, it seemed, had subsided to an easier level, thanks to

239

the media's attention having diverted to a story about the state of school lavatories. Children were wrecking their bladders and bowels, it seemed, by refusing to go to the loo during the school day. Long may it last, thought Phil, heartlessly.

CHAPTER SIXTEEN

Thea's account of her brief visit to Linda and the dogs was less than enthusiastic. 'She seemed to wonder what I wanted,' she reported. 'As if she thought I was spying on her.'

'Don't worry about it,' Phil reassured her. 'Linda's always a bit funny with people.'

'The dogs weren't much better,' Thea said. 'They weren't at all pleased to see Hepzie. You know how she gets – all waggy and ingratiating. They just *sneered* at her, the beastly things.'

'At least you tried,' said Phil, watching the road ahead with some nervousness. Gradually he relaxed, having persuaded himself that there was no chance of a repeat of the accident the previous evening.

For somebody so woefully lacking in historical knowledge, he often surprised himself by his liking for the Roman roads in the area. The Fosse Way, striking north-east from Cirencester, was his favourite. 'I love this road,' he told Thea, as they sped along the straight miles. 'It feels so *determined*.'

'I hate it,' she said calmly. 'The traffic goes

much too fast, and there aren't any interesting views from it. I can't wait to get off it and into the winding narrow lanes. The Romans had no souls.'

'Hmm,' was all he said to that. Then, in an effort to engage her again, he went on, 'I suppose Janey's saints would have known these roads. The Dark Ages came after the Romans were here – even I know that. Maybe St Kenelm walked along this very stretch.'

'Maybe he did,' she nodded. 'That's if he existed at all, of course.'

'Oh? Is there some doubt?'

'Very much so. Janey showed me his entry in that set of Baring-Gould books at her house. He's another one who's really just a legend. She prefers them to authenticated ones, I think. Easier to draw symbolic meaning from them, I suppose.'

'But he was killed by his sister? Did I get that right?'

'Yes. In fact she had several goes at it, but got there in the end. But he had magical powers and she was soon found out.'

'I still think it's uncomfortably close to things we've been hearing about the locals in Temple Guiting. And this St Melor, whoever he was. We should be researching him a bit more. Except I get the feeling Gladwin's got one of the girls onto that by now.'

Thea laughed. 'Gladwin's looking quite efficient, wouldn't you say? Considering this is only her first week, she's obviously got things under control.'

'Oh, yes,' Phil agreed as heartily as he could. 'She's very impressive, given how little there is to go on.'

'Did she say anything else about St Melor this afternoon?'

He shook his head. 'I suppose she's wondering how it could possibly fit the facts.'

Thea tapped a finger on the steering wheel. 'It must implicate Janey and her Saints and Martyrs.'

'Indeed,' he assented. 'Which neither of us can pretend would come as such a major surprise, now can we?'

Thea sighed and said nothing. He knew she was thinking that Janey Holmes would make a tragic murderer. Better, almost, to bury the whole idea and let the anonymous victim drift peacefully into forgetfulness.

As they approached Guiting Power, Thea threw Phil a quick look, and asked whether he felt equal to a bit of a detour. 'We could go and have a look at Hailes Abbey,' she suggested. 'Just from the car – see what it has to offer. Have you ever been there?'

He shook his head and valiantly agreed to her idea. She turned left and slowed to fish behind her seat for the map. 'You'll have to navigate,' she told him. 'I can't remember exactly where it is.'

The tortuous route lay through Guiting Wood, and then across a sweep of open farmland that felt like a private road. 'Must have been the farm's approach drive once,' he observed. 'It's called Salt Way.' There was something alien about the landscape, and the way the few vehicles they met seemed to slow for a good stare at them. Thea drove sedately, giving herself time to look around. 'St Kenelm's Well is just over there,' Phil told her. 'Feel free to park me and hike up for a look.' But they had already passed the steep hill with the well at the top.

'Another time,' she said.

Hailes Abbey turned out to be unimpressive, involving a walk that Phil felt unequal to and a fee to go in. 'I get the picture,' he said, peering at the row of stone arches which was all that was visible from the car. It was close to five o'clock, but the sun was still high, throwing dark shadows from the stonework and surrounding trees. 'But I'll wait if you want a better look,' he said again, feeling increasingly noble. All he wanted was to get back to his comfortably angled lounger. It was hot in the car, and his head was aching. The dog on the back seat was panting, too, obviously wanting to go home to some shade and a drink of water.

'Oh!' said Thea suddenly. 'Look!'

He followed her gaze and focused on a couple walking towards them, having just emerged from the abbey ruins. 'Um...' he said blearily. 'That's that girl from the other night – Soraya. Isn't it?'

'And she's with Rupert Temple-Pritchett,' Thea hissed dramatically. 'Holding hands, look. Good Lord, what an unlikely couple. He's twice her age.'

'Probably her uncle or cousin or something,' said Phil, trying to concentrate. 'And he's *more* than twice her age. We know he's early forties and she's twenty.'

'Don't let them see us,' Thea whispered, sinking down in her seat.

'Difficult to avoid. She'll recognise the car. Why does it matter, anyway?' He wanted to point out that kneeling on the floor of a small Fiesta was well beyond his capabilities even without a prolapsed disc, but he held his tongue. Instead, he watched the couple closely, trying to assess the nature of their relationship. The girl looked fit and well, for a start, which was a relief. Being knocked into a hedge by this very car could have led to quite severe injuries. As it was, Soraya was swinging the arm that was joined to Temple-Pritchett like a young child. She kept looking up into his face with the unmistakable glow of young love.

'They're in love,' said Thea, her voice full of astonishment.

Phil turned his attention to the man. His face was open and soft and somehow more genuine than during previous encounters. He smiled happily at the girl, and let her swing his arm as unresistingly as a doll. 'Yes,' he said. 'I think they are.'

The pair walked right past Thea's car without even seeing it. 'They're not interested in us, or anybody else,' said Phil. 'I haven't seen anything like that since – since – I don't know when.'

'It's rarer than you think,' murmured Thea. 'He looks so different, doesn't he? Do you think all that foppish stuff was just a stupid act?'

Phil flapped a hand to indicate his ignorance. 'Possibly,' he said.

'Like Lord Peter Wimsey,' Thea mused. 'Hiding his scheming mind behind a dim-witted manner, to put people off the scent.'

Phil recalled other references to this Wimsey person, where his abysmal failure to respond had given rise to disappointment. He still knew nothing whatever about the chap, but made a careful sound of accord.

'But – what about her father?' Thea continued. 'He can't be very happy about it. Rupert's probably older than him. How long has it been going on? Do people *know* about it?' She watched the retreating backs of the girl and her escort with a stare intense enough to bore holes. 'They're not trying very hard to avoid observation, are they?'

'I doubt if the locals ever come here. It'll all be tourists from other places, won't it?'

'Oh, well,' Thea sighed. 'I don't suppose it's important. And they do look terribly happy, don't they? That girl deserves some pleasure.'

Phil did a double take. 'How do you work that out?'

'Oh – she just seems the sort of person who always gets a raw deal. Ordered about by her father, getting knocked down right outside her own fields. I just see her as a victim, somehow.'

'But she's in love, and everything's all right.' He had a thought. 'She was probably mooning along in the lane the other night, never even hearing us coming, and not getting out of the way. All her own fault, you see.'

Thea laughed. 'That's right,' she agreed, and started the car engine.

As Phil navigated them back to Hector's Nook from the unfamiliar direction, his mobile went off. Fumblingly, he answered it, to find Gladwin full of eager information. 'We've matched the DNA,' she said, with scant preamble. 'But it's thrown up rather a contradiction.'

'Go on,' said Phil.

'Well, according to the lab analysis, the dead man is Rupert Temple-Pritchett. The sample matches the one we requisitioned from his mother's legal people.'

Phil grunted. 'Well, that can't be right. We saw him ten minutes ago, large as life.'

'Exactly. So we're wondering whether it might be his father, a man called Graham Bligh, according to our investigations. I'm not exactly clear on the science, but it seems a fair guess that they'd be very similar.'

'Hmm,' said Phil. 'Or maybe the labelling got mixed up – that's more likely, don't you think? Happens all the time. Though on second thoughts, it can't be the father, can it? The age doesn't match. Rupert's father–' he registered the jerk of surprise from Thea beside him, 'must be well into his sixties. I thought these bones came from somebody much younger than that.'

'Rupert is forty-one now. His father – wait for it – was only sixteen when seduced by the lady in question. Take five from forty-one – thirty-six – add sixteen – fifty-two. Deduct a little bit for the pathologist's margin of error, and it works perfectly well.'

'OK,' said Phil slowly. 'Well, I promise you, he's very much alive, which can only mean there's been some kind of mix-up at the lab.'

Gladwin made a tapping noise for a few moments. 'If so, that's going to make a mess of the legal proceedings. Although nobody seems to be in any great hurry to get it settled. Nothing's progressed for the past two years or more.'

'Well, the important point is that the dead man is part of that family,' Phil insisted. 'As we thought. That in itself gives you the green light to bring them all in for formal questioning.'

'Yes,' agreed Gladwin glumly. 'Plus we'd better look for Graham Bligh, I suppose.'

'Cheer up,' he adjured her. 'This is what you've been waiting for. And thanks for telling me – it's nice to be in the loop again.'

Despite these words, Phil felt irrelevant and superfluous, contributing nothing to the enquiry, a helpless onlooker, fit for nothing. All he'd accomplished during the past week was to thwart Thea in her planned explorations of the area and annoy various local people.

At the house, he almost rolled out of the car, stumbling painfully to the front door, the spaniel threatening to trip him up in her own dash for sanctuary. 'Honestly, you two,' mocked Thea. 'That's gratitude for the lovely drive I've just given you.'

Hector's Nook stood cool and inviting, the wood-panelled rooms suggestive of earlier times when the sun was so much less intrusive and the outdoors something to be avoided. Thea gave first priority to checking that the snake was still in its rightful place, and the horses well provided with water. 'Only one more day,' she announced, coming back from her chores. 'And all's well. I might as well keep quiet about the escapes, when Archie comes, don't you think? He doesn't need to know. I can write to Miss Deacon later on, and tell her a bit more. Of course, by then DS Gladwin might have solved the murder as well, and everything will have settled down again.'

Thea had been eager to hear the latest news as soon as Gladwin's phone call had ended. 'What was that about Rupert?' she demanded, and Phil had conscientiously repeated every detail.

'Well, that's that, then,' Thea had said blithely. 'Case closed. It was obviously Janey's father who did it – killing his wife's young lover in a fit of jealous rage.'

'Thirty-five years after the event?' Phil queried.

'Well he didn't know about it before, did he? According to Rupert, it was just vague suspicions until they had the DNA test done.'

'And cutting off a hand and foot for good measure?'

'That will have been to please Janey somehow,' she said confidently. 'Something to do with one of her saints. Once they'd got a dead body, it could come in handy for one of the Saint ceremonies.'

'Thea, you're being ridiculous. None of that makes the slightest sense. Apart from anything else, it would implicate Janey.'

'Well, Fiona, then. We both thought she was too normal to be true.'

'Did we? I just thought we found her refreshingly ordinary after all the other weirdos we've come across.' He heard himself revising his previous reservations about Fiona, presuming that by comparison with most of the other people they'd met, she was indeed a beacon of sanity.

'But Rupert and Soraya,' Thea said wonderingly. 'Was it *really* how it looked? Could he be an uncle, or even her real father, do you think?

Would that explain her adoration? It just seems so *unlikely* otherwise.'

'You know the answer to that as well as I do. Nobody looks at uncles or fathers like that. And it isn't so unlikely. It happens all the time.'

'Maybe you're right. I remember my sister Emily had a thing with a man twice her age, when she was twenty. He was a secondhand furniture dealer and had a glass eye. My father went ballistic about it when he found out.'

'Not because of the glass eye?'

'More because of the terrible old van he drove, I think,' she giggled. 'The point is – it does happen.'

'Of course it happens,' said Phil impatiently. 'But for me the point is that fathers almost always go ballistic about older men seducing their daughters. It offends their sense of what's right, somehow.'

'That's interesting, isn't it,' she agreed, clearly quite ready to discuss the socio-psycho-sexual implications if that's what he wanted.

But Phil had had enough. 'What's for supper?' he asked shamelessly.

The pieces of evidence, the stories and connections swirling around the village and the people he had met all combined to make Phil mentally restless but physically exhausted, even before factoring in his traumatic experience of that morning. 'I feel as if I've been sandbagged,' he said, as he sat in Miss Deacon's small courtyard, catching the westerly rays of the sun full on his face.

'It has been quite a day,' Thea said, with a sigh.

'I haven't really got to grips with the fact that you might easily have been shot and killed. I can't really bear to think about it.'

He felt a foolish flutter of pleasure at these words. She did love him, then, if she couldn't abide the thought of his death.

'Your initial concern was all for Giles,' he reminded her, knowing it was a daft thing to say, even as he said it.

'So it was,' she admitted. 'What a cow I am.'

'Not at all. Just true to your principles to the bitter end.' He threw her a smile, to show he was teasing.

'I keep thinking about Janey as well. She seems such a tragic figure, even though she's always quite cheerful when you talk to her. Everybody seems to like her, and she's got plenty of interests. But losing a baby – what a terrible thing!'

'People lost babies routinely, only a century ago. When did it get to be such a devastating catastrophe, I wonder? One child dies and the whole nation goes into mourning, now.' He assumed she would pick up the reference to a major news story during the past winter, when a small girl went missing in East Anglia and was eventually found trussed up and decomposing in a tiny cobwebby shed. The place had quickly become a shrine, with the usual mountains of cellophane-wrapped flowers. Phil and Thea had agreed that it was gruesome on every level.

'I think it was always desperately painful, but people had different outlets and distractions. Religion, lots of surviving children to focus on, other people in the same boat. If you read contemporary letters and so forth, the same lines keep recurring, about relief from suffering and God's will. Plus the stiff upper lip, which has a lot to commend it, if you ask me.' She paused. 'None of which does anything to reduce Janey's misery.'

'It must have been the First World War,' he mused, answering his own question. 'When just about everybody lost a son.'

Thea flipped a hand, as if to divert the conversation to a new topic. 'Stephen Pritchett's going to blame you,' she said. 'Don't you think? No sooner does his son show up, than you cause him to be half-killed. How must they be feeling – him and his wife?'

'Who knows?' It was asking too much of him, that he should empathise with the Pritchetts. 'I suppose I'll catch up with him over the next few days. For all I know, he's shaking in his shoes because he thinks Giles is the killer the police are looking for.' He remembered with a new jolt that Gladwin had discovered who the victim was. The anonymous bones in their tree-disturbed jumble, now had a family, even if some doubt hung over his precise identity. It made a huge difference, he realised. 'Why would Giles be so angry about my discovering the remains of somebody he probably hardly knew?'

'Who says he hardly knew him?'

Tiredly, Phil forced himself to think. 'The dead man must be twenty-five years older than Giles. No, wait a minute. This gets impossibly complicated.' He shook his head. 'I can't remember how Gladwin worked it out, now. Rupert and Janey are forty-one – we'd pegged them as older than that, hadn't we? Anyway, that means they were around thirty-six when the murder happened. Rupert's dad was sixteen, so early fifties when he died...'

'Stop!' Thea begged. 'I'm not following any of this. We'll have to write it down.'

Phil entertained a vision of the white board at the police station, where Gladwin and the team would have jotted dates, with arrows and lists and any relevant pictures. There'd be a timeline, with everybody's name and age slotted in as appropriate. He was trying to hold all that in his weary head.

'Or we could just leave it to Gladwin,' he said.

A few minutes after they moved into the house for a bedtime drink and a quick bit of tidying, Hepzie began to bark. She barked urgently and incessantly, which was unusual. 'That bloody snake isn't loose again, is it?' said Phil.

Thea had gone pale. 'If that's all you're worried about, then you've got thicker skin than I thought,' she said. 'I'm scared it's another man with a gun.' She had gone to each window in turn, peering out into the twilight. Neither of them was inclined to open the door.

'It's probably a fox or squirrel or something,' said Phil. 'You can't see anybody, can you?'

'You're not looking in the right place,' came a voice from the kitchen doorway. 'I just walked right in through the back.'

CHAPTER SEVENTEEN

It was Robin, father of Soraya, and he was not holding a gun. Nor a knife, crossbow or any lethal weapon. He was actually looking rather sheepish.

Phil's instant assumption turned out to be correct. The man had come to make a complaint about the accident of the previous evening. He began haltingly to express his concern and displeasure.

'But she's perfectly all right,' Thea blurted, interrupting him. 'We saw her this afternoon.'

'What? Where?'

The silence that followed was an abyss of regret at having given away what was quite probably a secret. 'Oh, well, she was at Hailes Abbey,' Thea pressed on unhappily. 'She looked quite fit and well.'

Robin blinked and then frowned. 'Well, yes, she works there sometimes,' he said. 'On the kiosk. Is today one of her days?' He addressed this question to a far corner of the room, and showed no surprise when no answer was forthcoming. 'Maybe it is.' He appeared to do a mental calculation. 'Friday,' he concluded. 'Yes.'

Phil gave the man a careful scrutiny. His clothes were clean but crumpled. The cuffs of the shirt were frayed. His hair was too long and there was a scab on his chin. He was very thin. Hadn't the

Fiona woman said something about him being ill? 'Sit down,' he suggested. 'Have a drink.'

It was ten o'clock in the evening. All three of them suddenly became aware of the oddness of a visit at such an hour. 'Sorry it's so late,' Robin said. 'I had a cow calving, or I'd have come sooner.' He rubbed a hand across his brow. 'And I'm to be up again at five, for the tanker.'

'Can I get you coffee or something?' Thea asked. 'I don't think we've got any booze.'

'I don't drink,' said Robin absently. 'Soraya, it is. She could've been killed. It's not right, is it?' His look was much more of a supplicant than an accuser.

'I know,' said Thea gently. 'And I really am terribly sorry. I was dazzled by the sun, and never even saw her. I was going very slowly, luckily. And she landed in the hedge, amongst a lot of cow parsley and stuff. It wasn't at all serious. We made sure before we let Fiona take her home.'

'You people,' the man went on. 'Stirring things up, doing what you like, not understanding anything. Getting away with it.' He looked at Phil. 'And you in the police, they say. Something high up, is it? Not answerable. It's not fair, whatever anybody says.'

It was delivered in a flat, hopeless tone, as if he expected the words to go ignored. Thea went to him, and laid a hand on his arm. 'Please don't think of us like that,' she pleaded. 'We never meant to stir anything up. Honestly, it's been as upsetting for us as for everybody else. And Phil's hurt his back. When I hit Soraya, the jerk hurt him more than her. You really shouldn't judge,

254

you know.' She injected a thread of severity into her final words, but the atmosphere remained tentative and strangely considerate. It was like the hushed mutterings around a hospital bed, Phil thought. Everyone afraid of the pain lying just below the surface. Thea moved away, followed closely by her dog.

Phil felt himself to be in a no man's land, between the professional activity of the murder enquiry and the sick bed he was forced to lie on because of his back. He knew little more than disconnected scraps about the investigation, and had no authority to formally question any of the Temple Guiting people. All he could do was pay very close attention to whatever came his way.

'Mr...?' Had he ever known the man's surname?

'Wheeler,' came the answer.

'OK, Mr Wheeler. Do you remember on Wednesday when Miss Deacon's horses got out, you told me some story about a vagrant you thought must be the dead man?'

'Aye.'

'Well, were you trying to divert police investigations away from the reality when you told me that? Did you say the same things to DS Gladwin?'

Robin Wheeler nodded. 'True, it was. Why'd I say anything different?'

'I see. And I suppose you've heard what Giles Pritchett did this morning?'

The man leant forward, his small hands clasped between his knees. 'D'you think it was him, then, who killed and buried that bloke under the tree?'

Phil tilted his head consideringly. 'What do you think?'

Robin sat up straighter. 'Not for *me* to say, is it? My girl and Giles Pritchett went to school together, on the same bus. She always had a bit of a liking for him. Then he went off somewhere and his Dad was forever badgering me and sorry about where he might have gone to. As if *we'd* know.'

Giles Pritchett went to the local comprehensive? Or did Soraya by some miracle get a place in a public school? 'Which school was that?' he asked.

'Not the same school,' Robin scoffed. 'Same bus, that's all.'

'Ah,' said Phil, obscurely satisfied that his assessment of the social standing of the young people had been right all along.

Thea was sitting in an armchair close to the fireplace, the spaniel on her lap. She played idly with its long ears, while the animal wriggled with ecstasy. Hepzie seldom kept still during the daytime, but she slept like a stone at night.

Robin Wheeler got up abruptly. 'Best go now,' he said. He seemed to be resisting an urge to say something humble and apologetic. 'I've had my say.'

'Yes, and we really do regret what happened last night. It could have been very much worse, and you're well within your rights to be annoyed about it.'

The farmer drew back his lips in a forced smile. 'Yeah, well annoyed doesn't really cover it. Panicked is closer, if you want the honest truth. If I lost that girl, it'd be the end of me.'

He doesn't know about Temple-Pritchett, then, Phil concluded, suddenly remembering how Robin had dismissed Rupert as a 'waste of space' the first time they'd met. All the same, he felt a profound pity for the man, as well as a dawning respect. He had made the effort to come here, when he would normally be in bed, and confront people who might well make him feel inferior. 'How did you get here?' he asked curiously. 'We didn't hear a car.'

'Oh, I came on the cob. He needed a turn, and these light evenings are good for a ride.' He spoke as if the use of a horse as a means of transport was still quite normal.

Phil looked through the uncurtained window. It was no longer light. 'It's dark now,' he said.

'He can see his way, don't you worry.'

'I'm more worried about car drivers seeing *him*,' said Phil.

'Don't you worry,' said the man again. And then he left, through the back door as he had entered. The horse, apparently, was tethered to a hitching post that had been there since the house was built three centuries ago. Thea followed Robin out and reported it when she returned.

'No wonder Hepzie barked so much,' she said. 'We've never had a visitor on horseback before.'

Saturday morning brought the first clouds for what seemed like months. Phil thought at first that it was still pre-dawn when he woke at seven and looked out of the window. Then, having checked the clock on the wall and looked again, he realised there'd been a change in the weather.

257

It made him sad to think that could be the end of the un-British heatwave; that from then on there'd be the usual drizzle and cool breezes, with only the occasional bright afternoon to remind itself that this was summer. Without the blazing sunshine, there would be no excuses for lounging in the garden. Work would once more be the norm. Except, he remembered with a stab of pain, there was still his back.

And there was still an unsolved murder to think about. Less than twenty-four hours earlier he had been staring at the muzzle of a pistol and wondering what it would feel like to be shot. He still had not spoken to Stephen Pritchett about his son's behaviour and subsequent severe injury. There was no pressing reason why he should, apart from normal human decency, based on their acquaintance. A kaleidoscope of local faces swirled through his head. They could all have known the man who'd been murdered – assuming it was Rupert's father, Graham Bligh. Certainly Janey's errant mother had known him intimately. The discovery of his probable identity must have created a major digression in police thinking, Phil supposed. The bizarre story of the genetic complexities resulting from Mrs Temple-Pritchett's behaviour had come across like a fairytale – something that was barely credible and yet was merely one of countless strange-but-true anecdotes. Life was full of them – coincidences, unexplained flurries of telepathy, chance encounters. The woman had conceived two babies on the same day, by two different men. Medically speaking, it was perfectly possible. For the family involved, the implications must have been beyond imagining. Hardly surprising, then, that the rogue inseminator should find himself slaughtered under a beech tree – except that his killing took place thirty-five years after his sin had been committed.

Meticulously, he went over everything he knew about the people concerned. Rupert had been the chief source of information, but he had disclosed no precise dates. Surely it was the case that the DNA test which had finally confirmed the decades of suspicion, had only taken place a few years ago? The technology had not existed before then. Perfectly likely, surely, that the murder had been committed at that same time. Which put all the suspicion onto Janey's father, Mr Temple-Pritchett, the cuckold wildly intent on revenge, on discovering that his son was not his son at all.

Gladwin would be following that line as a priority. She'd be tracking the man down in Tuscany or wherever it was he spent most of his time. She'd pore over the contradictory DNA test results that were in the hands of some solicitor or other, since there was an ongoing 'case' about it. What exactly, Phil wondered for the first time, did the case consist of? Who was suing who, for what? Was it to do with Janey's fabulous house and the trust who owned it? Was Janey's father charging Janey's mother with some sort of crime against their marriage? From what he'd understood, they still lived together as a couple in their Mediterranean hideaway.

Pared down to the basics, the murder had

suddenly begun to look very simple. There was ample motive, means and opportunity for Janey's father to have killed Rupert's – but the task of putting together a convincing prosecution case with evidence and witnesses looked impossible five years on. Plus there were the very untidy extraneous factors such as the behaviour of Giles Pritchett, the murky involvement of Robin and Soraya Wheeler, and the activities of the Saints and Martyrs Club, linking to the mutilation of the corpse. St Melor, he remembered. There had been a saint, killed by his uncle and deprived of a hand and a foot into the bargain. It would not be safe to ignore any of these elements. If Temple-Pritchett were to be brought to court, his defence would bring it all in, if only to muddy waters that were already far from clear.

And wasn't there something else? Something he and Thea had talked about, right at the beginning? Templars – that was it! The glaring detail of the family name, tied so directly to the village and its sense of ancient history still somehow surviving in the very air of the place. The mother of the twins had been a Temple. She had allied her name to that of Pritchett when she married. That meant, of course, that both Janey and Rupert were of the Blood Royal, so to speak. Their paternity hardly mattered, in that case. And, he thought helplessly, neither did the murder of one of their fathers. Graham Bligh was irrelevant to the Temple heritage. Which presumably removed it from the list of motives for killing him.

Thea came down at eight the next morning,

followed by the dog. 'Good night?' she asked him.

'Not bad, thanks. I've been lying here going over everything again. More as a sort of mental exercise than anything else.'

'So you haven't had a dazzling insight into who, why and how, then?'

'Not exactly, no.'

'Well, I have!' she announced with a broad smile.

'It fits perfectly,' she insisted for the third time, as Phil struggled to pick holes in her theory right through breakfast and beyond.

He found himself pushed into defending his own theory that Bernard Temple-Pritchett was their killer – a theory that Thea dismissed with provoking certainty. Her own solution was the only one she would now contemplate. 'But you'd never be able to prove it,' he argued. 'And without proof, it's useless.'

'So I'm going to find proof,' she said confidently. 'Smoke them out. I've done it before.'

It was true, he thought ruefully. Either by luck or design, she had more than once flushed out a murderer and thereby done a lot of the police's work for them. She wasn't afraid to get close to people who would frighten off most women of her size and background. Thea waded in where others feared to tread.

'I don't see how,' he objected. 'Especially as we'll be packing up to leave this time tomorrow.'

'Don't worry about that,' she said. 'A day's a long time when it comes to solving a murder.'

He knew he should stop her – tie her to a radiator if he had to; anything to keep her from

261

rushing off into the dragon's lair and probably breaking the law while she was at it. He had briefly tried anger. 'Don't be a bloody *fool*,' he had shouted. 'This isn't a game.' She had shaken her head wordlessly at him, leaving him at a loss.

Then he tried pleading with her. 'Think of my position,' he begged. 'Think of *Jessica*. If this goes wrong, you'll be such an embarrassment we'll both have to leave our jobs and change our names.'

'It won't go wrong,' she breezed. 'I promise.'

'It will if you've got the whole thing back to front. If you've made a fundamental mistake in your reasoning.'

'You don't think I have, though, do you?' she challenged. 'And you'll be grateful to me when I serve you up some watertight evidence with a red ribbon around it.'

'No,' he said stubbornly. 'I'll still be embarrassed. You're taking far too much into your own hands. I can't decide whether you think you're Superman or Batman or the Jolly Green Giant.'

'Don't be silly,' she said. 'I'm going in a minute. Look after Hepzie for me, and if I'm not back by one, raise the alarm.'

He could say it was his back, of course. That he had been powerless to prevent her from doing as she chose. He could even say she hadn't told him anything of what she intended. If it came to it, he could probably retain his position and his dignity by a few careful omissions and deviations. But it infuriated him that he would have to. It bothered him dreadfully that he was allied with a woman who could so blithely ignore his status in society, his obligations and assumptions. It was as if a bishop had married a Spice Girl, he thought sourly. It made him even more sour to realise he couldn't think of a more up-to-date airhead to use as an example. Unless it was Jade Goody. But Thea was worse than an airhead – she had plenty of brains. The fact that she chose to use them so irresponsibly made everything even more aggravating.

She had given him no real details of what she was going to do or where she intended to go. 'If you want to help, you can phone Stephen Pritchett,' she had suggested. 'Ask him how Giles is, and say you've got no hard feelings.'

'And what use is that going to be?'

'It'll tie up a loose end,' she said.

So he did it. Pritchett sounded groggy, as if still in bed. It turned out that he was. 'I sat in the hospital till gone midnight,' he said.

'Oh, did you? Then I'm really sorry to wake you. How is he?'

'Conscious. In tremendous pain. You'd think they'd be able to deal with it in this day and age, wouldn't you? Frankly, Hollis, I think the staff are working at dangerous levels of undermanning. You never see the same person twice, and they've got hopeless channels of communication. I don't mind admitting to you that it's frightening.'

'He's not in a private place, then?' Phil still clung to the idea that all the Pritchetts were rolling in disposable income.

'Of course he isn't. Private places don't handle emergencies, and don't take kindly to police officers standing guard over their patients day and night. Nor, I might add, could I afford it, even if they did.'

'But he's out of danger?'

Pritchett gave a rumbling sort of sigh. 'So it seems. Apart from facing prosecution for threatening to kill a police officer. That's you,' he added unnecessarily.

'And your wife? How's she taking it? She must be glad to know Giles is still ... well, alive.' It sounded stark in his own ears.

'Trudy doesn't know what to think. She's out of it, to be honest with you. Probably the best thing.' He sounded deeply mournful.

'You mean she's taking tranquillisers or something?'

'Doped up to the eyeballs. It's her usual recourse when life gets hard. I thought you knew that.'

'No,' said Phil. 'Although there have been a few rumours.'

'She's hooked on the damned things,' said Stephen. 'Has been for years.'

Phil made sympathetic noises, then, 'How well do you know Rupert Temple-Pritchett?' he asked, on a sudden impulse.

The man answered readily enough, though with a note of impatience in his voice. 'His father's my cousin. Until a few years ago, he and his wife lived in Guiting Power. Then they sold up and moved away.'

'So you were close until they moved?'

'Not at all.' The voice was less groggy now, Phil noted.

'But you *are* friendly with Janey, and she's their

264

daughter. And Rupert's sister.'

'What's all this got to do with anything?'

Phil took a major risk, then, with a sense of having little more to lose. 'You probably didn't know that the murdered man has been identified now. His name was Graham Bligh, and he was–'

'I know who he was,' interrupted Pritchett. 'But I had no idea he was dead. Somebody told me they'd seen him, come to think of it, not so long ago.'

Phil's heart lurched. 'Did they? Who? When?'

'Can't remember. A bit ago now. Somewhere like Birmingham or Coventry. We never knew him well, he was just one of the youngsters that hung round Jackie.'

Phil calmed down. For a man of Pritchett's age, *a bit ago* could easily be five years. And yet – there was still a nagging doubt as to the true identity of the body. The DNA said it was Rupert. Knowing it could not be him led to assumptions that actually had no firm evidence to substantiate them.

'You knew Bligh was Rupert's father, too?' It seemed too late to withhold the whole story from Pritchett. Besides, the man had somehow earned the right to be kept informed, even if his son was still under suspicion as a murderer.

The response was frigid. 'Gossip,' he said tersely. 'Idle gossip.'

'Um–'

'In any case, what would that have to do with anything? Rupert Temple-Pritchett is a wastrel, always has been. Made his sister's life a misery. Mocked all her interests, said it was her fault the little one died, tried to break the trust. A real

265

waste of space, that little beast. If he was a cuckoo in the nest, nobody would be surprised.'

'I think that's been proven,' Phil mumbled, trying to reconcile this description with the suave Rupert he knew.

'Well, that's not my business. If the dead man is Bligh – and I don't believe it is – then that lets my Giles off the hook. What possible reason would he have to kill a man he never knew?'

'But Giles does know something about it,' Phil insisted. 'Why else would he be so furious with me?' The glaring fact that he was speaking to the father of the man who had tried to kill him returned to Phil with some force. 'And he's in real trouble as a result.'

Pritchett made a wordless sound. 'No need to remind me of that,' he said. 'But first we've got to reconstruct his liver and much of his large intestine. Leave me alone, man. It was a bad day when you ever came to Temple Guiting.'

Phil rang off, feeling there was more than a grain of truth in that.

Outside, the skies continued to be grey, the thick clouds producing a sense of claustrophobia after the previous weeks. Phil worried about Thea, and then drifted into niggling away at the implications of his conversation with Pritchett and mentally revising the jigsaw that Thea had been so sure was complete. His focus was increasingly on Rupert – Rupert who was keeping company with a young woman, without her father's knowledge, and who was regarded by Robin as a waste of space and by another person as a bastard.

Robin and Soraya on his first encounter with them had said they 'saw him around' from time to time, presumably when he was visiting Miss Deacon, Soraya keeping silent about her intimacy with him. Nobody liked him, it seemed, and yet he'd come over as decent enough in his chats with Phil and Thea.

Thea believed she had worked it all out during the night. She had switched on the light and made notes, in the small hours. She had checked them again in the morning, adding arrows and more notes, until she thought she had the whole thing clear. She had remembered clues and small remarks that Phil himself had missed. But the real surprise had been her abrupt alteration in mood. All week she had irritably avoided the murder investigation as much as she could. Interested in Janey and Fiona for their Saints and Martyrs Club, she had taken much less notice of Rupert or Stephen. She had insisted that she didn't care who the bones had belonged to or how they'd got where they had. The catastrophe involving Giles, and Phil's brush with death, had not changed her mind. What had, then?

Seeing Rupert and Soraya together, he realised. Something about that unlikely couple had pressed a button for Thea and, from one moment to the next, she was engaged. Belatedly, inappropriately, passionately engaged.

Damn it.

Passion was where Thea had begun in her unravelling of the mystery. 'Everybody we've met seems to have a great enthusiasm about something,' she noted. 'Starting with Janey and Fiona and their saints, of course. But there's Giles – though with him *enthusiasm* isn't quite the word. Rage is more like it, from what you've said. Now there's Rupert and Soraya obviously crazy about each other. And Robin, a passionately over-protective father.'

'According to Fiona, that's not over-protective-ness, it's dependence,' Phil said.

'Same thing in the long run.'

'OK. So what about Stephen Pritchett? He's not passionate about anything, is he?'

She pushed out her lips thoughtfully. 'Not really. He seemed almost defeated by Giles going missing and his wife being so useless. Maybe Stephen's the odd one out, and really not part of the story at all.'

As a result of his telephone conversation, Phil thought Stephen sounded like a man with very little left to lose, and no secrets worth keeping. From the point of view of a police detective, this lack of affect would be a sign of guilt – a man with so much pressure and fear inside him that all he could do was keep the lid down tight and operate on autopilot. But Thea believed the opposite. She assumed that people with obvious passions were capable of murder. 'It was years ago,' she reminded him when he'd queried her assumptions. 'That's plenty of time to deal with the stress and get back to how you were before.'

'Is it?' He had tried to decide whether she was right about that. 'Doesn't committing murder change a person forever?'

'I suppose we'd all like to think so,' was as far as

she would go in reply.

Phil had listened intently to his lover's analysis of what had happened to Graham Bligh, trying to find flaws in her reasoning, trying to object that she had nothing concrete to base her theories on. She had waved it all aside. 'You'll see that I'm right,' she insisted. 'Always go for the simplest solution – I've learnt that much over the past year.'

He had puffed out his cheeks at this. He and Thea had been involved in a number of killings since they'd met, and, as far as he could see, not one of them had been explained very simply. Motives remained firmly hidden, the guilty covered their tracks and things were often not at all what they seemed. 'Simple?' he had echoed. 'You must be joking.'

'Not at all. I mean – once you know what everybody really wants, it all falls into place.'

'I see,' he lied.

If it hadn't been for his damaged back, there would never have been any question of letting her go off alone. She had taken shameless advantage of his weakness and he wasn't sure how long it would take him to forgive her. Even if everything worked out as seamlessly as she predicted, there would still be a nagging resentment at the way she had behaved.

But it wouldn't work out seamlessly – it stood no chance of doing so. Thea's hypothesis was that Janey's devoted friend Fiona had swung a pick-axe at Graham Bligh's head, in order to put an end to the paternity proceedings, then buried him, perhaps with the help of Giles or even

Robin, first having stripped him of all his clothes. She had convinced herself that Janey could not cope with any further family pressure, and that loyalty to her brother only made it worse.

'They were *twins*,' she kept saying. 'What greater bond can there be than that?'

'But why Fiona?' Phil demanded. 'Why not Rupert himself, or Bernard Temple-Pritchett, or even Janey's husband? Why on earth are you so sure it was Fiona?'

'I just am,' she persisted. 'And then I think there was a closing of ranks, so anybody who suspected what had happened made a pact not to give her away. And if they did assist in hiding the body they had even more reason to remain silent.'

Phil had grasped handfuls of his own hair in despair. 'My sweet Thea – normally I would listen to you. You know I would. But this time you've gone right off the rails. It absolutely doesn't hold water. Promise me you won't confront or accuse anybody. Go and talk to them, if you must. But have a care, because I'm perfectly certain you've got it wrong.'

She had at least undertaken not to make any direct accusations. 'I never intended to anyway,' she said. 'I just want to see if I can get her to incriminate herself. Don't worry – I'll be perfectly all right.'

CHAPTER EIGHTEEN

An hour passed, with Phil awkwardly pacing the ground floor of Miss Deacon's house, Thea's spaniel at his heels. 'She should be phoning us any minute now,' he told the dog. 'I'm not going to wait much longer. The stupid woman's going to get herself into all kinds of trouble, I know she is. She thinks she understands much more than she really does.'

Hepzie wagged her long tail slowly, looking up into his face. She really was a pretty dog, he acknowledged fondly. A good match for her lovely mistress.

The phone remained silent for a further half hour, at which point Phil could restrain himself no longer. He was going to take his car and track Thea down, however much agony it caused him. What kind of a man simply stayed at home waiting for his girlfriend to solve a murder single-handed? It was beneath his dignity. Besides, when the story finally emerged amongst his colleagues, the loss of face would be unbearable. Except, he reminded himself, Thea had it wrong. Every time he went through it, her theory acquired more holes, more false assumptions and dead ends. It even occurred to him that she might have deliberately invented the whole thing as a smokescreen. With a sinking feeling, he eyed the spaniel, and said, 'Damn it, I'll have to go and find her.'

Hepzie eyed him back, and wagged her tail slightly faster.

First he ensured that the back door was locked and all windows closed. Then he let himself out of the front, pushing Hepzibah back into the house and telling her to stay. Dejectedly the dog did as she was told and slunk off to the living room. Phil climbed carefully into his car, which smelt terrible. With disgust he soon tracked the smell to a quarter of a pork pie that he had left on the back seat a week ago, intending to fetch it for Hepzie soon after he arrived. In the sweltering heat it had undergone several transformations, until it was a sodden stinking mess that left a greenish mark on the upholstery when he gathered it up and threw it into one of Miss Deacon's hydrangeas.

He spent two minutes adjusting his seat, trying to find an angle that his back could cope with. There was no comfortable position, but some were slightly less excruciating than others. When he depressed the clutch, a new pain shot up his leg, all the way to his shoulder. 'I'm falling apart,' he gasped aloud. 'This is ridiculous.'

But he refused to give up. The engine started at the first turn of the key, and he reversed across the gravel, before turning up the drive. The act of pulling the steering wheel to the left sent the same pain up and down his entire left side. But once on the straight, with no gear changes, it subsided. Holding himself rigidly upright, he found it became possible. At the top of the drive, he turned right without undue anguish and proceeded sedately into the village centre.

His mind knew no rest, as he struggled with an unwholesome stew of logic, ethics, professional obligations and annoyance with Thea. As he came in sight of the ancient trees that seemed to represent Temple Guiting better than any of its buildings did, he was reminded of his first journey beneath them, almost a week earlier. In some ways too much had happened, and in others too little. He and Thea had not cemented their relationship as he had hoped, they had not been free of outside worries or uninterrupted in their hideaway. He had to force himself to concentrate on the business in hand – the identification and secure incarceration of the person who had murdered Graham Bligh. He was a policeman and it was his duty.

Once more, he ran through what Thea had said over breakfast. Somehow, her certainty had almost persuaded him that she was right. Her theory was riddled with holes, but the way she batted all his arguments away gave him a flickering confidence in her. Thea was not stupid, he reminded himself. She was good at seeing into people's hearts and minds. While he had been miserably nursing his back on the sunny lawn, she might well have been quietly mulling away at the murder, without letting him know. Certainly, she could not have been anything like as disengaged as she'd pretended.

And she liked Janey Holmes. She had taken to her right away, last Saturday morning, and consistently defended her ever since. Perhaps she understood something about Fiona's feeling that Phil could not. Perhaps all this Famous Five stuff now had arisen from no more than something she had seen in Fiona's eyes or heard in Fiona's voice.

His first stop was the village shop, where Thea had told him she might find Fiona, because she was on the rota for running the shop. Exactly what she planned to do after that had not been clear, even to Thea, but whatever it was must have taken place by this time. 'If that works out smoothly, the whole thing might be over by coffee time,' Thea had said. Neither of them had really thought it possible.

It took him a full minute to get out of the car, find his balance and move to the shop door. It was standing open, held by a man Phil had not seen before. 'We're ever so sorry to leave. You've been so kind – and the weather! Weren't we lucky?' He was addressing the woman standing at the shop counter, who nodded and smiled, but seemed anxious to deal with another man waiting to pay for a basket of goods.

'Well, I'll be off then,' said the man in the doorway. 'Oops! Sorry, mate. Didn't see you there.' He had nudged Phil's shoulder as he backed out, still beaming gratitude and farewell into the shop.

'That's OK,' gritted Phil, who had automatically flinched away, causing grievous consequences for his recalcitrant disc.

'You local?' asked the man. 'Haven't seen you before.'

Mind your own business, Phil wanted to shout. He gave an ambiguous waggle of his head and moved purposefully into the shop without a backward glance.

It was not Fiona behind the counter. And the man waiting to be served was another strange face. Phil understood how very few of the local residents he had actually encountered during the week. DS Gladwin would have met more of them, in her investigations.

'Gosh, I'm glad to see the back of that one,' said the woman. She smiled at Phil, almost as if she knew who he was. 'He's one of a group staying at the Manor, and they've been in here every day, thinking they're benefiting the local economy. In fact we've had to order in all kinds of nonsense for them, which has been a real pain. How's your back now?'

Phil blinked and gave her a closer look. No, he was sure he'd never seen her before. 'It's a bit better,' he said. 'How did you–?'

'Oh!' she laughed cheerily. 'We've heard all about you and your bad back. Besides, your lady friend said you might be in about now. She left you a message.'

'Did she?'

'She said to tell you she's gone to Janey's.'

'Right. Thank you. Er – did she catch Fiona in here, at all?'

'Fiona? Oh no. She doesn't do the shop on a Saturday. She's got her old dad to see to at the weekends.' The woman spoke as if Phil should have known this already. The implication was, he supposed, that a senior policeman should know

275

everything about the village and, by and large, this was no bad thing. The sort of woman who would happily vote for a CCTV camera on every corner of every street in the land.

'Well, thanks,' he said, turning slowly and contemplating the long walk back to his car, fifteen feet away.

The immediate question now was, did Thea want him to follow her to Janey's? The obvious answer was yes. Why would she have left the message otherwise? On the other hand, it might simply have been intended to set his mind at rest. No harm would come to her there. In fact, of all his many worries, harm to Thea was not amongst the top three. He trusted her not to provoke anybody into deliberate aggression – and with Giles Pritchett safely trussed up in hospital with imminent liver failure, she was unlikely to be under any real threat.

He drove slowly, resisting as far as he could any necessity for changing gear. Why hadn't he equipped himself with an automatic car, he wondered in frustration. How much easier life would be if he had. The seat was a fraction too far back for comfort, so he had to stretch his left leg to depress the clutch, and that hurt. With gritted teeth, he followed the tenuous lead his annoying girlfriend had given him.

Going to Janey's had not been part of Thea's original plan. Her quarry had been Fiona, the woman who knew everybody's business, and who had cast strange glances at Soraya, as well as at Thea herself. Many times that morning he had

276

wished he'd refrained from casting aspersions on the woman's motives. It turned out that his careless remarks had sparked the train of inexorable logic that had led Thea to her alarming conclusion. At least, it had if she had been honest with him. With every passing moment he feared she had not. And, unless she could supply a very good reason indeed for her deceit, he was going to find it hard to forgive her.

Her car was parked in the oval sweep of top-quality stone chippings; the house looked unperturbed. No shrill sounds of fighting women, no atmosphere of conflict. Phil stumbled painfully to the front door and rang the bell.

Thea herself opened it, with a smile that felt unpleasantly smug and superior. 'Perfect timing!' she said. 'You can drive then?'

'Are you all right? I've got something to tell you. It changes the whole thing.'

'Hush!' she warned him. 'Not now. Have a bit of sense.'

Why, he demanded of himself, was he in the role of the clumsy tyro and his untrained girlfriend so obviously in charge? He felt like shouting *Don't you know who I am?*

'We're discussing St Melor,' Thea said calmly, as she led him through to the conservatory. Under the much greyer skies, it had a more sinister atmosphere. The greenery of the plants dominated everything and the humidity made it difficult to breathe freely.

'Go on, then,' he invited. 'Fill me in on what I've missed.'

Janey Holmes was sitting on a cane sofa, her arms resting on the thick cushions, her head back. 'Hello,' she said. 'Excuse me for not getting up. Once I'm down, it seems such an effort.'

'I know the feeling,' he said.

'Of course you do. How is the back now?'

'It comes and goes,' he said vaguely. 'It helps if I can distract myself from thinking about it.'

'Of course it does,' she said.

He looked at her more closely. There was something dreamy about her, like someone spaced out on Prozac, not fully connected with the real world. He glanced at Thea for a hint, but all she did was gently raise one eyebrow, which he took to mean *Just follow my lead, OK.*

There was one of Janey's *Lives of the Saints* volumes on a low table, the pages open and held down with a glass paperweight. Thea went to it, and picked it up. 'Listen to this,' she said, and proceeded to read aloud: *'January 3rd, about AD 411. There was a duke, or prince, of Cornwall, named Melian, whose brother, Rivold, revolted against him and put him to death. Melian left a son, Melor, and the usurper only spared his life at the intercession of the bishops and clergy. He, however, cut off his right hand and left foot, and sent him into one of the Cornish monasteries to be brought up.*

'The legend goes on to relate that the boy was provided with a silver hand and a brazen foot, and that one day, when he was aged fourteen, he and the abbot were nutting together in a wood, when the abbot saw the boy use his silver hand to clasp the boughs and pick the nuts, just as though it were flesh and blood. Then it says, *Rivold, fearing lest the boy*

278

should depose him, bribed his guardian, Cerialtan, to murder him. This Cerialtan performed. He cut off the head of Melor, and carried it to the duke...'

'Right,' said Phil, slowly. 'Two murders, in fact.'

Janey stirred. 'We've never done St Melor,' she said, a new focus in her eyes. 'Honestly, we never have.'

'You've been in the Club since it was first started, have you?' Phil asked her.

'Absolutely. Fiona, me and three others started it.'

'And have you ever missed one of the ceremonies? Surely you can't have been to every single one.'

'I went on holiday once or twice, as well as visiting my parents in Tuscany every summer. And I did go to that horrible hospital a few times after little Alethea – well, you know.' She frowned at the floor. 'But Melor's day is in *January*. I've never missed a January.'

'It does say he died on October 1st,' said Thea, consulting the book. 'Maybe somebody thought it would be better to do him then.'

Janey's head went from side to side in emphatic denial. 'You shouldn't be accusing me like this. You're suggesting the Club really kills people. That's *wrong*. Of course it's wrong. You think Rupert–' She gave them an imploring look, 'I can't tell you anything. It isn't fair to ask me. I haven't done anything wrong, honestly. They just wanted to protect me, that's all. You can't blame anybody.'

'But Janey – the body we found this week had a hand and foot cut off, just like St Melor. Isn't

279

that too much of a coincidence?' Thea was holding one of Janey's hands, shaking it gently for emphasis.

The big woman made an obvious effort to reply sensibly. 'I don't know. I never heard of St Melor until now. I told you when you came before, there are loads of saints I haven't properly researched.'

'Hmm,' said Thea, flourishing the book. 'I find that a bit difficult to believe, to be honest. As far as I can see, the great majority of them are ineligible for your club for various reasons. I'd have thought that by now you'd be scraping around for somebody to focus on each month.'

'Well, we do some of them more than once. Like Kenelm. Because he's local.'

Phil let himself lapse into private thought as the two women discussed saints. He was still wondering about the confusion between Rupert and his father, Graham Bligh, and about the multitudinous comments to the effect that Rupert was a nasty piece of work.

'Janey,' he said, with a quick glance at Thea. 'How do you get on with your brother? He obviously comes to the village quite often, because he told us so. He drops in to see Miss Deacon, and we've seen him nearly every day this week. Does he come to visit you as well?'

Janey's frown deepened and she obviously thought hard before answering. 'Rupert and I own this house, you see,' she said. 'That is, the trust has to keep everything fair between us. Grandaddy said so. I need Rupert to be here, to keep everything running.'

'Yes, I see,' Phil lied. 'And you and he are good

friends, are you?'

'He's my brother,' she said. 'But he wasn't very nice about the Saints and Martyrs. He said some very nasty things about the Club, you know.' She met his gaze briefly. 'That was a long time ago, but it really wasn't very nice.'

Thea was still clutching Janey's hand. 'Some people don't like Rupert much, do they?' she said.

Janey pulled her hand away. 'Stop it!' she cried. 'Stop talking about nasty things. I told you before – I like to keep everything polite and happy in this house. We don't have arguments or bad temper here. It's a rule.'

Phil sighed softly to himself. The woman was plainly unreliable as a witness. The rich voice has turned into the simpering tones of a little girl, visibly regressing as he questioned her. Also, he was sure she was concealing something. She was being careful not to speak without thinking first. He was on the verge of giving up and persuading Thea to leave.

'Well–' he began. 'It's been good of you to talk to us. We should go now and leave you in peace.'

Janey cast him a look that carried flickers of panic. 'Oh, no, don't go,' she said. 'You could have some lunch. Fiona's never here on a Saturday, you see. And when Sammy phoned – well, I didn't know what to say.'

Phil looked again at Thea, with a minute flick of his head, indicating that they ought to leave. But Thea was giving all her attention to Janey.

'Sammy?' she repeated. 'Who's Sammy?'

Janey opened her mouth to reply, but the words

281

never passed her lips. A shattering crash interrupted her, and all three of them turned in panic towards the window, which had imploded all around them. Janey had a hand to her neck, and Phil, wrestling yet again with the anguish of his back, was slow to notice that there was blood between her fingers.

'Oh, my God!' howled Thea. 'There's glass everywhere.' Then she noticed Janey. 'What–?' she choked. 'What's the matter?'

'I've been stabbed,' said Janey, eyes wide. 'Look, I'm bleeding.'

'Phil! Quickly – she's got glass in her neck.'

Already he had his mobile out and was tapping keys with his thumb. A closer look at Janey had reassured him that no major artery had been severed. The blood was not jetting across the room, merely trickling steadily over the woman's ample shoulder, and down her fleshy front. 'Press something over the wound,' he ordered Thea. 'Unless the glass is still in there, of course.'

'Let me see,' Thea told Janey, her own lips drawn back in distaste. Grass crunched beneath her feet as she moved. Janey withdrew her hand an inch or two, to reveal a gash about an inch long, but not especially deep. 'It hurts,' she whined.

'Ambulance, Temple Guiting,' Phil was telling his phone. He gave the address, and then got himself patched through to a special police number, where he made it clear that the incident was part of an ongoing investigation. Much of what he said was automatic, virtually coded, intended to prevent ignorant uniformed officers clomping blithely across a scene that could be rich in much-needed evidence.

Thea peered at Janey's neck for signs of lurking shards, and deciding it was all clear, pressed a pale blue antimacassar to the wound, having snatched the makeshift compress from the back of an armchair. Phil hoped it wasn't too imbued with bacteria. It certainly looked clean enough.

'That's what did it,' he pointed at a large grey stone sitting in the middle of the floor. It looked innocent, if out of place. Almost all the glass had fallen between it and the window, but he could see a few pieces further into the room. 'Thrown with quite some force,' he added. 'Glass is lethal stuff – we could all be bleeding to death in here.'

'Am I bleeding to death?' Janey asked in a small terrified voice.

'No, no, of course not. Look, it's nearly stopped already. Nasty thing to happen, though.'

'Not too good for the carpet, either,' Janey giggled, valiantly trying for the customary British reaction to a crisis even in her traumatised state. 'We'll never get all this blood out of it.'

'It's not half as bad as it looks,' Phil said.

'But who did it?' Thea asked wonderingly, looking around at the devastation. 'Do you have any idea, Janey?'

'Oh yes,' came the muffled reply. 'I expect it was Sammy.'

'Not Rupert?' Phil queried.

Janey laughed, a gurgling sound of amusement mixed with pain and confusion. 'No, it wouldn't have been Rupert,' she said.

'Where's that ambulance?' Thea chafed. 'They're taking ages.'

'About four minutes so far,' said Phil. 'I'd guess we ought to allow at least twenty.'

'Well, thank goodness we've got you to keep the murderer at bay,' said Thea, who appeared to have abandoned any attempt at discretion or even common politeness.

Janey had remained in the chair, despite being showered with shards of glass. Now she began to struggle to stand up. Her manner was much more adult, as if the former childlike demeanour had fallen away like a coat. 'I feel silly now,' she said. 'I've only got a cut on my neck. I don't really think I need an ambulance at all, actually. I can't abide hospitals.'

The others made no reply to this. Phil was trying to peer outside through the shattered conservatory window. 'Not double glazed,' he noted with interest. 'I didn't think that was allowed any more.'

'It is if you're Listed,' said Janey. 'That glass has been here for two hundred years or more.' She stared at the broken pane in obvious distress. 'Doesn't it look dreadful,' she moaned.

'Double glazing would have kept that stone out,' said Phil. 'Probably.'

Janey ignored him. All three showed signs of impatience, the unreal suspension of time as they waited encouraging nothing more than small talk, despite Phil's strong compulsion to ask again who Sammy might be. But he wanted DS Gladwin at his side – it was her case, she ought to hear any important testimony. Anything Janey might say to him now would only have to be repeated under proper conditions. It would com-

prise nothing useful by way of evidence otherwise. But Thea was less inhibited by protocol.
'Giles,' she said into the silence. 'Tell us about
him.' It was an order, that Phil suspected was less
easier to defy than if he'd given it.

'Rupert's little friend,' Janey responded. 'Ran
off when somebody said something he didn't
want to hear. He was always a bit of a fool.' Her
voice was strained, her attention more on her
neck than what she was saying, her attitude
partly hostile, partly clinging.

'Rupert must be twenty years older than he is,'
said Phil, who continued to have difficulty keeping all the ages under control.

'You do know he tried to shoot Phil, don't you?'
Thea demanded, when Janey simply ignored
Phil's comment. 'Giles, I mean. What was he so
angry about? Where has he been all this time?'

'Stop it,' Janey pleaded. 'It isn't fair, questioning me when I'm like this. It's harassment.'

She was probably right, thought Phil.

CHAPTER NINETEEN

Phil went in the ambulance with Janey, since
nobody else had materialised and he doubted the
wisdom of letting Thea go. Her habit of asking
important questions with no formal cautioning
could wreak havoc with any subsequent prose-
cutions. Even though he might commit the same
indiscretions, he would know better how to deal

with the consequences.

Nobody from the police had yet manifested themselves, which struck Phil as rather dilatory after his urgent direct call. Thea was left with the conundrum of how to take two cars back to Hector's Nook. He handed her the keys of his and told her she'd work something out. 'Thanks very much,' she said crossly. 'Aren't you worried that I might get stoned as soon as I step outside?'

'Stay inside, then, until the police arrive. They can't be long now,' was his callous reply.

The truth was, he had lost his hold on what Thea was thinking and planning. The last conversation he had had with her had been all about Fiona as murderer, and a determination to prove it. Since then, his thoughts had run through endless hoops, until he was almost sure she was deliberately misleading him. 'Stay here and tell them everything that happened,' he ordered her. 'And stay close to Gladwin if you can. She'll make sure you're all right.'

A ginger-haired female paramedic had inspected Janey's neck and decreed that there could be residual glass to be washed out, and some delicate stitching called for. Phil had the impression that there was another quiet day in Cirencester Accident and Emergency.

Janey was not enjoying the attention. 'I hate hospitals,' she moaned. 'They don't listen to you – and at some point I'm sure to get a lecture about my weight.'

Phil nodded sympathetically. They called it preventive medicine, when they nagged people about their habits so relentlessly. No doubt Janey would be offered a 'programme' with counsellors and nutrition experts, poor woman.

'So, did Thea say anything to you about Fiona?' he asked rashly. The need to resolve the issue was too strong to resist. 'I believe her thinking was along the lines of Fiona having killed Graham Bligh as a kind of favour to you. It did make a sort of sense when she first explained it to me.'

Janey frowned in utter confusion. 'Graham Bligh? My mother's old boyfriend? He isn't dead.'

'Oh, yes, he is. That's who the bones belonged to. I mean – it was his body buried under that tree.'

She was lying flat on a fixed trolley, her bulk overflowing the sides, the flesh of her arms and cheeks vibrating slightly as the ambulance traversed the small country lanes. Phil could see her thinking hard, and wondered again just what level of intelligence there was beneath the rolls of fat.

'Who told you that?' she asked.

'They matched the DNA,' he said. 'They've got your whole family on the database, you see, because of your father's legal case.'

'And they think those bones are Graham's?'

'Well, yes. Actually, it's a bit more complicated than that, because there must have been some mix-up. But yes, that's what they think.'

'Then they're stupid,' she said flatly.

'Oh?'

'They've got it so wrong, it makes me feel tired,' Janey said. 'What you just said is pure nonsense.' She exhaled a *huff* of frustration. 'I won't talk to you any more. If you'd just left things as they were, everything would be all right. It's all your fault.'

'That's what Giles Pritchett said.'

'It's what *everybody's* saying.'

'But I didn't make the tree fall down. Isn't that where it all began?'

'You didn't need to go crawling all over it. Robin was going to cover everything up again when he'd finished milking. But instead, you had to go and stick your nose in. It's all your stupid fault.' And she closed her eyes, saying no more. Tears started trickling down her cheeks and running into the papery covering of the trolley. The paramedic, who had been watching over Janey with an air of disapproval, said 'Hey! You're not meant to make her cry.'

Phil held up his hands in apology and shifted a few inches along the plastic bench they'd allocated him. The ambulance was driving fast but smoothly, his back no more than a dull ache. He thought about what he knew of Janey Holmes.

He had once heard a theory that very fat people are trying to draw notice to themselves, often after a childhood spent being ignored. Perhaps a twin would feel this need more strongly than most. Or a middle child in a big family. Or somebody consigned to a day nursery from their first few weeks. Distractedly, he thought he might have suddenly stumbled upon an explanation for the epidemic of childhood obesity – but he brushed it to one side.

'We're nearly there,' he noted. 'We ought to call somebody to come and be with you, and take you home again. I doubt if it'll take very long to deal with your neck. In the olden days, they've have sent a GP out to the house to patch you up.'

'The good old days, eh?' she said, with a brave effort at maintaining her aplomb. He wondered at her flurry of tears. Who was she weeping for?

At the hospital, Phil phoned Thea and ascertained that she was well protected by two uniformed officers, and was trying to explain to them just what had happened. 'It isn't much of a story,' she said. 'All I can think to say was that a stone came crashing through the window and a shard of glass got Janey in the neck.'

'That's about it,' he agreed. 'Which is why I didn't think I'd be needed there as well. Plus–' the full truth of this only now became clear to him 'while I'm here I'd better talk to Giles, if he's well enough.'

'Officially or unofficially?'

'Both,' he said. 'I mean, I don't think there's any real distinction.'

'You think he might confess to the murder?'

'Unlikely. As I see it, he's never really been on the list of suspects.'

'I could have been right about Fiona, you know,' Thea said stubbornly. 'It did make sense.'

'We're a long way from closure yet,' he said.

'Closure! Please!' Thea begged. 'I thought we'd agreed that was on the banned list.'

'Sorry,' he muttered, quelling the irritation at her continuing flippancy. 'Look – I'm going now. I'll try to keep you posted.'

'Are you phoning from inside the hospital? You know that's against the rules.'

'Not any more. They gave up trying to enforce

289

it a year ago. Bye, love. See you soon.'

Giles Pritchett looked young and very poorly. From the chest down, he was a mass of technological enhancement – tubes, monitors, dressings. It was dreadful to witness the consequences of just one bullet fired into a man's abdomen. 'Hello?' Phil said quietly. 'Giles?'

The eyes opened blearily, and took some time to focus. 'Hello,' he said, with a frown. 'What do you want?'

'Just a quick chat.' He kept his voice light and friendly, trying to erase any implication that he had come for recriminations. He need not have worried.

'Your people *shot* me,' the young man whimpered. 'I could be dead now.'

'That's true,' Phil nodded. 'It's what happens, I'm afraid, when you come at a police officer with a gun. The rules change quite a lot from what you might regard as normal. You must have known you were doing something absolutely unacceptable. I don't think you're stupid.'

'I was blind with rage,' said Giles, his voice thin and breathy. 'Blind with rage.' It was a phrase he must have opted for at an earlier point – it came off his tongue almost as a single word.

'But *why?* I still don't understand what made you so angry.'

'I *told* you. You put everything back to how it was when... How it was a few years ago. You brought it all up again, just when it might have been safe to go back. I missed my mum, you know. Those pills have turned her into a zombie.'

They both glanced around the room, as if they might find Trudy Pritchett huddled in a corner.

'Well, you're back now anyway.' Phil was as puzzled as ever. 'What exactly happened two and a half years ago, when you ran away?'

A sly look came into the reddened eyes. 'I had to keep myself safe. If I'd stayed at home, he might have got me as well. They didn't trust me to keep quiet.'

'Who might have got you? As well as who?' Phil leant forward urgently. 'Are you talking about the man who killed Graham Bligh and buried him under that tree?' Something was wrong in the question, he knew, but sometimes getting the facts wrong was an effective prompt to a witness.

'Not Graham Bligh, you fool,' Giles suddenly snarled, showing a brief burst of energy. 'Nobody cares a shit for Graham Bligh. Besides, he isn't even dead.'

'So people keep telling me. But at the moment, that's the official identity of the murdered man. They've done a DNA test...'

'Oh well, that proves it then, doesn't it? A hundred people seeing him and talking to him. But the lab says he's dead and DNA can't be wrong, can it?'

Phil had enough doubt of his own to take this attack calmly. 'OK. So when this man was killed, whoever he was, you were afraid you might be next? So you went into hiding. Wouldn't it have been possible to send at least an email to your parents, telling them you were still alive? Your mother's been worried out of her head.'

'They never really believed I was dead. That

291

was just a stupid panic when they heard what you'd found. I sent them a card at Christmas. That's more than a lot of blokes in my position would have done.' He was weary again, a lost boy. 'And then you mucked it all up.'

'It makes no sense to blame me,' said Phil angrily, belatedly remembering that Pritchett Senior had mentioned the Christmas cards. 'Why does everyone keep doing that?'

'It does though. If anyone local had found those bones, they'd just have covered them up again and kept quiet.'

Phil sat stiffly back in his chair, staring at the white face and thinking about the words that had just echoed what Janey had said to him in the ambulance. 'Oh,' he said.

There were a dozen urgent questions he wanted to ask, and almost no time to choose the most important one. Fiercely he forced his brain to work. 'Soraya,' he said. 'She was your friend. She knows what's been going on, doesn't she?' Giles said nothing, his gaze on the blank TV screen on the wall facing him.

'Did you know she's going out with Rupert Temple-Pritchett?' Phil said, following a hunch that had no immediate logic to it.

'Don't be stupid,' came the languid response. 'That's impossible. Even if it could be true, Robin would kill them both.'

A nurse told him he must stop tiring the patient. In the corridor outside he met Stephen and Trudy Pritchett, walking slowly, holding plastic carrierbags of shopping. Stephen lifted a hand in greeting, but Trudy ignored him. Her head was shaking slightly, and Phil wondered whether she might have Parkinson's Disease, as well as all her other problems.

Phil's back was a constant distraction. It made every move an ordeal, the urge to simply find a sofa or even a bed where he could stretch out and relax was growing stronger by the minute. He could call Gladwin and pass on the message that Soraya Wheeler might be at risk from her irate father. He didn't have to do everything himself. He just needed to sit down and think, anyway, after all the scraps of information he'd gathered that morning. The dead man was not Graham Bligh. That much seemed certain. In fact, the obvious implication was that it must be Rupert Temple-Pritchett after all, as the DNA said, which meant the man he and Thea had spoken to, claiming to be Rupert, was somebody else. But who? And where did that leave Soraya who was in love with the man who claimed to be Rupert? And who was almost certainly loved in return, because surely nobody could have faked that look of adoration he and Thea had seen on the man's face? Why would he, anyway? He hadn't known he was being watched. If he was intent on seduction, perhaps, he'd enjoy working on the girl's affections first – but that sounded very old-fashioned. It hadn't looked as if there'd been any resistance from Soraya, although that could simply indicate a successful outcome to the overall plan, of course.

In any case, regardless of his growing anxiety, there was no way he could march in (march in *where*, anyway?) and order the man to leave the girl alone. Janey Holmes might inhabit a world where knights on white chargers dashed to the rescue of damsels in jeopardy, but the reality of the twenty-first century was altogether different.

He needed to speak to Gladwin. That was the priority. Parallel investigations were obviously stupid, neither knowing what the other was doing. She would not thank him if he had discovered more than she had and never deigning to share it with her. He tried to review the hours since he had last compared notes with her, and the facts he had gleaned in that time.

Not a lot of facts, he admitted to himself. A whole heap of hints and arguments and wild theories, but scarcely a single fact. And yet he did feel much nearer to – *closure*. The word fitted, whether Thea liked it or not, and he felt a bubble of defiance against her implacable scorn for such words. He did his best to speak plainly to his officers, to give clear instructions and set them tasks with real goals – but jargon was inescapable. Sometimes it was useful, anyway. It avoided premature judgements and prejudicial attitudes. It did actually sometimes make people stop and think.

He was stranded, he realised, although it would be easy enough to get a taxi to the police station and see what was going on. And from there it was only a couple of minutes to his flat – which had seemed so far away all week. Confined to Temple Guiting, he had felt cut off from his own familiar world, he realised now. He had missed his dogs and his colleagues, and the normal pace and pressure of work. Now, he could simply call a cab and be transported effortlessly to his own firm bed, where he needn't worry about Temples or Pritchetts for at least the rest of the day.

He brought these thoughts up short. How could he be thinking along such self-indulgent lines? What about Thea, valiantly striving to keep so many balls in the air? Miss Deacon's house, for a start. And the various residents of the village, creating a maelstrom of confusion and violence – she had let herself be sucked right into the heart of it and nothing was going to persuade her to climb out again until all questions were answered. He couldn't just abandon her at this stage. One more day, that was all. Tomorrow Archie would arrive and he and Thea could be excused. Gladwin would pursue the murder investigations in her own capable way, and Phil could rest his back with a clear conscience.

Just one more day... He fished in his pocket for the Ibuprofen and swallowed two of them dry. Then he phoned for a taxi.

There were still so many questions he should have asked Giles while he had the chance: random mysteries that kept popping into his head with little or no logical thread to them. How completely had he actually disappeared – would a cursory search have located him, via credit cards or council tax payments? True disappearance took planning and persistent hard work – even leaving the country was no guarantee of success. Money was the stumbling block – if you wanted to live anything resembling a normal life, you had to be in the system. And the system kept remarkably close tabs on people nowadays. Had his parents colluded in some way, slipping him cash and reassuring themselves that he was at least alive? Only when a dead body had materialised had they panicked, perhaps after a longer-than-usual silence, and approached Phil unofficially to ascertain that it was not their dead son.

The taxi took him to his flat, which was airless and smelly from the hot weather. He had fully intended to return on Monday morning at the latest, and here it was, Saturday, with milk standing sour in the fridge and the waste bin unemptied under the sink. Despite his conscientious brushing and grooming of the dogs, there was evidence of their presence in the air. An earthy scent from their muddy feet on the rugs and the rumpled dusty hairy bedding in their baskets struck his nostrils. It was a *male* environment. No flowers or chemical air fresheners mitigated the smells. He made a mental comparison with Hector's Nook, which had bowls of pot pourri on the window sills, and plants in every room. There was beeswax polish and open windows and real sheepskin to fill the place with echoes of fresh fields. Here in town, it was frowsty and stale and he didn't like it.

He phoned Thea again. 'Where are you?' she said, a trifle breathlessly. 'You've disappeared on me.'

'I came back to the flat. I need some clothes.'

She accepted the mendacity without comment. 'OK. So what next? Out here it feels as if a bomb's about to go off. Everything's gone quiet and tense and I have no idea what I ought to be doing.'

'But why? What can possibly happen?' It all seemed a long way away to him, as if Temple Guiting had shifted to a parallel universe that he could no longer reach.

'Phil – somebody threw a dirty great stone at us, two hours ago. Remember? We could all have been badly hurt. Doesn't that feel like a crisis to you? As if the person out there might try again?'

'It was Janey's house. She must have been the target, not us. Besides, it was a relatively harmless stone, not a bomb. Relax. I'm staying here tonight, and I'll speak to you tomorrow. I need to get my car back sometime.' He didn't care that he was failing her in a big way, that he had said no words of affection or concern. He was too drained, too befuddled to say the right things now.

'All right,' she said. 'If that's what you want.'

Then he did what his body had been urging him to do for some hours past. He arranged all the cushions he could find in one corner of his leather sofa, shook off his shoes, put his feet up, closed his eyes and sank instantly into a restful slumber.

The relentless ringing of his front doorbell roused him after what felt like seconds. When he realised what it was, and heard the associated shouts of his name, he tried to sit up and only succeeded in rolling off the unyielding leather onto the floor. Forcing his back into submission, he stood up and shuffled to the door.

Gladwin was standing there, with two uni-

297

formed officers. 'For Christ's sake, where have you been?' she shouted at him. 'We've been looking everywhere for you. Your phone's not working. We thought you must be dead.'

He blinked stupidly at her. 'The phone's fine,' he said. 'What do you want?'

'There's some sort of siege going on in Temple Guiting. You know the people – we want you there.'

'Thea! Not Thea?' He remembered other times, other crises where his beloved had got herself into danger.

'Thea's all right. She called us. She's been trying to call you. She thought you must have gone out.'

'But the phone's fine,' he repeated. 'Let me go and see.'

Before they could stop him, he had gone to the small alcove where the landline phone sat on its own small shelf. The receiver was askew, where he had carelessly dropped it after Thea's abrupt conclusion to their conversation. He nudged it back into place, feeling foolish and guilty.

'What time is it?' he asked.

He got no reply to that. Instead Gladwin had followed him and was staring angrily into his face, 'Phil, we've wasted ten minutes or more already. If you don't come right now, we'll go without you.'

'All right. I'm coming.' He patted his pockets for wallet and mobile. With another pang of guilt, he remembered switching it off before collapsing onto the sofa. How many more absolute rules had he managed to break that day? A glance at the clock on his mantelpiece told him it was a few minutes short of five in the afternoon.

In the car, Gladwin tried to bring him up to date. He listened with an effort. 'The DNA was not wrong,' she began. 'The body isn't Graham Bligh after all.'

'No,' Phil agreed. 'I think I'd come to that conclusion. Is it Rupert then?'

'Seems it must be. The man you've been thinking was him is an impostor. And he's causing a whole lot of trouble up at Wheeler's farm.'

'Rupert's dead,' Phil repeated. 'Does Janey know? What about his parents? And the Pritchetts?' It was as if the whole house of cards had collapsed yet again. He could not shake off an image of the foppish visitor to Hector's Nook lying under the roots of a tree, steadily decomposing. 'He *said* he was Rupert. We believed him.'

'As anybody would.'

'Have you got it all straight now? Are we going to arrest the person who killed him?'

Gladwin leant her head against the side window of the car. 'I'm making no promises,' she said.

But Phil was rapidly waking up. 'Do you know who he really is?'

'Not for sure. We're going on the theory that it must be Graham Bligh, more by default than anything else. After all, the only motives that make any sense are to do with the paternity case and who inherits the estate. If Bligh never had any contact with his son, he might not have found it too hard to slaughter him. And he must have thought he'd have a claim on his share of the property.'

Phil gave this some serious thought. 'But why impersonate him?'

'No idea,' she said. 'Except there's the other matter of the descent from the Templars. Young Jinnie at the station seems to think there'd be enough fame and glory for anybody able to prove they carried Templar blood to warrant committing murder. I can't say I'm altogether convinced.'

'Jinnie's the one who tracked down St Melor as well, I suppose?'

'That's the girl. Special talents, you might say.'

'So how would that fit? The hand and foot business?'

'No idea again. That's what we're hoping to discover when we get to the farm. I warn you, I'm not going to take the orthodox route this time. I'm still facing investigation for what happened yesterday. This time there'll be no guns or sudden rushes. I'm taking it very slowly and calmly – OK?'

He gave her an appraising look. 'Why haven't they taken you off the case? The IPCC oughtn't have let you carry on.'

'Because there isn't anybody else,' she said. 'Other than you.'

He absorbed the barb and applied his mind yet again to their destination. 'I really need to know what to expect. You said it was a siege.'

'I exaggerated,' she admitted. 'Although–' she looked away from him at the long stretch of the A429 ahead, 'I *am* taking a bit of a gamble. If it goes wrong, I'll have to kiss goodbye to a promising career.'

'Then don't involve me,' he said angrily. 'Stop playing games and let me have a proper briefing.'

She shook her head. 'I can't. If I tell you now, you'll have time to stop me. If you don't know, they can't blame you. I realise it's a lot to ask on such a short acquaintance, but you're going to have to trust me.'

Any man would be angry, he told himself, being sidelined by a woman in such a cavalier way. 'So what's my role? Why have you brought me here at all?'

'You might come in useful,' she said. 'As a witness. Don't get too close – with that back you'd only be a liability. But another pair of eyes and ears could be invaluable.'

And he had to be content with that.

CHAPTER TWENTY

When they arrived at the house he remained in the car, on Gladwin's orders. 'I'm sorry, but it's for the best,' she told him. 'You're here purely as a bystander. I want you because you're known to these people and it helps to have a familiar face on the scene.'

'All right,' he said, forcing himself to relax on the back seat. For the third time that day he felt he'd been diminished. He was beginning to believe it himself – that he was ineffectual and slow-witted. 'This is Wheeler's farm, then, is it? I thought it was closer to the village.' He had been surprised when they'd driven almost a mile beyond the spot where Thea had knocked Soraya into the hedge, until he realised that the road had curved so sharply that the real distance was much less. 'It must be milking time,' he added inconsequentially, remembering the reference to a herd of shorthorns.

'Looks as if the cows are having to wait.' Gladwin tilted her chin at a yard full of brown and white speckled beasts, shifting restlessly, eyes fixed on a square building with a firmly closed door.

The new detective superintendent marched off across the yard to two unmarked cars, where she conversed inaudibly with a gaggle of men who had obviously been patiently waiting for her. Phil knew the procedures for a siege: the immense care to be taken to protect the lives of all officers, the triple- and quadruple-checking necessary before any action was taken. Gladwin had blithely asserted that there were no firearms involved, but after the incident the day before with Giles Pritchett, Phil was not inclined to take her word for it. Farmers had guns – everybody knew that.

Without being told, he assumed the man at the centre of the so-called siege had to be the one he and Thea knew as Rupert Temple-Pritchett. From the location and the restless cows, he thought it safe to assume that Soraya or Robin or both were his captives. Just why this was happening remained entirely obscure. Phil had half-suspected Robin Wheeler of being capable of bad behaviour. He believed the man had deliberately loosed Miss Deacon's horses, and equally deliberately told the story of a nameless vagrant being the body under the tree in the hope of diverting police attention from the truth. Janey had implicated him by her revelations in the ambulance. But surely Robin Wheeler was no murderer. Instead, it seemed he was currently in the role of victim.

As he watched, Gladwin left the knot of police people and began walking towards the house. Tension tightened every muscle, his fists clenched as his instincts screamed at him to stop her.

The farmhouse was constructed of the usual Cotswold stone, the mellow colour suggesting it must be at least two centuries old. The yard was weedy and there was no sign of a properly kept garden. The front door had a large thistle growing beside it, and a creeper straggled across the top, several tendrils bridging the join between doorframe and the actual door. It was obviously very seldom used. Had Gladwin noticed this, Phil wondered?

She came to a halt some ten or twelve yards short of the door, and leant her head back to see the upper windows. 'Hello?' she called. 'Will somebody please speak to me?'

Had they tried telephoning the house? That was the recommended practice these days – to attempt a rapport with the hostage-takers while maintaining a safe distance.

Nothing happened. In frustration, Phil wound down his window and called, 'They'll be at the back. Try the back.' As soon as the words had flown, he wanted to recall them. The woman surely knew what she was doing. He had only betrayed his own presence by his noise.

But it seemed the order was a good one. Smoothly, Gladwin made a ninety-degree turn and marched off towards the side of the house. She gave a little flip with her hand to indicate she accepted his advice. She was far too relaxed, in Phil's view. Was she wearing a protective vest? Didn't she know she could be killed by other weapons than a gun? A crossbow bolt or even a well-aimed knife could come whistling down on her from an upstairs window as she stood there so defenceless.

She disappeared around the back of the house, and he heard her calling again. 'Please will somebody come and speak to me? We've had a report of some trouble.'

Who had reported it? How much contact, if any, had she already had with the people inside the house? How come she was being so damned calm about the whole thing?

The other police officers were alert, but did not have the twitchy demeanour that was usual in such situations. They muttered quietly amongst themselves and one spoke into a radio inside his car. After three more minutes, Phil could endure no longer. Stiffly he got out and walked across the yard. Several backbones straightened as they realised he was approaching. Evidently they knew who he was.

'Sir,' said one of them. 'DS Gladwin wanted you to stay in the car, sir.'

'Maybe she did, but I'm tired of being kept in suspense like this. Exactly what's going on? Is she safe, going in like that?'

'We've been speaking to the young lady, sir – Miss Wheeler. She sounds quite relaxed, but simply claims that there's a man keeping her and her father inside the house against their will.'

'How? How's he doing it?'

'She says he's got some powder that's poisonous. If they make a move he doesn't like, he'll throw it in their faces. She's not sure he's serious, but is inclined to believe him.'

'So how did she manage to call you, without him knowing?'

'He did know, but he thought she was calling her friend, not us. He ordered her to do that, you see. He was listening in the whole time and prompting her as to what to say. He wants her to run away with him and leave her father, but she refuses. So he's doing what he can to force her.'

Phil rubbed his aching spine thoughtfully. 'I've never heard anything so bizarre,' he said eventually.

'Nor me, sir,' agreed the officer. 'She carried it all off brilliantly, though. You could tell she was upset. She pretended to be telling this Fiona the whole story, when really she was speaking to DS Gladwin. She kept warning her on no account to call the police, but just get here and deal with her dad.'

'How long ago was all this?'

'Must be an hour or more now. We've been here since four-forty, and not seen any sign of life.'

'So what if they've gone? What if he has already poisoned them and himself?'

'That's what the super's gone to find out now, sir,' said the man, with just enough forbearance to show Phil he was being annoyingly slow on the uptake.

Anger seized him. Why hadn't the woman explained all this to him in the car? She had deliberately withheld important details – in particular the powder. 'But it could be ricin,' he exploded. 'We need special biological suits, the hospitals alerted – what the hell is the woman playing at?'

'Here she is now, sir,' said the man, with obvious relief. 'You'll be able to ask her.'

Phil was aware of a certain delicacy in the situation. Gladwin was indisputably the SIO, with authority over the team working on the Temple Guiting case. But he, DS Hollis, was equal in rank to her and superior in experience. He could pull her up if he saw her making mistakes, and would, at the last resort, be expected to report her to the chief constable if she broke any rules. But senior CID officers did have considerable leeway. The primary task was always to acquire solid evidence before charging anyone with a crime, and methods for doing this could sometimes be devious. Watching his colleague's face now, he knew he had to trust her for a while longer.

'They wouldn't answer me,' she said, matter-of-factly. 'The door's locked and I couldn't see anybody through the windows.'

'So how do you know they're still in there?' Phil demanded. 'This chap tells me there was half an hour or more when nobody was watching the house.'

'Not strictly true,' smiled Gladwin. 'I had somebody stationed at the road gate, who would have seen if anybody left. Besides, the vehicles are all still here.' She waved a hand at a battered pick-up and a red Puma, both of which Phil recognised.

He shook his head helplessly. 'So what now?' he asked. 'Am I right in thinking he's using a biological substance to threaten the Wheelers?'

'So he claims. I expect it's just washing powder. Since all that ballyhoo last week, everybody's thinking about ricin as a means of mass destruction. People really don't have much imagination, do they? I mean – where would he get ricin from, anyway?'

'There's a plant at Hector's Nook,' Phil remembered. 'For a start.'

'What? A *ricin* plant? How did you recognise it?'

He explained about castor oil plants and the ease with which their seeds could be turned into toxic dust. 'But it's a bit early for seeds yet. They'd have to have been gathered last year, when nobody was talking about the stuff.'

'So it's washing powder, bet you a hundred pounds,' said Gladwin.

'But we can't take the risk, can we?' said Phil, feeling like a dull old uncle, hearing Thea's voice in his ear chiding him for being so timid, while at the same time knowing it was the only professional stand he could take.

He changed the subject when Gladwin didn't respond. 'How did Soraya know your number? Did she call your mobile? It sounds very clever of her.'

'One of my sergeants gave it to her. We realised this morning that she was associating with a man we had reason to mistrust. I sent Hilary over for a quiet word. All this isn't entirely unexpected, you see.'

He stared at her. While he'd been stumbling around the village, thinking he knew everything there was to know, Gladwin had been ahead of him. He remembered Giles's anxiety for Soraya. He reran the complicated story about Graham Bligh and Rupert, his son.

'So–' he began, intending to ask once more just who the man with the suspicious powder was. But the sentence was never completed. Another car came hurtling into the yard, hooting its horn. Phil winced and cast a worried look at the farmhouse. The one thing you *never* did was startle a volatile criminal when he was holding people hostage.

'Who on earth–?'

Two women scrambled out of the car and Phil wasn't entirely surprised to see his girlfriend emerge from the passenger seat. The driver was just as unmistakable, festooned with a broad white bandage around her neck. Janey Holmes stood huge and determined, her gaze on the house.

'Leave this to me,' she said. 'He isn't going to do me any harm.'

Gladwin, to Phil's relief, did her best to intercept the woman. 'The doors are locked,' she said. 'You won't be able to get in.'

Janey eyed the front door with its unused appearance. 'I don't think so,' she said. 'Have you actually tried it?'

Phil and Gladwin's eyes met. He had diverted her before she'd tried the door. They had simply assumed that it was locked. Both shook their heads, Phil feeling yet more of a fool than on all the other occasions that day.

'Right, then.'

Short of summoning two or three of the by-standing policemen to physically restrain her, there was little anyone could do to stop Janey Holmes. Even Phil was starting to believe that this was a very tame little siege, appropriate to the quiet country village. Almost as much urgency arose from the unmilked cows as from the goings-on in the house. Janey put her meaty shoulder to the door and easily heaved it open. There was a scraping noise, and a rustling from the disturbed creeper, but it made little genuine protest. Only when she disappeared inside did Phil turn to acknowledge Thea, standing at his side, watching Janey intently.

'Hello,' he said. 'Fancy meeting you here.'

She didn't smile. 'Do you know who that is in there?' she demanded.

'Not Rupert,' he said. 'That's as far as anybody will tell me.'

'Rupert's dead, you idiot,' Thea said.

'Right. Can I just say, in my own defence, that this is not my case, I am not the SIO and that I have hurt my back? In these circumstances, I think I can be excused from following the very strange behaviour of the people here.'

'Shut up,' she told him. 'You were lucky I persuaded Gladwin to bring you along in the first place. She didn't want to spare the time going to fetch you, but I said you'd be extremely useful back-up.'

'And she believed you?'

'Obviously.'

'And now Janey Holmes has entered the dragon's den, while a large bunch of police officers hangs back, scared of their own shadows. And I include myself in that.'

'It makes very good sense. Janey knows him better than anybody, and is convinced he won't hurt Soraya or Robin.'

'But *he* – whoever he is, killed Rupert. Is that right?'

'So it seems.'

'Which in my book makes him dangerous and desperate. He's facing arrest and the most serious criminal charges.' He smacked a fist into an open palm, in a parody of frustration. 'This is the most ludicrous piece of police work I've ever seen.'

'No, Phil, it isn't.' Thea spoke earnestly. 'Gladwin's really being very clever. She's got all these men here for if things get nasty. But there's no rush, is there? We've stirred things up a bit now, hooting the horn and sending Janey in. You'll see – it'll all be over in a minute.'

'And why isn't Janey still in hospital?' he grumbled, knowing he'd been defeated yet again.

'Because she's only got a cut on her neck, for heaven's sake. They've stitched it up and bandaged it, and let her go. Oh!'

Sounds of raised female voices were coming from the house. Everybody in the yard held their breaths and waited. There were no screams for help, but Phil noticed that two of the waiting policemen were calmly putting on face masks. So, he thought grimly, they were taking the ricin threat seriously after all.

'Come down here *now!*' he heard Janey shout. 'There's to be no more mucking about. As usual, you haven't thought anything through, have you?'

'Dad!' came a cry from Soraya. 'What's the matter?'

Evidently the whole group was coming down the stairs, their voices increasingly audible as they approached the front door. A new tension gripped the people outside, and the police officers stood straighter, some taking a few steps towards the house. Gladwin flapped a hand at them, her own gaze firmly on the open door.

It seemed to be over. Janey emerged first, and called, 'He's coming.' Then she added, 'Robin's been taken ill. Looks as if he'll need a doctor.'

Phil realised, for the first time, that there was no waiting ambulance, as there ought to have been. Again he felt an angry horror at Gladwin's lackadaisical methods. 'So how–?' he began, but again he was interrupted.

Everything sped up. Janey was just clear of the door when a blurred figure dashed past her. With astonishing momentum, the man they'd known as Rupert Temple-Pritchett almost flew out of the house, head down, legs at full stretch. He headed blindly towards the farm drive and the road beyond, with every prospect of complete escape.

But Phil could not let that happen. Here was a clear and obvious challenge which required no conscious thought. The runaway was bound to pass within a few feet of Gladwin's car, against

311

which Phil had been leaning ever since Gladwin had returned from her fruitless trip to the back of the house. All he had to do was launch himself at the right moment to intercept the flying figure.

Which is what he did, making contact with his quarry at roughly knee-level. The headlong dash took them both rolling violently onwards for some distance, before Phil's limpet-like hold on the man's legs brought him to a halt. A hail of blows from the man's fists descended on Phil's head and shoulders, but he kept his arms wrapped tightly around the struggling legs, until reinforcements came and took over.

'Wow!' said Thea, in his ear. 'My hero!'

Janey appeared, the acres of skirt material blocking his view of anything else. 'Oh bother,' she said, in a voice that contained profound regret. 'I didn't think anybody would catch him.' She reached down and gave Phil a hearty slap on the cheek. Then she did it again, saying, 'And that's from Soraya. She'd do it herself if she wasn't seeing to poor Robin.'

Her victim tilted his head enough to look at her face. 'You wanted him to get away,' he gasped. 'You planned it so he would.'

'I tried to give him a sporting chance,' she admitted. 'Just for old times' sake.'

A *huff* of amusement came from the flattened fugitive. 'Good old Janey,' he said. 'There'll never be another like you, old girl.'

Thea was crouching close to Phil's head. 'Can you get up?' she asked.

He carefully started to try. 'No,' he said. But his attention was still on Janey and the man she had

tried to liberate. 'Who *is* he?' he asked. 'Somebody please tell me.'

'Sammy Holmes, of course,' said Thea. 'This is
Janey's husband.'

CHAPTER TWENTY-ONE

Although they couldn't be sure until proper
analysis had been done, Phil forced Gladwin to
concede that the powder that Holmes had been
brandishing was indeed very much like ricin.
Some of it was sprinkled on the floor of Robin
Wheeler's bedroom, but it seemed none had
been imbibed or inhaled by anybody. Robin had
been taken away, breathless and shaking, but
Soraya insisted it was his pre-existing condition,
and nothing to do with being held hostage by a
murderer.

DS Phil Hollis was suffering for his act of
heroism in more ways than one. Primarily, his
back had been jarred and twisted to such an
extent that he had been told to lie flat for at least
three days. 'By rights you should stay in hospital,'
the doctor told him, after a night spent in a side
ward at Cirencester General. 'But if you've got
someone at home, you'll probably be just as well
off there.' Thea, with no discernible hesitation,
had volunteered to nurse him, on condition the
dog could come too.

Secondly, the general reaction amongst the
people at the scene had been decidedly frosty.

Janey had slapped him; Soraya had wrung her hands and wept; and Fiona – who had appeared moments after the capture of Sammy Holmes – had given him a cold stare and told him he'd ruined everything right from the start.

Thea had defended him angrily. 'What are you talking about?' she had flashed at them. 'He's just caught a killer, who was holding two people hostage.' Her fury had effectively silenced their accusations, but Phil felt the effect of their reproaches, despite her efforts.

Order had slowly been restored from the farmyard chaos, although the wretched cows had not been milked until far into the evening.

Thea had handed Hector's Nook over to Archie, who had arrived on schedule in the middle of Sunday, blissfully ignorant of the excitement that had been going on in the village over the past few days. Now she was in residence in Phil's flat until he could fend for himself. 'I know I'm a lousy nurse,' she said, 'but I can't just abandon you, can I?'

They talked obsessively about the events of the past week all through Sunday evening, and Phil lay awake that night going over it in his mind. It was Monday morning before the final piece of the jigsaw fell into place and a revelatory light went on in his brain.

'I've got it!' he announced.

'What? What have you got?' Thea had resorted to drawing diagrams in an effort to make sense of the whole tangled business, with nearly a dozen elements ringed and linked with wiggly lines.

'Saints and Martryrs', 'Soraya and Rupert/ Holmes', 'Templars', 'The Manor', 'Janey's house', 'Janey's baby' were just some of them. She'd added dates and likely motives, but still it wasn't apparent just why Sammy Holmes would have murdered Rupert Temple-Pritchett.

'It was something Giles Pritchett said. Plus the way everybody behaved towards me yesterday. It suddenly dawned on me that they *all* wanted Rupert dead, for a whole lot of different reasons.'

'Oka-ay,' said Thea slowly.

'Except Stephen Pritchett. He genuinely had no idea what had been going on. He must have been supplying cash to Giles on and off, and been alarmed when the boy went quiet for the past six months or so. But Giles knew about the murder, as well as the rest of them.'

'And was so furious with you he tried to shoot you – I remember,' she said wryly.

'The thing we've been so confused by was the way Holmes wandered so openly around the village, while telling us he was Rupert.'

'Well, yes. That *is* confusing.'

'But you see, he only told people who didn't know him as Holmes. That's obvious, of course, but it's also a clever way of keeping Rupert officially alive. He used his credit cards every now and then, as well. There was never a death certificate, or a body. That's the most important bit, do you see?'

'Not really.'

'They needed him to be alive so that Janey's parents in Italy could keep on the legal case against him and his biological father. They thought Rupert was still alive, and Holmes probably sent them emails or letters as if from him.'

'But why?'

'The trust. I'm only guessing, but I bet you there's something in it to Janey's detriment if her brother dies.'

'Like what? Surely it would be to her benefit to inherit the whole place?'

'Trusts are funny things. It could well be that if only a sole legatee survives, the whole thing has to be wound up, and she'd have to find the cash for maintenance and all the rest of it out of her own pocket. It seems quite likely to me that the thing was set up in the first place to keep an equal balance between the twins. If one of them dies, there's no further need for that.'

'Yes – she said something like that, didn't she? When she was being so dopey and little-girlish. I assume it can be checked?'

'Easily. In fact, I think you'll find Gladwin's already done it, knowing her.'

'So what about Soraya?' Thea had been especially enraged by the girl's ingratitude on Saturday afternoon.

'I think she and Holmes were genuinely in love. Janey and he have been separated for four years, and although they're still on friendly terms, she doesn't seem to want him back. So there was no need for them to keep it secret, other than from her father. Robin and Rupert were much the same age, probably knew each other all their lives. We know Robin didn't like him, from what he said when the horses got out. Didn't he call

316

him a waste of space? So he'd have gone along with the general protection of Holmes, even if he didn't want his daughter getting entangled with him.'

'But why would Holmes have taken them hostage like that?'

'I can only assume Robin found out about him and Soraya and tried to put a stop to it.'

'And Rupert – I mean Sammy – fought him off with ricin?' Thea was openly sceptical.

'I admit I don't understand the ricin, other than that with it being so much in the news, all kinds of lunatics are going to try making it, and using it for their own ends. As a murder weapon it has some appeal – painless, bloodless, that sort of thing.'

'But very stupid – he could have breathed it in himself at the same time as using it on them.'

'Maybe that was the intention. If Robin stopped him having Soraya, maybe he was happy to die along with them. Don't you think there was a sadness about him, right from when we first met him?'

Thea gave this some thought. 'Not really,' she concluded. 'But he was acting a part then. It's difficult to separate the actor from the real man.'

'Do you remember, when he was talking about the baby, he said something about it being his. We thought he was its uncle, when really he was its father. The acting lapsed then, at least.'

She nodded. 'That's true.' After a moment, she added, 'So where is Graham Bligh?'

Phil shrugged. 'No idea. He's not part of this at all, is he? There's no need to look for him now.'

317

She paused. 'Except he's lost his son. Shouldn't he be told?'

'He might never have known he *had* a son. It's probably best to leave him in peace.'

'Hmm,' she said, and they lapsed into silence for a while.

Finally, Phil stirred himself to round it all off, before they moved onto more intimate matters. 'So there we have it, more or less. Giles told me that if anyone in the village had found the bones, they'd have quickly covered them up again and said nothing. That's why I've been the object of such fury. They were all desperate for me – and you – to shut up and stop trying to uncover the truth.'

'But Gladwin would have done it, without us.'

'Maybe she wouldn't. Maybe the whole thing would have slipped further and further down the priority list until it was virtually forgotten.'

'But can she prove it was Holmes who killed Rupert?'

'Very probably not. He'll be charged with holding persons against their will and using a dangerous substance – assuming it really was ricin. Unless he confesses, there might never be official closure on the death of Temple-Pritchett.'

Thea shrugged. 'I'm not sure that would matter too much, would it? The whole village can't be wrong. Maybe it was a necessary evil, bumping him off.'

'You might think that, but I couldn't possibly comment,' said Phil with a grin.

The publishers hope that this book has given you enjoyable reading. Large Print Books are especially designed to be as easy to see and hold as possible. If you wish a complete list of our books please ask at your local library or write directly to:

Magna Large Print Books
Magna House, Long Preston,
Skipton, North Yorkshire.
BD23 4ND

This Large Print Book for the partially sighted, who cannot read normal print, is published under the auspices of

THE ULVERSCROFT FOUNDATION

THE ULVERSCROFT FOUNDATION

... we hope that you have enjoyed this Large Print Book. Please think for a moment about those people who have worse eyesight problems than you ... and are unable to even read or enjoy Large Print, without great difficulty.

You can help them by sending a donation, large or small to:

**The Ulverscroft Foundation,
1, The Green, Bradgate Road,
Anstey, Leicestershire, LE7 7FU,
England.**
or request a copy of our brochure for more details.

The Foundation will use all your help to assist those people who are handicapped by various sight problems and need special attention.

Thank you very much for your help.